D1568965

BEST FRIENDS, FANTASY LOVERS

Dicey Grenor

Published by Dicey Grenor
Independent Author
www.DiceyGrenorbooks.com
Copyright © Dicey Grenor, 2014
All rights reserved

Cover Designer: Najla Qamber Designs.
www.najlaqamberdesigns.com

ISBN-13: 978-1502353566

ISBN-10: 1502353563

Dedicated to Billie Jean Godley Powell: You always believed in me. You never hesitated to tell me you were proud of my accomplishments and "barracuda" personality. I'm happy to have called you "boss" and "friend". I'm so sorry I didn't call back. I had no idea we had run out of time. It will haunt me for the rest of my life. Please know I'll always remember, love, and miss you. Be at peace now, my friend. I know you would have loved Tommy and Capri, so this one's for you. *Smooches*

Friendship has never been so tempting...

ACKNOWLEDGMENTS

Natalie Berry, Bill Fowlkes, Kendralyn Jasper, Danyahel Norris. My lovely, lovely beta readers… I am so grateful to you for taking this long, agonizing journey with me. I thrive off of your feedback and support. Thank you, from the bottom of my heart.

I went to many awesome rock concerts within the past few months, including the Queen + Adam Lambert one I'll never forget. Special shout out to guitarist, Glenn Gilbert (Vanity Crimes) for letting me hang out at several of yours. Also shout out to guitarist, Doomstress Alexis (Vendetta Diabolique) for putting together the smoking hot Bayou Doom Fest. Wishing your bands much success.

Jaies Baptiste, you already know. Thank you.

To my millions and millions of fans—Hey, it could happen!—thanks for being daring enough to read another of my twisted works. I tried to make this one lighter and more mainstream…but we must all accept that I'm not wired that way. At least I know you'll be okay with that. Newbies to my books— watch out there, now! That's the only warning I'm giving this time.

CHAPTER 1

Capri closed her eyes—just for a second—when next thing she knew, chairs began scraping across the tile floor, waking her as students filed out of the auditorium-size classroom. With the midterm coming up next week, there couldn't have been a more inopportune time to nap. But dammit, she was tired. All those sleepless nights spent studying for the midterm she took last period were finally catching up to her.

Wiping drool from the side of her mouth, Capri looked next to her where Sasha's head lay on a desk, her eyeballs swimming left to right under her eyelids as she dreamt of things Capri dared not even imagine. Asleep. As expected. After another long night of partying. Sasha wouldn't even have shown up if it weren't for the professor's attendance policy, and that Sasha had already missed too many days. One more absence and she'd start dropping a letter grade. That did not bode well since Sasha's parents had conditions on whether she continued to reside on campus. Grade conditions.

A new set of students were already marching in

like a herd of cattle for the next class starting in ten minutes.

Capri kicked her sneaker into Sasha's black boot, jerking her awake.

"What? What!" Sasha's head spun around, her eyes struggling to focus on the chaotic swarm of students vacating and entering the classroom.

"We're being invaded by aliens." Capri zipped her books in her backpack, adjusted the waist of her low-riding jeans, and stood to leave. She paused for a moment while Sasha oriented herself with her Martian surroundings.

Sasha's face went from shock to panic, confusion to skepticism, and finally— "Ah. You're joking." She swept hair from her eyes and started gathering her things. "You really have to learn to smile when you're joking. Your poker face is hella creepy."

Capri handed Sasha an ink pen that had fallen on the floor then hoisted her backpack to one shoulder. "And you really have to learn to pay attention in class." Never mind that Capri had slept as well. At least she'd caught *most* of the review, which would come in handy. Capri would need the leverage for—

"You and I both know that's not going to happen, so name your price."

Bingo.

Capri was all about bartering. She didn't have a lot of money and resources, but she had other valuables that Sasha did not. Like a serious attitude when it came to studying...and notes to study with.

"Let's see..." Capri started towards the exit, pretending to think it over as she walked. "You can have my notes from today's review if you give me a ride to work in the morning." Capri could always walk or catch the university bus, but why be inconvenienced when her roommate had a car with heated seats and the early morning temperature would be somewhere around too-cold degrees? Helping Sasha ace another test would be worth it for the comfort of roundtrip curbside transportation. "I have to open the computer lab at nine. I'll need you to pick me up too. Around six. That cool?"

"Cool." Sasha, showing no signs of fatigue now that class had ended, caught up with Capri as they walked out into the brisk, cool morning. "Why do they insist on torturing us with shit we'll never use in the real world anyway?"

Capri tucked both hands in her denim jacket pockets. "I think they just want us to prove we're teachable. We'll go before an employer, show our credentials and grades, and they'll immediately know: I can teach this one how to do the job and they'll do it well. This one, not so much."

"No wonder I'm not interested. I don't want a job." Sasha swept her long stringy blond hair off her neck. She had a habit of doing that. "Hey, let's go out tonight. Don't you have the night off?"

Capri shook her head. "No way. I'm tired." Being off of both jobs tonight was an early Christmas present. She intended to make the most of that time doing something she didn't get to do much of— sleeping.

"Of course you are, Ben Stein. All you do is work and study. That's why we have to go out. It's Friday night. Let's make the best of it. You have the rest of the weekend to study."

"Stop calling me that. And some of us have responsibilities. I have to work in the morning, remember?"

"So what? Down a Red Bull and you'll be fine."

Ha! Easy for Sasha to say. She'd be happy with a B in Psych 101. That's all her parents expected of her. Capri didn't come from a wealthy family like Sasha. Not working was not an option. She needed to have the best grades to get the best job.

Capri's golden opportunity to have uninterrupted time to herself had come. "Or...*you* can go out, have a blast, and tell me all about it tomorrow." Capri could actually get to bed early and wake up refreshed then study for next week's exam while at work tomorrow. Working in the campus computer lab really was a great gig for a student. Her second job at the library wasn't too bad either. Both were perfect places to study. Since she had to work all weekend, she'd get a lot of studying done and get paid for it.

Sasha was right. All Capri did was work and study. That's all she could do if she wanted to be successful in life. And she did. Nothing would stand in the way of her dreams. She had it all planned out.

"Girl, you better live now while you're young. Pretty soon you'll have kids and saggy tits. You'll wish you had taken advantage of natural vaginal lubrication now."

Capri laughed. "I don't have time to lubricate my vagina. I'm going to be a professional therapist, not a prostitute."

"Honey, we're all prostitutes. Don't kid yourself. The better your vagina is, the better your clientele. And by better, I mean wetter."

Capri laughed as Sasha got on her usual soapbox about the birds and the bees and the flower and the trees, and all of her twisted ideals about gender roles and feminism, sexual liberation, and pussy empowerment. Capri had heard *Life According to Sasha* before. To be honest, she found it all contradictory. With a wet cooter, she could get a wealthy man…and be more independent? What the hell?

Sasha realized her monologue was going nowhere fast. "Okay. How 'bout for an hour? You haven't gone out with me since our second day of orientation."

Oh, there was a reason for that. Capri couldn't hang with the elite party girl. Not when they had different aspirations.

Nevertheless, Capri cocked her head. Maybe Sasha had a point somewhere in there about only living once. Going out for an hour wouldn't be the end of the world, would it? She really could stand to break the monotony of her schedule. Just this once.

"Okay," Capri said, thinking of how literal she would be. She would even set her watch to notify her when the hour was up. "I can go for an hour."

Sasha froze with her mouth gaped. "Really? You're giving in that easily? And here I was all prepared to bribe you with chocolate." Sasha pulled out her cell and started punching the pad. "I'll RSVP us. Frat party starts at eight. We can get there at nine-thirty." She tucked her phone back in her jeans pocket and nudged Capri's side with an elbow. "Getting laid tonight isn't a bad idea either." Sasha laughed as Capri pulled away. Sasha had to jog a little to catch up with her. "You're going to have to give it up to somebody sometime. Best to go ahead and get the bad lay out of the way now so you'll be ready for—"

"Don't push it. We're just going out to do some underage drinking, stand around so all the upper class girls can point fingers at us and call us whores, dance once or twice with some guys who probably don't even go to school here but front like they do so they can get some college pussy," Capri took a deep breath and continued. "And then I'm going back to the dorm to sleep while you actually fuck one or two said guys and later stumble in our room and pass out on your bed."

Sasha's eyes widened in mock horror. "Thank you very much for showing me my shortcomings." They walked inside their dorm building and started up the first flight of stairs to their tiny room. "I'll go for a record of three guys tonight to shake it up a bit. Can't be all predictable and shit."

They laughed.

"You're laughing now," Sasha flipped her hair, "but it's true. You need to get laid, and this frat party we're going to tonight—plenty of hotties. You're hot. You're eighteen. A freshman. It's time to give it up."

Capri shook her head. "You sound like a guy. Should I be worried? You trying to fuck me?"

"Only thing you need to be worried about is me pushing you down the stairs to your death so I can get an automatic four point oh for the semester."

"That's just a myth, you know. And why do you care about a four point oh anyway?" Capri faced their room door and started digging around in her backpack for her keys.

"It'll make the parents happy. They may even let me trade in my car."

"Right. Because last year's model is so outdated."

"Exactly." Sarcasm was lost on her. Sasha's attention had already drifted elsewhere. "Helloooo, stranger."

"Hello, yourself. Do you ladies have a moment?"

"Damn straight." Sasha's voice had dropped an octave in an attempt to sound seductive.

Capri, too busy trying to figure out which of her keys matched their door, didn't bother turning around to see who Sasha was hitting on now. It wouldn't surprise her if Sasha brought the guy inside and did him on their puppy paw welcome mat as soon as Capri unlocked it. That kind of easy access to fucking was the reason Sasha had wanted a coed dorm. Capri had wanted the dorm because it was the only one with a laundry room on the same floor and no curfew. They were both practical girls, though one of them was more of a free spirit than the other.

Capri continued trying keys in the door while trying not to listen to Sasha get her mack on.

"See, my band's playing tonight, if you two can make it. Here." Papers rustled as it sounded like he was handing a sheet to Sasha. "We need all the support—oh, hell—who am I kidding? We need all the beautiful girls in the audience we can get to cheer us on and stroke our egos while we perform. I've been passing these flyers out all day, and I have yet to invite one lad." Then he laughed. Sort of. It was a breathless, light sound that gave out as if he didn't have the energy to put into it fully. He sounded genuinely happy, and his foreign accent came through thick with a strong lilt. Scottish, maybe? No, Irish. "So what do you say, ladies?"

"What kind of music is it?" Sasha asked.

"Doesn't matter. Do it for a good cause. That way, even if our music is shite, you would have done your civic duty of helping to build self-esteem in today's youth."

"I can see you've worked on your pitch."

Capri could hear the excitement in his voice and the interest in Sasha's, so she hated to be the one to burst their bubbles. She didn't want Sasha to unilaterally change their plans for the evening and answer affirmatively for them just because Sasha wanted to fuck the guy. "Actually, I have to work in the morning. We're going out for a hot minute then I'm—" Capri inserted the correct key then turned around expecting to gently let down a chubby redhead with itty bitty green eyes, a full body of freckles, the palest of skin, and thin lips…maybe one that was four feet tall, dressed in all green, and carrying a pot of gold and a four-leaf clover.

She was not prepared.

And she couldn't remember the last time she'd stared…at anybody.

"Then you're…?" He waved his hand exuberantly, letting Capri know to get on with it. She didn't speak, so he finished for her. "Then you're going to bed like a seventy-five-year-old woman in a nursing home?" He smiled, and it was brilliant, bright as the sun. Nothing else mattered but his ethereal joy. "Wait." He put long fingers up to his lips, which drew her eyes there. "My mamó's eighty, and I do believe she's Skyping in to support my band tonight. You know what that means? That means you're lamer," he put his fingers in the shape of an L in front of her face, "than an old lady in a nursing home. Is that really how you want to be known around here? Is that really the legacy you want to leave?" He put his hands on his hips and waited. His eyes twinkled with amusement as his perfect pink lips widened into a smile.

Jesus. That smile.

Those eyes.

That hair. The mass of unruly dark curls on top of his head…and the thick eyebrows he used expertly to make countless facial expressions. Even his skin, the same natural tan as hers…and those delicate cheekbones that cradled his straight nose were awe-inspiring. Capri stared up his tall, thin frame to his androgynous features because there was so much unexpected beauty to take in.

"Uh…" Capri couldn't utter a coherent word if she tried. She tried again anyway. "Um…" Oh, he had green eyes, all right—olive green—but that's where her preconceived image of him, based on a handful of foreign films, ended. A couture high fashion show in London was missing a model.

Maybe it was time to give up her virginity.

Where the hell did that come from?

"You're staring," Sasha whispered to Capri.

"My photograph's on the flyer, love," he taunted as he extended a sheet to Capri. "So you don't have to memorize my face."

Capri swallowed the saliva that had accumulated in her mouth and took it from him. Was she really salivating? Her face heated with embarrassment.

To get his attention, Sasha shook the flyer she'd gotten from him in front of his face. "Eh, what's your name, pretty boy?"

He didn't take his eyes from Capri. Mirth was written all over his face as he studied hers. He even popped the collar of his gaudy orange leather jacket before answering. "Thomas. My friends call me Tommy. Seventy-five-year-old women call me Tom because they forget the other half."

That accent. Capri shivered.

Sasha laughed. "We just *love* supporting youth in the community, Tommy." Sasha grabbed Capri's arm, turned the key dangling from the door and opened it. After Sasha shoved Capri inside their room, Sasha turned to him, leaned against the open door and grinned. "I'm Sasha, by the way. That's Capri. And we'll both be there."

"Good," he smirked. "Then you'll find out what groupies get to call me when they're screaming my name."

CHAPTER 2

The lavvy door swung open. "Hey, man! What's taking you so long?"

Tommy jerked from his self-assessment in front of the medicine cabinet mirror to find Spirit, his band's drummer, at the door sporting an angry face and stiff shoulders. Spirit was always rushing Tommy to do something or other. Spirit had no patience. "What the fuck, mate? Is the house on fire?"

"Not yet, but it will be if that's what it'll take to get you to come out." Spirit had no sense of humor either. He was not joking.

"I said give me five."

"And that was *forty*-five minutes ago." Spirit exhaled noisily like he was seconds from blowing his cool. No one wanted that to happen. Spirit may have been shorter than Tommy, but he had iron-pumped arms and metal-spiked rings on his knuckles. He also had a frightening tat on his neck, midnight black Hitler youth-cut hair, and an *I'm-a-badass* attitude. At the band's insistence, and lucky for Tommy, Spirit had been working on controlling his temper. He started again, calmer than before. "I don't want to rush in and start performing without doing a final sound check, you know?"

"All right, all right. Get your knickers out of your fanny. I'm coming." Tommy turned back to the mirror and gave himself another inspection. Damn. He should have flat ironed his hair. The messy brown mop atop his head was everywhere. "Just give me five more minutes." He started trying to tame a stray curl.

"Man, you're worse than a bitch." Spirit had had it. He stormed over to Tommy, grabbed his arm, and dragged him out of the bathroom. "Time's up."

"Heeey!" Tommy squeaked as he went along with Spirit out into the living room, out the front door, and to the mini car where the other two band members waited. Tommy snatched his arm back from Spirit and straightened his leather jacket. "Stop manhandling me, you big twat."

"I would if you'd act like a man and stop primping so much," Spirit growled as he held the driver's seat down for Tommy to climb in the back. "Your hair hasn't looked any different since I've known you. Five more minutes in front of the mirror is not going to change that."

"Since when did maintaining one's exterior become a negative thing?" Tommy squeezed into the backseat. "You said yourself we should cater to our female fan base since they generate the most buzz around male rock bands."

"What fan base?" Spirit adjusted his seat until it cramped Tommy's legs then got behind the wheel. "We won't have one if we don't make it there in time to play."

"Bitches don't care how you look as long as they think you're famous." Divine, the band's bass guitarist, imparted his personal words of wisdom.

Tommy settled in uncomfortably beside him. "Oh, yeah? This, coming from the geezer who has worn the same pair of britches for ten weeks straight and not been laid once." Tommy's nose crinkled and he shook his head to indicate he'd encountered an offensive smell. "When was the last time you even took a bath, mate?" Every male in the car broke out in laughter, with the exception of Divine. Tommy held his sleeve over his nose. Next time, he'd be sure to get dressed first so he could sit shotgun. "Think I'll pass on fashion advice and advice about bitches from you, Divine. Nothing wrong with playing well *and* looking fit while doing it." Tommy did his best to make sure no part of his body touched Divine, which proved difficult in the close confines of the mini vehicle. "That goes for smelling fresh, in case you're wondering. You should give that some thought, yeah?"

Sneers and jeers directed toward Divine about his hygiene didn't last very long as they zoomed down the road toward their first gig as a solid band. Divine traded a few verbal jabs, but none of the teasing mattered. He couldn't be shamed into cleaning himself up because he just didn't give a shit.

Next, they all ragged about how it took Tommy as long as the girliest of girls to get dressed. Switching from Divine to Tommy was like going from one extreme to the other, but Tommy didn't care what they thought of him either. There was a method to his madness. Obsessing over his looks prevented him from worrying about their first live performance. It helped calm his nerves. Displaying coolness was the rock star way. Fake it till you make it, right? The constant chatter between his mates—even at his own expense—helped to hold his bellyflies down. At least they'd invited a shitload of hot babes. No matter what, he was guaranteed to get laid tonight. He'd need to release all his pent up energy soon.

Chicks dug him.

Chicks dug rock stars even more.

Chicks dug that he rocked a guitar, and stardom would come soon enough, starting with this gig.

First, his band would rock the house then he'd be balls deep, pumping hard in some A plus pussy before the slag could shout, "We will rock you!" Maybe even two or three pussies. He had the stamina for it.

Oh, yeah. It would be smashing. He grinned.

"What the fuck you grinning about, girlie?" Savior, their lead singer, reached from the front passenger seat and popped Tommy on the forehead before getting out of the car.

They had arrived.

See—Spirit had nothing to worry about. The pub they were playing at had been in spitting distance from the house they rented.

"I'm smiling because it's a fine night out and we finally get to sample the fruits of our labor." Fruit, pussy, same thing. Tommy had never had trouble getting girls, but rock star girls were on a whole new level. They became groupies who would do anything to be with the rocker. He was ready for that side effect of being a musician. He'd been playing solo for a long time before hooking up with the band. Long enough to know he didn't just play for the sake of art or self-expression. He played for the accolades, for the recognition, for the idolization.

For chicks.

Shit-eating grin plastered on his face, he exited the vehicle and looked around before following his mates to the car boot to get his "instrument of love" from its protective case. He called it that because he would never love anything or anyone more than he loved his guitar. He only took it out when he meant business, and he never shared it. After the performance, his instrument of lust, tucked away safely in his stretchy black pants, would come out to play. He gave that instrument away freely. Every chance he got.

There was no chauffeur to open the door or valet to park the car. No line wrapped around the building with eager fans. No red carpet to pad their journey up the gravel walkway. And once they went inside, there was no wall-to-wall, standing-room-only crowd. Instead, a quaint and cozy atmosphere greeted them. Smooth jazz filled the room as diners spoke intimately with their dates. Bar seats were full. Most of the tables were taken. It wouldn't have impressed U2, but the scene was nice for a local, newly-formed band to make their musical debut.

Tommy looked around to see if he recognized any of the customers as his hand-picked invitees. That would make his selection process even easier after the show. Spirit stopped abruptly, causing Tommy to run right into his back.

"I told y'all to be here at eight o'clock. Not eight oh five. Not eight ten. And I damn sho' ain't say eight thirty." Uh oh. The pub owner sounded irate. Even the bald spot on the back of his head was red with anger.

Spirit held his hands up. "Hold on now, Mr. Steely—"

"Here I was doing you a favor. This is a jazz

cabaret. I don't even play that head banging noise in my establishment. I made an exception for you."

"And we appreciate that. What had happened was—"

"I have a reliable jazz band coming on at nine-thirty. They need to start setting up at nine." Mr. Steely put a hand on Spirit's shoulder. "Sorry, kid. Maybe next time." He turned towards a muscle man standing near the entrance and waved him over. "Security!"

"But Mr. Steely…" Spirit didn't seem alarmed yet. He was still in reasonable discussion mode.

Tommy ducked away and headed towards the stage. Spirit could handle the pub owner. He was not only the more business minded of the group, he'd been the one to secure the venue. Businesses weren't hurting for talent to showcase. Getting this gig had taken months of begging. After all that hard work, they hadn't come all this way to get thrown out with their tails tucked between their legs. Not before they had a chance to wow the audience. They came to play and that's what they were going to do.

Tommy ignored the bouncers approaching the stage. He hooked up his electric guitar into the equipment onstage, took a deep breath, and hit the first chord. The room stilled.

Now that he had everyone's attention, he struck another chord and another, adjusting his system as necessary. Customers started shifting their bodies toward the stage from where they sat. He plucked a few more harmonious keys until Mr. Steely held up a hand to stave off his goonies from throwing the band out. They were just warm up chords that told Tommy his guitar was tuned just right. If he'd expected some immediate cheering from the audience, well, that was just not going to happen. The deadpan look on their faces indicated they'd need a bucket of lava dumped on their heads to warm them up. He adjusted the amp volume and struck another chord, intending to wake their arses up. At least, Tommy's notes had unfrozen Mr. Steely, who started nodding his head at Spirit.

Mr. Steely walked towards the stage. Tommy kept hitting notes. "Fine. Play. But you no longer have a full hour," Mr. Steely shouted. "You have the remainder of the hour. Once time is up, it's up!" He was being a twat, but he'd made a concession. That was something.

Spirit rushed onstage, staring Tommy down with a fumy death eye. His body language spoke loudly of his thoughts: if Tommy had dressed a little sooner, they wouldn't be in this mess. Tommy was to blame.

Tommy thought it was best not to joke about their predicament since he liked to keep his ballsack. Attached to his body, preferably. "Uh…sorry, mate."

"Fuck off, Tommy."

"Uh uh uh. I'm onstage with my guitar in hand." He plucked a particularly impressive succession of notes and reared back on his heels. "Which means you can't call me Tommy right now." They had all agreed to call each other by their stage names while onstage. In fact, that's why he always called them by their stage names. Much easier to remember that way.

It looked an awful lot like Spirit was about to throw a drumstick at him.

"Testing, testing." Savior's voice echoed too loud and too grainy through the speakers at that moment. He didn't have time to get it perfect. "Ladies and gentlemen, thank you for coming tonight and welcoming our band, Holy Nesters! Who in here loves rock-n-roll?"

Customers returned to eating and drinking and waffling on like they hadn't heard a thing. Others actually got up to leave, meaning rock wasn't their favorite genre...and there would be fewer chicks for Tommy to seduce later.

Best to start playing for real then.

Tommy strummed a few notes of one of their original songs and hit a few chords that signaled Savior's intro. Savior couldn't begin singing yet because he still had to fiddle with equipment. A few ear piercing streaks when his microphone got too close to a speaker saw the backs of other customers' heads as they made haste out the door. Tommy ignored the open disregard for his band, especially since it made room for more people to enter the pub. He even noticed some girls he had spoken to earlier that day come in and stand near the stage. The ginger one smiled at him...and rose to number one on his list of potentials for tonight. Encouraged, he transitioned back to the beginning of the song, hoping the rest of his band would catch up as they could. The sands of their hourglass were running out on their time onstage.

Savior stood next to Tommy, holding a microphone between them while he began singing in his usual drop-your-knickers voice. Tommy closed his eyes and accompanied that voice through the band's favorite song. At that moment, he didn't care if none of the other band members could join in. He and Savior together were pure holiness.

Spirit's drums gradually entered, and it seemed planned. When the beat dropped, the rhythm took over, and before Tommy knew it, he'd tuned the world out around him. Nothing mattered but his guitar, the music, and what they both did to his soul. He felt it from way down deep, boiling up and pouring out into his fingertips. And while he played, he knew nothing meant more than this very moment. Every moment he held the guitar in his hands were magical and the best moments of his life. This proved to be another one of those glorious, spiritual moments when he wasn't just a pretty face and a great lay with great one-liners. He was music personified.

He threw his head back and let his fingers work as they'd been intended.

Then he heard it.

It.

That note.

What the fuck was that?

It was off. Wrong. Ugly. An ear sore. Anything but magic.

It wasn't Spirit's drums or Savior's voice. It was a guitar. Not his. It was coming from Divine, the bass guitarist. He was fucking killing it. And not in a grand way. In the worst way possible. It caused Tommy to lose his focus, his magic. He got off, and not in a good way either. He started hitting notes to match the bad notes in his ear instead of the melody in his heart.

Fuck it to hell. The band was supposed to join in with him and play the piece they'd been practicing, the piece Savior had written, not create some bullshit while they were onstage. In front of so many potential fans. In the midst of their first gig. The gig Spirit had taken weeks to secure.

Tommy opened his eyes once he felt the warm, wet, soft particle hit his face. A French fry. Great.

Another hit his shoes. Another and another hit the stage around him, until he realized he was not in the middle of some freak storm dropping manna from Heaven, but having the equivalent of rotten tomatoes being thrown at him.

No, no, no. This was not how it was supposed to go. This performance was supposed to make them stars.

Tommy, being a glass half full kind of lad, took notice that people had left the bar and their tables and had come closer to boo and throw things. Since the area surrounding the stage was full of bodies, it hadn't degenerated into a total fail yet. He had to do something to shake things up and turn the bad around. Quickly.

After unstrapping his guitar and laying it at his feet, he dropped his jacket on the floor next to it. He pulled his light gray t-shirt over his head and began swinging it around to Spirit's drumbeat. Whether the crowd was laughing with or at him didn't matter. He'd gotten a rise out of them. Any attention was better than none. And this attention was better than having food thrown at them. So he twirled the shirt in the air, grinning as he did so, since no one could resist his smile. After that short break, he hoped to be ready to find his magic again. He picked his instrument of love back up and began hitting...more bad notes.

Damn. He just couldn't get right.

Without provocation, one of the cuties he'd met earlier hopped onstage and took off her shirt, exposing a lacy red bra. She tossed her stringy blond hair off her shoulders and started gyrating to the music—if it could still be called that. Tommy couldn't remember her name, but he was grateful for her participation. It took some of the heat off them.

He wondered where her hot friend was. The mute.

One by one Savior, Divine, and Spirit rid themselves of their shirts as well. A wave of ahhs hit the stage when Spirit unveiled the results of hours spent in the gym. Sure, the scene had turned into a circus act, with more focus placed on their bodies than on their music. With the way they had sounded, that was a blessing in disguise. At least it was a fun circus where the boos had turned to whistles and laughter. Holy Nesters would be talked about around town. They would not be soon forgotten.

It was great craic.

Feeling buzzed from the pub's high energy, Tommy picked that moment to stop playing and dive backwards into the audience to body surf. It was a miscalculation on his part, however. The sea of people standing around the stage divided and he landed on his head on the floor.

The music didn't stop. Spirit continued to bang on his drums. Savior continued to sing. Divine continued to strum his guitar. And they actually sounded well good. They hadn't even noticed he was missing from the stage.

Wankers.

Maybe this band thing was a terrible idea. He couldn't believe he'd landed on his head. That didn't happen to rock stars. Ever. Elvis was mooning them in his grave.

But if Tommy hadn't landed that way, he wouldn't have looked up and seen her.

It was her. Extending a hand to help him up.

She'd taken her hair out of the braids she wore earlier, and it stood out like an adorable corkscrew curly mop like his. She was adorable. With her lips pursed to hide a smile, her dimples were pronounced, her brown eyes mischievous. The implication that she was probably laughing at him underneath all that cute should have grated his ego, but it made him curious instead. How could she be so shy earlier in the day yet so approachable now?

He rubbed the spot on the back of his head. Approachable? Jump to conclusions much there, Tommy? She just was a kind person, willing to help a raging lunatic from the floor. After being the only one to care that he'd gotten there.

He took her hand and stood. "You came." And there he was stating the obvious, well, shouting it over the music. "I mean, you managed to change your old lady plans for the night. I'm honored."

"I wanted to know the name your groupies shouted." She let go of his hand and looked downward. He was certain she was trying to suppress a laugh. "You could have just told us it was Boooooo."

He smiled despite being the butt of the joke. "Ah. She speaks. After the way I stunned you with my hotness earlier, I didn't think you'd be able to speak around me, let alone hold a full conversation."

She could no longer hide her laughter, and the way her face lit up, warmed him way down to the pit of his exposed abs. "It's difficult to be stunned around a guy you just watched bust his ass and make a fool of himself."

Haha…and ouch. "That hurt worse than my fall."

"Cocky thing like you, I'm sure you'll recover quickly." She looked around. "So…I sure hope your grandma didn't Skype in for this. And if she did, hopefully, she has other grandchildren to make her proud, because you…your band…well…" She just let her thought trail off.

Funny girl. He liked…and despised that. With a passion. He was the jokester. No one would out-joke him. Except she'd done nothing as utterly ridiculous as he had tonight. First, the horrible playing. Then the strip show. Then his disagreement with the floor. He'd never live this down. "Nah. Mamó's dead. She died while body surfing at a rock concert several years ago."

Well, that wiped the smile off her awfully cute face. "I'm sorry."

He debated dragging the lie out a bit, juicing it for comedy a while longer. Then he realized they didn't have that kind of time. Mr. Steely was heading toward them, the general direction of the stage. Another group holding instruments walked closely behind him. Holy Nesters' five minutes of fame were up.

Tommy bumped her cheek with the knuckle of his index finger. "I'm just fucking with you. I mean, she's really dead, and she'd probably shoot me the finger if she would have heard or seen this performance tonight," he shook his head, "but she died from a heart attack. My brother and I pulled a prank on her and it didn't sit too well with her heart condition."

Her hand covered her mouth in horror. "Oh, God. I'm so sorry."

Wait. This wasn't coming out right.

Never mind.

Tommy looked up to see Spirit tousling with another guy holding drumsticks. Spirit wasn't ready to stop playing. The other band's drummer was ready to physically dismount Spirit from behind the drum. Oh, no. If Spirit was the Hulk, he'd be turning green right now.

And there went the first punch.

And the music ended.

It was replaced with shouting, bodies flying, and complete chaos.

Tommy watched as the stringy blond chick lifted the underwire of her bra and flashed the whole room from the stage. "Hey, isn't that your roommate up there?" Nice rack. He would totally hit it.

"Yeah. Sasha. She said she was going to do that tonight. I didn't believe her."

"I'll get you a drink if you flash yours too." He couldn't help eyeballing her covered chest as he said it. Forget the blond.

"I don't drink."

He leaned down closer to her ear so only she could hear. "We need to change that starting right now."

"I have to work in the morning." Her voice showed an edginess that hadn't been there.

"So? Lots of people go to work wasted or hungover."

"Not me. I have to study while I work. Besides, it takes more than a drink to see my boobs."

"I'll kiss a guy," he ducked a bottle soaring through the air, "if you flash your boobies."

"Why would I care about that?"

"Because I'm not gay. And you like seeing me make an arse of myself."

She smirked. "Okay. You're on."

"You first."

"Do I look like I was born yesterday?" She cocked an eyebrow. "You're first, and I get to pick the guy."

Shit. Were her boobs worth all this? He looked down at the cleavage peeping out of her black leather jacket and back up to her puffy lips and brown eyes.

Time to man-up. "Let's get on with it then. Which one?"

She pointed.

Tommy looked out of the corner of his eyes at the fella approaching him then back to her for reconsideration. *I mean, come on.*

She cupped her boobs through her jacket to remind him of the stakes. Tommy took a deep breath before turning to the Hercules clone standing next to him, who just so happened to be sporting a black SECURITY t-shirt, and kissed him square on the lips. He immediately ducked to the floor and slid through the bouncer's bowlegs to escape the impending blow.

Tommy was a lover, not a fighter…who was about to get his arse kicked in here thanks to her. But it was all worth it. When he emerged a few feet away, the cute curly-haired girl ran over to him. She lifted her blouse and flashed a pair of breasts that made him bite his bottom lip. Hard.

Those big brown nipples.

I'm fucking her tonight.

"Out! You, you, you, and you, all of you out right now." Mr. Steely pointed to each of Tommy's former band members while two of his bouncers held each of Spirit's arms. "I want you and your band gone. Don't ever come back."

Tommy dropped to the floor and scoured through French fries and broken glass for his t-shirt and jacket. It was also a great place to avoid the bouncer's swinging reach, except Tommy didn't see his clothes before the bouncer caught up to him. Probably best to run for it while he still had pants and legs.

He rose from his knees and grabbed his instrument of love and her hand. "Hey, let's get out of here!" He took off running with her fingers entwined in his. They were nearly out the door before he decided to double back. Tommy ran up to the bar and grabbed two bottles of something that would get him tipsy and her shitfaced then legged it out of the pub.

"Wait. Sasha's in there. She's my ride."

Throwing the guitar strap over his neck, Tommy held the bottles in one hand and grabbed her hand again with his other. "We don't need a ride. I live right around the corner." It wasn't the best place for a lady, but it would get him some more time with her tonight. A good hour would be all he needed.

Even though she ran with him to the alley, she stopped once she realized they weren't being chased. "I can't go home with you. I have to work in the morning."

Excuses, excuses.

Tommy felt disappointed until he saw her look at their clasped hands with longing. She didn't want to leave him yet. She just needed a little convincing. "I can't promise I'll have you at work on time in the morning. I *can* promise you won't regret phoning in sick."

Her eyebrows rose and she gulped. "I need the money. I get paid by the hour."

She'd talk herself out of entering Heaven if St. Peter required her to spend a few minutes at check-in.

If he was a true rock star, he could offer to pay what she'd make tomorrow, but he wasn't. And he couldn't. He was barely making it himself. Even though he was half-tempted to lie and tell her he would anyway, he decided against that. He had to step his game up. What would convince a girl like her to come back to his place? "I'm a good cuddler. I can keep you warm on this chilly spring night." Chicks liked that affection shit.

Tommy shifted his guitar to hang on his side in order to wrap his arms around her. Bottles together in one hand, he pulled her face against his bare chest so she could feel his warmth. Actually, he was pretty cold. Frigid, even. But skin to skin contact was always a good thing when you were trying to get a girl. Eye contact, smile, and touch. Seduction 101. Tasting would be next.

"Dude, you're cold. Where's your shirt?"

"No idea." He was used to cold weather and didn't need to layer up like most Americans he'd met. He also didn't expect to be standing outside in the frigid temperature trying to convince a girl to come back home with him. And there it was. "Won't you share your jacket with me?" He pretended to shiver. "It'll be a cold walk for me to make alone. I could catch my death out here." He glanced toward the street where pub customers passed and said a silent prayer that Spirit didn't show up wagging the key to his mini car.

"How will I get back to my dorm?"

He did his best to keep his eyes on her face and not let them drift to her cleavage. "I can borrow Spirit's car later or you can call your roomie." Emphasis on *later*.

She looked at her watch, and he just knew he'd lost her. She surprised him. "Okay. I don't want you to catch a cold." She opened her jacket and wrapped her arms around him. With her warmth seeping into his body, they started walking in the direction of his house. "But only for an hour. I need to get to bed so I can get up in the morning."

He smirked. "Sure, sure." He'd make sure she was in bed, all right. He leaned his head on hers and got as close as he could to her while maintaining a brisk walk and balancing his guitar and bottles. Any sign of a ride right now from Spirit or Sasha would completely derail his less than pure plans. "By the way, what was your name again?"

"Capri."

"Capri, I meant to tell you—you've got one beautiful set of tits."

He felt her smile on his arm. He felt like high-fiving himself.

"You kissing that security guy?"

He cringed. "Yeah, what about it?"

"That was funny as hell. You should have let him punch you. That would have been even funnier." Her body shook as she giggled.

Next time he would. He'd do anything to make her laugh. The sound of it on her lips was simply sin. In fact, if she wanted to see him get beat up, she'd get that chance real soon. Once Spirit got ahold of Tommy later, Capri could get her fucking hysterics on, and maybe Tommy wouldn't mind his arse-whipping so much.

CHAPTER 3

Capri took one of the bottles from Tommy and tucked it under her shirt as much as possible to avoid attention from law enforcement. They loved catching people leaving the club, and they weren't too fond of teenagers carrying alcoholic beverages for some reason. She could join the military and kill a man with a gun right now with no problem. But getting caught with booze would land her in the slammer. She had yet to figure out the logic behind that one.

Tommy concealed the other evidence of larceny next to his body, using his guitar as covering. They walked clumsily underneath her jacket, leaning on each other with his arm draped across her shoulder, her arm around his waist. As his guitar routinely bumped into her, Capri was too engulfed in his embrace to care. Plus, he kept talking, like someone who didn't know how to turn himself off. Tommy liked hearing the sound of his own voice, which happened to work out perfectly for her. The way he spoke was nothing short of ear porn. The way words rolled off his lips like musical lyrics sent chills through her body that had nothing to do with the cool evening breeze. She'd discovered the titillation power of the Irish accent from watching the movie *The Commitments*, and it had stuck with her ever since.

Capri had been sitting at a corner table in the bar when Tommy's band had arrived, so she knew he hadn't been onstage long. Still, it had been long enough for him to work up a faint sweat. His damp hair and skin should have turned her off due to it being a stranger's body fluid and all, but she found it…arousing. The skill and passion he put into playing his guitar until he perspired epitomized hotness. It helped that his scent was pleasant too. Not too overwhelming. Prevalent enough to make her curious about how he tasted. Then there was their close proximity, the brushing of his hip against hers, the rise and fall of his chest. Her sexual awareness had heightened, and nearly all of her senses were engaged. With so many factors influencing her attraction to him, Capri couldn't put her finger on any one particular thing that sealed her fate for tonight. She had no doubts about what she was going to do when they got to his house though.

She gripped his torso tighter. They needed to be as close as possible under her jacket so he wouldn't be too cold. Yeah, of course, that was her only reason. Kindness, altruism…

He looked down at her face and smiled.

It was his smile that did it.

She looked in his eyes and smiled back.

No. Definitely his eyes.

Regardless, Capri had made her mind up about what would transpire between them. She'd have sex with him, plain and simple, sans emotion or commitment. To ensure she remained casual about the intimate act, she wouldn't even kiss him. It didn't matter that his olfactory cues indicated he probably tasted sweet like honeydew. She couldn't risk an attachment to Tommy. Afterward, she'd go home, go to sleep, go to work in the morning, and carry on like nothing ever happened…except hopefully, she'd feel like a real woman.

She could do this. She would. "So…you're Irish, right?"

That launched him into another sexy monologue.

Fine by Capri.

Sasha may have been the free-spirited one, but Capri operated on logic. Logically speaking, hooking up with Tommy tonight made sense. What Capri planned to do with him had nothing to do with female liberation or some bullshit like that, though she did feel liberated enough to make her own decisions without checking them against social norms. But really. Capri's plans revolved around one simple, undeniable fact: she wanted him, and she couldn't say that about any other man on the face of the earth. He was the one she'd been waiting for.

To pop her cherry, that is…because Capri had no time for a permanent guy in her life.

She glanced at her wristwatch while he described his home in Ireland. He'd come here to enroll in the university because that was the only way his parents would pay for his trip to America. His goal had always been to play music, not get a degree, so he wasn't particularly upset about being on academic probation and not graduating on time. Truth be told, he *wanted* more time here because he had no intention of returning home until after he made it big. Bon Jovi big.

All of it sounded lovely. She appreciated ambition as much as the next person, but shit. How much further did they have to walk? He'd made it seem like he lived only a couple of blocks away. Here they were, a lifetime or so later, walking on a busy sidewalk in a non-residential area. Perhaps that detour through the alley hadn't been a shortcut at all but a way of hiding from his band and her roommate as they drove by.

Umhm. Tommy thought he was slick.

Capri was on to him and his unnecessary seduction tactics. Getting Capri on her back required no effort on his part, but he didn't know that for certain. From his perspective, this long walk gave them some alone time. Some time to woo his latest target, to soften her up for his upcoming advances. Considering he could be with any girl he wanted right now, Capri found his attention flattering. However, she didn't have all night to lollygag about the city with him plotting how to get in her drawers.

She sighed in irritation. How much of a whore would she be if she just asked him to take her up against the wall of one of these stores? *Let's just get it over with already.*

"...and that's my story. I've traded lush greenery for traffic jams and smog, but America's a sound place to be. It's where I'm going to get rich and famous." Tommy pulled the jacket tighter around her shoulder. "You all right? I know this isn't the night you envisioned, walking home in the cold with a shirtless stranger after the most embarrassing moment of his life. You can hop on my back and I'll carry you, if it'll make it better. I'm stronger than I look."

As hot as he was, he looked about as strong as a grasshopper. She shook her head. "I'm fine." Except his thoughtfulness did nothing to ease her agitation. She didn't want to get to know his sensitive side for the same reason she didn't want to kiss him.

Walking home with someone she'd basically just met should have been scary. It would have been for most girls, she imagined. But present sexual frustration notwithstanding, Tommy put her at ease. If a car full of thieves and rapists drove up next to them, he'd get his skinny ass kicked. At least she felt comfortably certain that *he* was no thief or rapist. He didn't pose a threat to her safety, though her virtue was in serious danger.

He looked down at her again. "I've done all the talking. Penny for your thoughts."

Damn his face was close.

That accent though. "Thoughts" sounded like "taughts"…and the word had never sounded hotter.

Uh…

No. She would not lock up again. She would not start sounding unintelligible like she belonged in a *Beavis and Butt-head* episode. She just needed a second to get her "taughts" together.

He cocked an eyebrow. "Thinking that hard about shagging me, eh?" He smiled, and she melted. "Unless you tell me what you were really thinking, I'll be forced to assume I'm correct…and that would inflate my ego to monstrous proportions."

Like any more inflation was possible. "You're used to that aren't you?"

"What?"

"Smiling and getting your way."

He shrugged. "Maybe. If that doesn't work on you, I have a stare that might. I've been told my eyes will make any bird drop her knickers. Imagine what else it could make you do." He narrowed his gaze to smoldering levels.

She laughed because he'd made a joke out of absolute truth. "And you have no shame."

"None a'tall." He squeezed her shoulder. "So tell me what you were thinking and you won't have to know the full weight of my eyes." His long lashes fluttered vehemently. "I will spare you the devastating effects of my weapons of mass destruction."

Good thing she didn't have to play coy about her intentions. And good thing she knew Tommy's expectations. Guys like him didn't invite girls over to his house for a chat and latte on a Friday evening. There was nothing wrong with letting him know they were on the same page. Maybe it would cut down on some of the games and bullshit, and most importantly—time. "Okay, you got me."

"No, really. Tell me," he whined. "I want to know what's on your mind. You intrigue me."

She stopped walking, forcing him to stop too. "That's *really* what I was thinking. In fact…" Capri looked around at their surroundings, "I was wondering if there was a nice, comfortable spot for us to get it on now."

His brows furrowed as he stared at her. It was his turn to be stunned silent.

Now that her point had been made, she started walking again, dragging a perplexed Tommy with her. "Now what are *you* thinking?" she asked.

"Truth is—I can't tell if you're winding me up. 'Cause if you are, that's a shitty thing to do to a man who's seen your boobs." He licked his bottom lip. "If you're not, I'm not used to a girl being open and honest about her thoughts, so I don't know what to make of that either."

"You'll have to wait and see then, won't you?" She sure hoped he wasn't one of those guys who took forever to orgasm. Sasha had told her about those guys who screwed like they had something to prove. "How's your head from that Olympic backflip you did earlier?" She used that as an opportunity to touch his soft, thick curls, easing her fingertips through his mane to the knot on the back of his head. Thinking of how she'd love to hold on tight to a handful of it while he penetrated her caused her to remain in his hair way beyond an appropriate check for injuries. "Maybe you should get that looked at." She reluctantly let go.

"No. My head is made of steel, as my mum always says." He tucked Capri's arm back around his cool, slim waist. "Now, let's get back to what you were thinking. I want to know more. Like…" Tommy looked around and pointed at a building. "Are you a do-it-up-against-a-brick-wall kind of girl or…" he pointed to an empty parallel-parked car, "a break-into-someone's-car-and-shag-in-the-backseat kind of girl?"

Actually, she was neither. Yet. "I've never done anything like that." She noted the hopeful look on his face. "I'm not opposed to it though. You into that sort of thing? Doing it in public places?"

His eyes twinkled. "Fuck yeah."

"Which do you prefer? Brick wall or empty car?"

"I have no clue. I haven't experienced it yet either. Girls have too many restrictions. They're afraid of getting caught or that beetles and sand will get in their twats or comets will fall from the sky and crush them for fucking somewhere other than a bed. Spontaneity is the spice of life. Nothing more sensual than going with the flow and being adventurous."

Wasn't variety the spice of life? It was one thing to have sex as the mood struck and another to chance serious consequences associated with it. "Sounds more like you enjoy living on the edge. Danger excites you not spontaneity."

He looked as if he needed to think about it a moment. "It's a wee bit of both, I suppose."

Capri glanced in the back of another parked car as they passed. Could she be that reckless?

She wouldn't have to test her limits tonight, since it was at that moment they began walking up a driveway, presumably the one to his house.

"This is me." He looked annoyed at the car in the driveway. "Looks like my housemates made it back before us."

A bummer, yes, but not unexpected. "Driving's usually a faster mode of transportation in this country than walking." She hid her smile, not her sarcasm. "Were you expecting them to go somewhere other than home?"

"No. I knew they'd be here. I'm just mentally preparing myself for Spirit's wrath."

"Which one is that?"

"The beefy drummer with all the ink."

"Yikes. How'd you manage to piss off the alpha male of the band?" Spirit looked like someone that didn't take any shit.

Tommy explained how he hadn't done the band any favors tonight by taking his time getting dressed. "Let's just say—it may get intense. I've decided to quit the band. They won't like that, but I'm better off by myself. Once I get that out of the way, you and I will get to know each other better."

"You shouldn't quit the band. The name Holy Nesters has to go, but you guys—" Wait. Thinking of the last part Tommy said, Capri stopped midway up the steps to his house. She had to address this now. "Just so we're clear—I'm cool with how much we know each other already. I don't need a three-month courtship complete with flowers and pretentious wooing. I don't need to go through all the bases to prove to myself and you that I can hold out for the big payday of a serious commitment. I don't have time for all that. My motive is simple: sex. All I need for that is you, opportunity—which we now have— and…maybe some liquid courage."

His eyebrows rose as he whistled once. "You don't mess around. Very direct. I fancy that." Tommy nodded his approval. "So you were just taking a piss earlier when you said you didn't drink?"

"I don't usually take the time to drink would have been a more accurate statement." Capri didn't take the time to do much that didn't directly further her goals. She had nothing against libations. In fact, she'd have a whole lot if that's what it took to still her nerves. She may have been calm on the outside, but her insides were a wreck now that they were at his house, mere steps from his bed, where she'd actually have to put her plans into action.

They walked up the rest of the steps. She could hear music coming from inside.

Tommy stopped, swinging the guitar to his side, and pulled Capri around until she stood directly in front of him pressed against his chest. He was no longer under her jacket, and she felt the loss of his skin as if a layer of hers had been removed. Twisting off the top, Tommy turned the bottle he'd been holding up to his lips and started guzzling. His head tilted so he could maintain eye contact with her, and he didn't move again until the bottle was empty. It only took a few seconds. He twisted the top back on then grabbed the bottle she'd been sheltering. He twisted the top off and held it to her lips, watching them with an intensity that screamed lust as she sipped from it.

He cleared his throat. "I'm twenty years of age. We all have fake IDs that say we're twenty-one in order to play in pubs. I see the stamp on your hand. How old are you? Eighteen? Nineteen?"

"Eighteen." She sipped some more. It didn't taste as bad as she thought it would. Way better than beer.

"Good ol' underage drinking," he smirked. "Always good to have something worth rebelling against. This is year numero uno for you?"

She nodded even though he was totally ignoring her speech about not wanting to get to know each other.

"What's your major? All that studying, you must be premed or prelaw."

"I want a doctorate, but not in medicine or law."

He continued watching her lips on the bottle as silence fell between them. Maybe this was a good time to warn him about it being her first time. She'd need him to be gentle. Patient. Skilled. And not squeamish about blood.

He bit his bottom lip. "So you're going to spend all those boring years in university? You'll go to bed early and alone, then get up early and work all day just to graduate and live that worker bee lifestyle permanently. The American Dream, yeah? That's no dream to me."

"Not all of us can be the next Bono. We don't all have your gift."

He smiled, seeming to enjoy the praise. Duh.

She needed to steer him back to why she happened to be standing on his porch. Time was ticking. Perhaps she should flash her boobs again before he asked more get-to-know-you questions.

His voice was low when he spoke again. "What are you thinking about?"

She swallowed the lump in her throat. "I was thinking I haven't had anal sex…yet." That should do it.

His bushy eyebrows rose, but he was otherwise silent. Was he shocked, disappointed…challenged?

She sipped from the bottle as they stared at each other. Not the worst way to kill sleeping time.

He wrapped his hand around hers on the bottle and raised it to his lips for a sip then raised it to her lips. It was the closest their lips had been all night, and that thought didn't escape either of them.

"Any special requests for where I should provoke Spirit to hit me?"

"No, I don't want you to get beat up. I need you at your optimum performance. Maybe I can talk to him while you…go get ready." She smiled then sipped. *That's right. Keep it flirty. None of that heart-to-heart bullshit.*

"Bollocks." His tongue swiped his bottom lip. "You keep talking like that and we're not going to make it inside." Tommy gave her The Stare, and oh, what a weapon it proved to be. His eyes moved to her lips again. Hers moved to his, watching his lips move closer to her lips.

Fuck. Nerves leapt into her throat. She felt

panicky. They were close. Then closer. He was going to kiss her.

She hadn't prepared to have her first kiss outside his door, like right now. Her heart started beating out of her chest in anticipation. His lips beckoned to her so strongly, like they were magnetized against resistance. But Capri was a girl of strength and willpower, who had already decided locking lips with him wouldn't be a good idea. She didn't need to kiss him to have sex. This was just another of his seduction moves, a trick to break her down. She wanted to give in, but her instincts said no. Not kissing Tommy would help her compartmentalize the sexual experience in her head. Unless she wanted to become Tommy's naïve conquest instead of a girl in charge of her own destiny, she had to remember that.

Capri moved as if to place an arm around his neck. Not to hug him or draw him the rest of the way to her lips. She looked at the time on her watch instead.

Tommy stopped within inches of her face. "Did you just peek at your watch?" he asked in a low voice. "You did. You totally just looked at your timepiece." He moved away. "Am I that boring? Should I wear a Spidey costume, dangle from the roof, and attempt a snog upside down?"

She shook her head. "You know I'm on a time crunch."

"Right. You've got to work in the morning. Will you be timing me when I'm inside you too?"

She laughed in spite of the tingle that landed low in her body. "I hadn't planned on it but...that's not a bad idea."

"All right," he smiled. "That can be the second thing you brag to all your girlfriends about, my sexual prowess. Prepare yourself for marathon sex, me vixen."

Oh, brother. "What's the first thing?" She sipped again.

"My instrument of lust is ten inches."

Jesus. Liquor sprayed out of her mouth before she had a chance to swallow, landing all over his chest.

He threw his head back and laughed.

Perhaps she shouldn't have skipped the frat party to see his band play after all. "I think I better go." No way would her first time be with someone that big. He was too thin and too white for her to have guessed it. *So much for Sasha's theories on determining penis size.* Capri turned to leave the porch.

Tommy grabbed her arm and spun her around tight to his chest again. "Hey, you said you were going to sort it out with Spirit on my behalf to save my arse. That sounded a lot better than the alternative. We need to stick to the plan." He tugged her tighter to his bulge. His tight pants did nothing to hide his excitement. "Besides, we have that opportunity for sex you spoke so openly about…and you still don't know my stage name. I have roughly…" he glanced at her wrist, "forty-five minutes left to show you how I earned it."

His face was barely an inch from hers, but he didn't bridge the gap between them. He waited for her to acquiesce, to get her head back in the game. Any other time she wouldn't have appreciated being overtaken, but her resolve to leave had been shaken. She'd felt the pull of his seduction in every move he'd made. The way he'd exerted himself and grabbed her had made her pussy clench in response.

What had she gotten herself into? "Okay," she

nodded.

His lips grazed across hers light as a feather. "Okay then," he whispered. He let her go and turned the doorknob. The door opened to a well-lit, well-trashed living room full of half-naked people.

CHAPTER 4

Tommy had never considered himself an upstanding lad. He was closer to a shithead to be honest, but that didn't make him gloat in the fact he was about to shag this beautiful young lady. Capri may have talked a pile of shite about anal sex and getting plowed up against walls, but Tommy didn't buy her cavalier attitude for one minute.

Sure, like most humans of the female persuasion, Capri responded to him sexually. He had noticed her shallow breaths when he held her, and her extra hard swallowing when he stared into her pools of deep brown. Her attraction to him could have been because she fancied guitarists. It could have been about his gorgeous bouffant hair and dazzling eyes that other ladies seemed to fancy. It could have been all of the above…or if he was lucky, just his crude sense of humor. Either way, whether she wanted him or not wasn't the question.

Capri had turned a bit green when he'd mentioned his cock size. Since Tommy had never measured himself, he couldn't be certain of anything except that ten inches was more than likely…a tiny exaggeration.

That was beside the point. What woman hot in the knickers for him and in to casual sex would be all googoo-eyed over him playing the guitar one minute, put her hands in his hair and stare into his eyes the next, then be scared to death at the mention of his actual cock? None. That's how many. Any slag wanting a good hard bob would be overjoyed at the mention of a massive cock, not terrified.

Was she *ready* for him? That was the question.

And Tommy bloody well knew the answer. Hooking up casually was not the sort of thing Capri did much of, if ever. Tommy could bet a game of pool billiards on it, even if he was down to a broken cue stick. Capri wasn't as scrubby as her roommate, and for some strange reason, he didn't mind. As horny as he was, he'd have to take it slow with this one. But not so slow that Capri and her watch ran off like a princess's carriage turning into a pumpkin at the stroke of midnight. He needed just enough time to make her proper ready. Considering her time constraints, convincing Capri that it would take longer than forty-five minutes to ready her saddle for his horse would be a major challenge. More of a challenge than just laying her down and ramming himself in.

The visual that came to mind at that moment made blood rush to his cock.

Time to get this bullshit with his former band over with so he could move on to sexy things. Ramming things and such.

Tommy held Capri's hand as he entered the noisy scene at his house. He hadn't intended the gesture to stake his claim; he just enjoyed touching her. He supposed letting his mates know to keep their grubby paws to themselves worked too. He certainly didn't have time to warm Capri up to the idea of being shared.

The party scene occurred nightly at their residence. What else were they going to do in between rejections from local pub owners? Study? Christ no. All of them took bullshit courses and none of them were enrolled for more than nine hours anyway. At least they used the parties to practice songs when the mood struck…and before the guards came to enforce the noise ordinance. A bunch of red-blooded, artsy males with time, creativity, and testosterone on their hands—it was a wonder they ever did anything more than throw parties. The parties weren't orgies, per se, but sometimes fucking went on. Sometimes the fucking involved people that didn't intend to fuck each other but got carried away in the moment. Well… Tommy looked around at all the tits and arse. Lots of fucking went on. Lots of boozing. Lots of music playing. Even more fucking. Maybe the parties were orgies.

He shouldn't have brought her here.

Tommy looked back at Capri and almost told her she should call her roommate to pick her up. He stopped short when Capri took a long drink from her bottle and smiled.

All right then. Who was he to deny her the pleasure of his company?

Tommy closed the front door and led her further inside as they adjusted to the warm environment.

"If it ain't the motherfucker that screwed us out of our first real gig," Spirit, wearing only underpants and chest hair, shouted over the music from the couch by the window. He reached over one of the girls on his lap and turned the stereo volume down.

Tommy set his guitar down by the door and laid Capri's jacket over it before answering. "*Real* gig? You call that a real gig?"

"First, only...whatever you want to call it. You screwed us. That's the bottom line." Spirit eyed Capri from head to toe then narrowed his glossy eyes on Tommy again. "I hope you're happy with yourself, playa. All that primping may have scored you a hot girl, but you could have had hundreds if you had proven how much better your bitch ass can play than how good you can look."

The girls sitting on each of Spirit's thighs snickered.

Hadn't Tommy already shagged the ginger with the big knockers? While that made a solid argument for why Spirit didn't need to lecture Tommy on getting laid, there was no need to mention it. Tommy couldn't even remember the bird's name...and it looked like Spirit had been drinking tons already. Plastered hotheads did not need extra provocation. "*Last* is more fitting, because I won't be playing with you fucktards again."

Capri exhaled noisily prompting everyone to look in her direction. "Guys, it was just one bad performance. You'll do better next time. You have to get used to playing together under pressure."

"Nobody's worried about Tommy quitting," Divine said from his usual spot on the floor in the far corner. He never participated in the party action. He also never missed an opportunity to watch. "He says the same thing after every practice."

"Ohhhh," Tommy wagged his finger, "but I mean it this time." He meant it every time, dammit.

"And you…" Spirit pointed his empty shot glass at Capri, "…your roommate was looking for you. She said you were really smart, valedictorian of your high school class. But you can't be that smart to leave with a stranger without letting your girl know where you're going." Spirit's eyes flickered to Tommy as he shook his head and cranked a thumb in Tommy's direction. "Especially leaving with this pervert."

Tommy couldn't argue with the pervert part, but saying Capri wasn't smart? "Fuck off, Spirit. If you would have gotten us on with a legitimate rock establishment, things would have gone differently and you know it. They would have been begging us to stay."

"Well, let's see, Tommy. How many rock establishments have you booked us at?" Spirit rose to his feet, dropping the girls on their arses on the floor. They just stayed there. Wasted out of their fucking minds. Spirit's naked arm and chest muscles bounced.

Beefy motherfucking show off.

"Aw, what are you so upset about anyway? Looked like it worked out well for you. You got some drunk whores to come back with you."

"Hey. I'm not drunk," the one Tommy hadn't fucked said from the floor.

Neither of them took exception to being called whores though. Classy.

Spirit made an aggressive step toward Tommy. "What am I so upset about? Are you shitting me right now?"

"My guts are fine at the moment, but thanks for asking, yeah?" Tommy prepared himself to throw the first punch before Spirit knocked him on his arse. Punch and run, Tommy's big plan. Blocking would just get him hit with a left jab. He'd learned the hard way from running his mouth one too many times and not being able to back it up.

"Sasha's left me before. She'll understand. I don't have a cell phone, so I couldn't call her." Capri moved Tommy's hand to her chest just above her breasts to get his attention off Spirit. "Tommy's been so sweet to me so far. His pervy side is the one I came here to meet." She had Tommy's undivided attention now. "And thanks."

Spirit's eyes narrowed with curiosity. "For?"

"Saying I'm hot."

Spirit smirked.

Tommy's eyes went back and forth between them and he didn't fancy—

Grunting noises from the sofa where Savior and a girl were going at it under a blanket distracted him. "Get a room, you dick. And take Divine with you. I don't need a peeping Tom tonight. I'm the only Tom who's going to see what's in this one's knickers."

"I rather watch him anyway. You take too damn long," Divine said.

"Hey, asswipe." Spirit made a sudden move out of the corner of Tommy's eye." Here are your clothes." Spirit tossed Tommy his shirt and jacket, but it was too late. They landed on the floor.

Tommy, concerned with preventing his prized face from being damaged, struck Spirit in the nose. Some would call it a sucker punch. Tommy called it self-defense. Only he'd fucked up on the defense part. Spirit had just been handing Tommy the clothes he'd left at the pub. Tommy had mistakenly thought Spirit was about to pound him with his spiked rings.

Jesus Christ. He was going to get it now.

Spirit held his nose as blood ran down his chiseled arm. "What the fuck you do that for!"

Tommy ran around the couch Savior had made himself too fucking comfortable on. "I thought you were about to hit me."

Spirit charged around the couch at Tommy, who leapt over the couch, bounced on Savior's back and hit the floor near where Spirit had been. "Sorry man!" Tommy meant it for Spirit and Savior.

Savior emerged from the blanket looking none too happy about being disturbed.

Tommy continued running around the room, bumping into anything and anyone that stood in his way. There would be a mess to clean and damage to repair when it was all over.

"This has the potential of being incredibly emasculating," Tommy said as he ran past Capri and noticed the confusion on her face. If she was looking for a stud, he'd proven himself to be unworthy. "I'm feeling bullied and unloved here. Can't we just pretend you already pummeled me to the ground and call it even?" Tommy picked that moment to trip over a stack of books on the floor as he attempted an escape to the kitchen and out the back door.

Books? What the fuck? A nerdy traitor had infiltrated the house.

He didn't have time to analyze that, however. Spirit had caught up to him and lifted him by a handful of his hair from the floor. "Ow! Bully much?"

"Get up, punk."

"Just hit me already, you big cunt." Tommy thought about it. "Just not the face. Heavens! Not the face!"

Savior had thrown on his underpants and had come to stand next to the action. He offered no assistance. "How is that you were the last to be ready to get to the gig but first to leave it?"

"I don't mean to be rude mate, but can you wait until after my beating before asking me to come up with a witty response to that? Jesus." Tommy made a half-ass attempt at hitting Spirit in the chest and missed.

Capri put her hand on Spirit's arm, the one with a hand tangled in Tommy's hair. "Okay, okay. Tommy's a selfish dickhead who should have been ready an hour before all of you. But come on. I'm sure you already knew that. Aren't you as responsible for not dragging his ass out of here sooner?"

Everyone, including Tommy, the one she'd been defending, looked at Capri like she had swallowed squirrel cum.

"You're saying this is *our* fault?" Spirit looked incredulous.

"I'm just saying, you all know what you're dealing with. I just met him, and even I know he's the kind of guy who likes to put a little extra attention into superficiality." Capri put her hands on her hips. "Next time he'll be ready early."

"Like hell," Tommy said.

Capri glared. "Perhaps you'd like one green eye and one black one?"

"Aye," Tommy sighed. "I'll be early."

"And he's sorry he punched you," she said to Spirit, "and used your back as a trampoline," she teased Savior.

Tommy hesitated since he'd always wanted to punch Spirit…and if Savior had been humping in his own room none of this— "Aye!" he shouted when Capri thumped the back of his ear. "Sorry for hitting and stepping on the both of yous."

Spirit let him go and cracked his knuckles.

Savior went back to the couch and sat next to his companion.

And Divine lit a spliff like nothing had ever happened.

Sons of bitches.

Capri clapped her hands together. "By the way, I've been thinking about a better name for the group. It should be something with Celestial in it. The band sounded angelic before…it didn't anymore."

"What do you know about naming bands?" Spirit's bare chest muscles bounced again.

Capri's eyes followed the movement. "I know I skipped a frat party tonight to go hear yours stink up the joint."

Spirit erupted in laughter.

Tommy picked himself up from the floor and stood between them. "We should probably…you know. What time is it anyway, Capri?"

"Wow. Capri. Tommy must have really made an impression on you to change your plans from hanging out with hot college jocks to listening to our discordance. And then to walk in the cold to our house?" Spirit whistled.

"I wouldn't say discordant. Actually, you guys sounded really good…before you didn't. The band needs some work, sure, but there's obviously some talent and passion there."

"You think so?"

Tommy tried again. "I don't mean to interrupt here, but—"

"Hell yeah," Capri ignored Tommy and answered Spirit. "Who wrote the song you played? It was an original, right?"

"I did." Spirit's chin lifted with pride. "I have lots more where that came from."

"Great. I'd love to hear them sometime."

"Capri, you have to work in the morning, remember?" Tommy was not feeling the way they'd exed him out of the conversation. Spirit had ginger and what's-her-face to fuck tonight. Tommy had Capri. And with all the tension raging in his body next to the adrenaline of being chased, Tommy needed her right now.

Spirit's brows rose. "Work? Where do you work?"

"At the campus comp—"

"Yeah, yeah, yeah. You two can talk about that shit laters." Tommy grabbed Capri's arm and pulled her down the hall to his room. Then he locked the door and stood with his back to it.

They stood like that for a while, eyeing each other.

"An attention whore, yes, but I didn't peg you for the jealous, possessive guy."

"I'm not." Not usually. Tommy started walking toward her, backing Capri up until she reached his futon and couldn't go any further. Getting her to lie on it was the general idea, so hooray for being one step closer to that. "I have a confession. Nothing's gone the way I've wanted it to tonight. This…" he pointed an index finger back and forth between them, "this, I want to go right. You and me."

She gulped. "Okay." The bottle she'd been holding the whole time lifted to her lips and she drank long and hard. When she'd nearly emptied the bottle, she wiped her mouth. "I have a confession too. I'm nervous as fuck."

No shit. He loved that she spoke her mind and expressed her feelings, but… "I don't need to be Sherlock to see that."

She had practically thrown herself at him at first—no complaints from him on that, by the way—but now she looked like she was going to barf in his lap. "Relax." He smoothed hair back from her forehead. "Pegging comes later when we have more time." Perhaps he should take that bottle from her before she finished it and really killed the mood.

"Huh?"

"Nothing." Hard to ease her tension with a joke she didn't get.

Instead of explaining, he took the bottle and drank the rest of its contents. Her barfing would be bad, yes. He also couldn't have her hammered beyond her ability to consent.

Tommy sat on the futon next to where she stood and patted next to him for her to sit.

Time to make her forget all that band nonsense, and overall unmanly behavior on his part, and turn back on his charm. Once she sat, he leaned closer to her and gave his best eye seduction. "Another confession: I really want to kiss you." He touched her chin gently and turned her face toward him. "I don't just mean a peck. I mean a full-on clash of our tongues. A sword fight without the swords…or fight."

If her skin had been a wee lighter, he could have been certain of whether she'd just blushed.

Capri moved her head when he tried to close the distance between their lips. His head followed hers, and she dodged again. He sat up straight. "Are you playing hard to get or have you lost interest?" He dropped his hand from her chin. "Fuck. It's because I ran, isn't it?" He slapped his knee. "I should have known you'd think less of me if you saw me running like a bitch from drummer boy. Truth is, I've never been good at fighting. If you want," Tommy stood, "I'll go in there and call him a rat bastard motherfucker to his face. I'll stand my ground. I won't win the fight, but at least your last image won't be of me running with my tail between my legs."

She laughed. "No, no. That's not it." She pulled him back down next to her and looked away. "Confession...I've decided it's best if we don't kiss." Capri put her hand on Tommy's thigh once he frowned. "Rest assured, I still want to be objectified. The sex is still on."

Tommy frowned even more.

"Touch me," she whispered.

"Hey, I'm all for kinky, but you're throwing out mixed signals. You want me to—"

Capri grabbed his hands and shoved them under her shirt until his hands covered the bra over both of her breasts. "I said 'touch me'. Haven't you ever had sex without kissing?"

Not that he recalled. That was *the* prelude to sex or else he'd be known as an insensitive jerk and get nothing.

"I need to do this before I lose my nerve," she slurred then lifted her shirt over her head and dropped it to the floor. "Your shirt's already off so..." Capri stood again and pulled her jeans off.

Tommy sat there in awe as she shimmied out of the top layer of her garments. Finally, she sat next to him in a white bra and striped knickers looking like a sex kitten ready to lick milk from her fingertips. As a young lad still capable of getting a boner upon sight of a naked girl, he was instantly ready to plug every hole she had. Except…he wasn't supposed to kiss her. For once, he actually wanted to, and not just to warm up to sex, but just for the sake of connecting. She'd need the warm up for how he wanted to give it to her: hard and fast.

He leaned in again.

She ducked before he realized what she was doing.

"Let's stop all the bullshit," she said as she swayed toward him. The effects of her drinking had never been clearer. "You have five minutes before I need to find a way back to my dorm."

As she wished.

Tommy sank his face in her cleavage and wobbled his head around on her soft pillows. Capri was so fit, her boobs so lush. He wanted to explore her nipples. A tug here, a lick there. If the shagging went well, maybe she'd give him another chance to savor them.

Hands on both slits of material on her waist, Tommy prepared to pull her knickers down. Capri had the same thing in mind for him, however, her execution was clumsy. When she rushed to pull his zipper down, he didn't feel pleasure as one would expect a horny teen to feel. Searing pain ripped through his groin. Capri hadn't managed to get the zipper down too far, just enough to do something worse than barf in his lap. She'd gotten the backside of his cock's skin jammed in the zipper.

For the first time in all his years of dreaming about stunting like the next big rock star, Tommy wished he hadn't gone commando. That might have saved his instrument of lust from such trauma.

"Aaaaaiiiiieeee!" he screamed, doubled over, and bit his lip until he drew blood.

Capri screamed too. "Oh, God! Oh, God!" She reached for his zipper again and retracted her hands just in time before Tommy bit them off. "I'm so sorry, Tommy!"

He'd have to revel in the way she screamed out to God later. Right now, the temptation to throw her out the window was too strong. "Fuck! Fuck!" He couldn't stop screaming. He should at least thank his lucky stars he'd been hard, otherwise, she may have castrated him.

"Please let me help."

"You've done enough!" He shook off her hands wherever she touched his back, shoulders or neck in some useless way to comfort him. "If you didn't want to shag, you should have just said so."

He continued to clutch at himself and boil over in pain. It hurt too much. Not just the pain, but the mere thought that his instrument of lust could be out of commission for a while. Oh, the cruelty.

There was a knock at the door. "You all right in there?"

For the next thirty minutes, they—Tommy, Capri...and Divine—used butter, olive oil, and Vaseline to grease the zipper and scissors to cut the fabric. They were finally successful in ruining a perfectly decent pair of tight rocker pants and freeing him from the worst pain he'd ever known. It was right up there with getting his testicles crushed under a boulder, which thankfully had not happened yet.

Fuck worst *pain*. This was turning into the worst *night* of his life. Definitely the worst hookup.

Once his mates had gotten a hearty laugh at his

56

peril and left his room, he and Capri were alone again.

"Oh, my God. I'm so, so sorry. Please forgive me. Please." Capri had her apology on automatic repeat. While he literally froze his nuts off with a bag of peas. And dressed in soft cotton pajama pants. And took two Advil, peeled back the covers of the futon and got in.

"I am like the worst lay ever," she mused.

"No argument from me there."

"Technically, I can't be considered a lay since we…oh, never mind. Can I see it?"

"See what?" Tommy's voice was hoarse from screaming.

"It."

Hope wisped through his haze of pain to the possibility he could still perform if she wanted to, until he realized the absurdity of it. "Aren't you the sadistic freak, wanting to see your handiwork?"

"You said it wasn't bad enough to go to the ER. I just want to see if I agree. This is your second injury tonight. I'm worried."

He studied her face, especially those puckered lips. She could at least give him a blowjob for his trouble. Then again…nah. He didn't want to chance an erection so soon after applying Neosporin. And apparently, trying to fuck her was bad luck. "Look, but don't touch. I will not be abused by you any further tonight." He removed the ice and adjusted his underpants so she could see the damage.

His cock skin was broken but still intact. It could have been infinitely worse.

Capri cringed. "What's that?"

"What? My fucking cock?"

"Not that. That." Capri swiveled her finger to

57

indicate the area above the zigzagged red skin she was responsible for.

"Don't be a twat. Haven't you ever seen an uncircumsized cock before?" Tommy eased his underpants back up.

She shook her head. "No."

"I'll never understand Americans and their mass genital mutilations," he murmured.

"No, that's not it. I've never… Never mind." She laid her head on his shoulder and rubbed his chest with her fingertips. "I'm so sorry, Tommy. This isn't how I wanted the evening to go either." She looked up at him with those intense eyes and half-opened mouth. After a moment, she kissed the tip of his nose then laid her head back on his shoulder. "At least you'll be okay in a day or so." She seemed truly sorry and embarrassed and guilty. Which was good for her. It didn't make him feel better a'tall.

Her cuddling up next to him, closing her eyes, and going to sleep even though she still had to work in the morning, did. He didn't care that she stayed out of guilt or obligation, as long as she stayed. He needed affection more than sex now, and he'd never thought he'd feel that way.

Hopefully, he'd be ready to give her a proper fucking tomorrow.

Or a hard spanking.

CHAPTER 5

Capri slowly awakened to the feel of warm, taut skin under her cheek and draped across her arms and legs. Even though she hadn't fallen asleep in this position, she knew immediately the sweet, masculine scent and toned limbs tangled with hers belonged to Tommy. Gorgeous, funny…injured Tommy. He'd been right when he said he was a good cuddler. The best, she would imagine. Her first time sleeping next to a guy was nothing short of heaven, even if it was on a futon instead of a RoyalPedic, and even if there had been no sex. The real surprise—Tommy had held on to her like his life depended on whether he let go. Capri was no psychologist yet, but the openness and desperation associated with that gesture showed a vulnerable side to him, if not a wholly endearing one.

Capri could get used to this. Being in his arms…

Fuck. She shook her head as if someone had asked her if she wanted to be gutted and used for shark bait.

She would *not* get used to this.

Capri slid Tommy's arm from her shoulder and her leg from between both of his. She took a minute, maybe more, to watch his lashes flutter. Then she studied the perfect shape of his lips and cheekbones…and chin and eyebrows. She ran her fingers through his hair and watched the thick curls fall messily across his forehead. *My God, how could a guy be so beautiful?* Even in a room with the barest spot of light, his beauty shined brightly. Watching him in this unconscious, innocent state had to be right up there with kissing on the list of things that would fuck her head up.

Goddamn.

Luckily, the call of nature became insistent, and she needed to search for a bathroom. Some aspirin would be nice too, because her head was killing her. She could ask Spirit for some since he was the inconsiderate asshole banging the loud, rhythmic noises outside Tommy's bedroom. Spirit's need to share his talent with the whole neighborhood was probably the thing to wake her in the first place. Damn him. *Who plays drums at this hour?* It had to be late, late night or early morning, considering how dark it was in Tommy's room.

Capri looked once more at the beauty lying next to her with his mouth agape before putting on her clothes and going into the hallway. She closed Tommy's door then looked down the hall. She could see Spirit giving his muscles a workout as he hammered away on his drum set in the living room.

Spirit held the cymbal he'd just hit to cut the sound short and looked at her, his face puzzled. "You're still here? I thought you had to work this morning."

"I do." Capri opened her mouth to fuss about Spirit drumming while his roommates were trying to sleep, when panic rushed into her chest. "Wait. Wwhat do you mean?" She looked down at her watch and shrieked. "Holy shit! It's after eleven!" Eleven thirteen, to be exact. Shit! Shit! Shit! Shit!

"Didn't you set an alarm?"

She shook her head and busted back into Tommy's room. "Tommy!" She shook him hard to wake him. "Tommy! I overslept! I'm late for work. Tommy!" She shook him harder, scarcely penetrating his deep sleep. "Tommy, please! I've never been late before." He mumbled something that sounded like *bitch tried to cut me cock off*, but he would not fully awaken. She smacked his jaw twice. "Tommy, is there a university bus stop near here?" She waited to see if he would respond coherently. Fuck. Her head was about to explode. "Tommy?" She poked him in his ribs. Nothing. It was no use. It would take her that much longer to get to work if she spent more time trying to rouse him.

"You can forget trying to wake him. He's a corpse until noon." Spirit stood in the doorway wearing a black leather jacket and jeans with no shirt, dangling his keys. "I can give you a ride."

Capri exhaled more air than she could possibly hold in her lungs. "Thank you so much! I was supposed to open the computer lab at nine. I'm so fucked." Without a backwards glance at Tommy, Capri stopped to use their filthy bathroom. *I mean does anyone actually pee in the toilet?* Then she and Spirit ran out to his car and sped off.

Spirit raked his fingers through the buzzed side of his head. "I take it you don't usually drink when you have to work the next day?"

Capri shook her head. "Not at all. And I didn't intend to spend the night. I just wanted to make sure

Tommy was okay." Fuck. She'd left her jacket, and it was too cold for this shit. "It's so dark in there; I thought it was still night." Plus, she'd been extra tired, and Tommy had been extra cozy.

Spirit laughed and wiggled out of his jacket. "Girl, we have industrial curtains in the windows to keep it dark all the time. We're like bats—up all night, asleep during the day." He handed his jacket to her and turned the knob to crank up the heat.

She stared at his offering for a moment before accepting it. She didn't feel so bad about putting it on once he put on a t-shirt he retrieved from the backseat. "Well, this would have been good to know last night. I have *never* been late."

"Shit happens." He handed her a pill bottle from the glove compartment. "For your headache."

She didn't hesitate to open the bottle and consume two tablets. She didn't have water to go with her pain relief, but no one ever said she lived in a perfect world. "In addition to being a mind reader, you seem to have everything in here. What about breakfast?" To her surprise, he pulled a granola bar from his sun visor. "Okay…how 'bout a comb?"

"Sorry. Last girl I rushed to work from Tommy's bed took that and the toothbrush."

Capri rolled her eyes and used her fingers to comb through her hair. "I'll try not to hold that against you."

Spirit reached over with one hand to help tame some of her stray curls. "Your hair's so soft."

Capri cut her eyes at him. "Keep your hands on the steering wheel, please."

In defiance, he put both of his hands in her hair and tousled it. "There. Now you match Tommy."

"I'll take that as a compliment," she laughed, "'cause he has great hair."

On the way, Spirit and Capri discussed his songs and creative process, her school and work schedule, and what they wanted to be when they "grew up". Spirit actually wanted to be a music producer more so than a performer. He was in school for business, not music. As surprised as she was about his aspirations, he also seemed surprised that Capri's focus on her future went beyond finding a husband and being a soccer mom. He said he hadn't ever met a girl so young so interested in entrepreneurship. While Capri wanted to have her own mental health clinic, his former girlfriends had no hobbies, skills, or interests of their own. They'd just wanted to be his main squeeze.

Conversation with Spirit flowed with ease because she felt no pressure to keep things casual. Casual and friendly were a given with Spirit since there would be no sex. She and Tommy, on the other hand, had unfinished business. And once it was finished, she needed to be able to maintain her composure and detachment.

Spirit screeched in the parking lot in front of the student center entrance.

"Thanks so much for the ride." She made a motion to grab her books before realizing she didn't have any. This day had really started out shitty.

"Don't mention it. It was my good deed for today. What time do you get off? You need a ride?"

"No, I'll be fine."

As she got out, Spirit took a pen from the ashtray. "Let me give you the house number so you can get in touch with Tommy later. After breaking his penis last night, you owe him a call." He kept the pen suspended in midair, waiting.

Capri looked at the pen then at him. "Don't you have paper to write it on?"

"Hell no. What I look like, a secretary? You and Tommy are the only ones in this century without cellphones. Give me your hand." He scribbled numbers inside her palm. "Be sure to call him. He'll want to hear from you."

She looked at the mess Spirit had made of her hand. "Last night you were ready to kill him. Now, you're looking out for his best interest."

"If you think I'd ever do anything other than look out for Tommy, you haven't been paying attention. He's like a brother to me." Spirit reached over to close the door as she backed away. Then he threw up the peace sign and drove off.

Um...guess she'd have to give his jacket back later. She sniffed his lingering scent. Leathery...and all around more masculine than Tommy's, but not as alluring.

So work was work. Other than having to apologize to a handful of students waiting to get into the computer lab, it was uneventful. The weekends were never packed considering all the students that had an extracurricular life and friends and lovers to spend it with. The director didn't even know she was late until she called him to explain. She'd gotten lucky this time with only a verbal reprimand. Since she had a reputation for always being on time, even early, she could still keep her job, minus pay for the two and a half hours she'd missed. That may not have been a lot of money for some folks, but it was half a fortune for her. She'd have to pick up some extra hours at the library.

Capri tried to study some, using a program on the computer, but her mind just wasn't on it. After reading the same sentences over and over without retaining any info, she gave up. Meeting a boy she liked and deviating from her routine had already started causing her problems. And it hadn't even been a full twenty-four hours yet.

She decided not to call Tommy. She called Sasha instead to cash in on the benefit of their bargain, a ride back to the dorm in exchange for Capri's study notes.

As she got in Sasha's car, Capri began regretting the decision to call her. Sasha would not stop questioning Capri about her time with Tommy. Since Capri didn't have anything to brag about, her answers were just embarrassing. Sasha's laughter didn't help one bit. Walking would have been less stressful with the added benefit of exercise.

When they began walking up the stairs of their dorm, Capri's heart dropped down to her heels.

Tommy sat at the top of the stairs. Grinning, he held out both hands for Sasha and Capri to grab and help him up.

"Good to see you in one piece, Tommy," Sasha smirked.

"Aw, a bit of tape and some glue, good as new."

"And the back of your head? No concussion?"

"No. I did go to the campus medic for a pass from class though." He looked down at his feet. "May as well make the best of such a vigorous night."

Sasha mussed Tommy's hair. "At least nothing happened to your hair or face."

"Yeah. Exactly." Tommy gave Sasha Capri's smile.

Capri felt a sudden stab of jealousy. To hide it, she turned the corner and headed towards the room.

Tommy grabbed Capri's arm and made her face him. "Where are you going? Don't you want your jacket back?" He handed her the jacket she'd left in his living room. They seemed to be making a habit of leaving clothes behind.

The way he'd assertively grabbed her arm sent shivers down her spine. "Should I punch you in the nose now for returning it to me?" *And for flirting with Sasha?*

"Come on. You know I thought Spirit was about to hit me." He toyed with the fuchsia scarf around his neck, an odd accessory for his green and white plaid pants. "I was being proactive."

"No, you were about to get your ass handed to you." Capri laughed. "Well, it's a good thing you're here."

His brows rose in a question.

"I need to return Spirit's jacket. And...I still need to know your stage name."

"I'm pretty sure you called me by name a few times last night, not in the way I'd imagined, unfortunately."

Capri's eyes went to the ceiling as she tried to remember the names she'd mentioned. None other than "Tommy" came to mind. She doubted he'd go by "I'm sorry" and "forgive me". She shrugged.

"It'll come to you," he licked his lips, "when you come."

Sasha cleared her throat and unlocked their room door. "Do I need to get missing for a little while then?"

Capri caught the hint. "That won't be necessary. I

didn't have my books with me today. I have to study."

"I specifically remember you promising to make your assault up to me," Tommy moved to block Capri's route to the door.

Capri looked away. She couldn't take The Stare at the moment. "I will. But not tonight. I'm on scholarship, Tommy. Studying is not a suggestion."

"Okay. I'll study with you then. I can help you get good marks."

Capri twisted her lips in disbelief. "You'll just distract me. Sorry, but you can't come in."

Tommy looked to Sasha for help.

Sasha mumbled something, went in the room, then came right back out. "I'll be back in a couple of hours," she said to either, neither, or both of them. She had clearly taken Tommy's side though.

Capri made the mistake of looking into his green, imploring eyes, and against her better judgment said, "Fine. What do you know about psychology?"

He followed her inside and hung his jacket across her desk chair. "I know that I'm mad in the head and will need a shrink one day. I can be your subject. I'm completely mental."

She wasn't that far along in her studies to conduct a case study on him. Despite her ideas of detachment where he was concerned, Capri did find herself curious about the demons that lurked underneath such a gorgeous outer shell.

When it was just the two of them in her small room with the two twin beds, Capri started feeling nervous again. It showed.

"If you're worried I'm going to try to bone you, don't. Because of some man-hater with penis envy, I still need a few days to heal." He plopped down on her bed and stretched out, guessing correctly that hers was the one made. "I just want to get to know you. The you that Spirit drove to work this morning and impressed him so much."

Yeah. That's the problem.

And it continued being a problem. She studied some while he flipped through her books and photo albums, but mostly, they talked. A lot. Until they fell asleep. To make matters worse, Tommy returned the next night, and the night after that. He found his way into Capri's twin bed and talked to her until they both fell asleep again and again. She started looking forward to the time, which was really an issue. So she started scheduling time with him. That way, she could still get other things done. Some nights, she went to his house to hang out with the whole band and listened to them play. Some nights they ate together. Some nights they pranked unsuspecting folks. Some nights he waited for her at her job until she got off work. Work passed much more quickly and with loads more excitement on those nights. Before she knew it, a whole two weeks had passed of the same distracting routine. No matter how well she tried to be responsible and follow a schedule, Tommy had a way of hijacking it.

She was setting herself up for failure with a capital F. She had the decline in her grades to prove it. She'd gotten a B on her midterm. A fucking B! Unacceptable. And yet, he'd become a habit. Someone she relied on to shoot the shit with. Her schedule now consisted of work, study…and fucking off with Tommy. But still no fucking.

Huh.

She was still attracted to him all right. Maybe even more so, if that was possible. On top of being easy on the eyes and ears, he made her laugh until her lungs ached. And he was still attracted to her, if that incessant erection of his was any indication. But none of that would ensure the future she had to work hard to earn for herself.

Tommy giggled in that cute way of his as he rolled closer to Capri so she could hear what was being said on the other end of the cordless phone. The other person was irate, shouting obscenities and threats. Tommy giggled again at his latest prank. He'd picked a random number in the phone book, blocked Capri's landline number, and told the person who answered that he was going to have their car towed if they didn't stop parking it in the street. That's what their garage was for. The receiving caller said he could park it anywhere he damn well pleased, including Tommy's mother's coochie.

Capri held her side as Tommy continued getting under that undeserving, unlucky person's skin. The click from the other end came much later than either of them had guessed, but she'd been closer to the time. "I won. It took over seven minutes before they hung up. You said it would be two."

Tommy sighed, reached in his pocket, and handed her a dollar. "Not fair. Let my objection be noted on the record. I told you it would have been a better laugh if I would have pretended to *be* the tower after a complaint had already been charged." He looked over and down at her where she lay stretched out on the bed next to him. "You cheated me out of that dollar, sweetheart, and I aim to get you back."

"Noted...but suck it. You lost."

He spoke low. "Suck what?"

She looked into his eyes...and electricity sparkled between them.

Goddamn he was fine. And looking at her lips like that...

Maybe it was time to give him what he had worked so senselessly to get. He still hadn't realized he didn't need to befriend her to bed her. Sure, she enjoyed the cuddling and pranks. She enjoyed listening to him play guitar and watching him talk nonstop about Ireland. The wooing was just unnecessary. Maybe if she finally had sex with him, he'd disappear and leave her alone to achieve her goals in earnest. At this point, she couldn't lie to herself and say she wouldn't miss him. She would terribly. But if spending so much time with him meant she'd continue to sacrifice things more important to her, he had to go. Her mother did not sacrifice it all for Capri to blow it on a boy.

But being this close to Tommy stirred new feelings in Capri, guiding her towards untrodden territory. The sweaty palms. The racing heart. The shallow breathing. The disconnect from her brain that made her believe she'd be better balanced if she studied less, slept less, worked less, and hung out with him more, could only mean one thing. Capri was ready to break the seal of her vagina. She had no moral reasons to fight against her natural desire to have intercourse. And underneath that was an undercurrent of rationale—she would feel less insecure in herself and more mature as a woman if she'd just do it with him already. Time to bring on the white, uncircumcised cock.

Tommy reached for her hand next to his on the bed and held it. His other hand traced her jaw.

Capri swallowed all the saliva that pooled in her mouth. The gulp could be heard in China. "You didn't have to spend all this time with me just to have sex."

He smiled. "You really think that's why I've been hanging out with you? I told you, you intrigue me." He sat up on his elbow and looked down at her. "It's a drag that you don't play video games, but you make up for it every time you laugh at my jokes."

Capri licked her lips, fully prepared to let him kiss her. He'd broken her bit by bit, night by night. And perhaps that had been his goal. He was one of the worst kinds of player—one that made you do everything you said you wouldn't do just for the sport of making you eat your words.

Well, fuck it. He'd won.

Tommy descended on her slowly, with the care he'd give a disabled or elderly woman. Capri just wanted him to plunge in and take it. To command her to do his bidding. To ravish her and give her everything he'd been saving for the past two weeks. She wanted his eagerness, his sexual aggression, his unbridled horniness. It would help subdue her nervousness.

She lifted her head to Tommy and connected their lips for her first kiss.

Capri felt his groan all the way in the back of her throat. His pleasure turned her on. She also felt a sense of relief. This was it. She was going to do it tonight. With him. She'd learn what all the hype was about regarding sex, then she could move on to something else, like getting A's on her finals.

He pulled away and smiled down at her. "That was nice."

It sent a shockwave all the way to her nether regions. Something she'd never experienced before. She felt lightheaded, scared, and excited all at once. "You really have a great smile."

"You've said that before." He touched the corner of her mouth with his thumb and slid it from one end to the other. "I like that you say what you think. You have a great smile too." He kissed her again, this time with tongue and wandering hands before pulling away again. "Confession: I'm not the type to commit to a relationship, and you said you weren't looking for that. I like being with you. I do. I just don't want things to change. Is that still okay?"

She slapped his arm. "It's because of you that I've gotten off track. I definitely do not want more. I like the way things are."

He lifted her shirt up and unsnapped her bra. Her breasts were exposed for his attentive hands and eyes. "Jesus. You have perfect tits. I just want to…" He couldn't even finish his sentence as his mouth found its way to both nipples.

Her back arched of its own volition and her pussy throbbed.

The sexual tension had been thick enough to slice with a butter knife since the first time they'd met. It still cackled like electricity in the air. She didn't want the moment to end, but she didn't want to delay what would happen next. They needed to get on to the deed.

Capri sucked in a mouthful of air as his body got more comfortable between hers. "Confession," she said in a hoarse, aroused voice. "I don't want you to be gentle. I want you to just take it. Don't hold anything back. Overtake me."

He stopped and looked up from her bosom. "That sounds a lot like rape. I'm all for kink and dominance play, but I'm not trying to—"

"It can't be rape if I'm consenting to it, can it?"

"When you use words like 'overtake', I get confused."

"It's a fantasy of mine. I want to be ravished like the girls in the novels. Take charge and make me yours."

"You like it rough, the sex?"

She nodded and licked her lips. Given Tommy's penchant for sex in unusual places, she was pretty certain he couldn't turn down what she offered.

He took another moment to decide whether it would be worth the risk. He stared at her face, then her breasts. He kissed her gently one last time, then grabbed both of her hands and pinned them with one of his underneath her back. He groaned with excitement and rocked his hips into hers.

The contact pushed his erection into her soft spot and sent trimmers throughout her core with pleasure she'd never known. "Mmm. Do that again."

He did and they moaned in unison. "Confession," he whispered. "I am so fucking turned on right now. You make me so hard."

She struggled somewhat with her uncomfortable position, but she didn't complain. He was giving her just what she'd asked for. When she bit his lip, he groaned even more.

Panting, he reached for the zipper of her jeans. "I'm going to fuck you hard. I can't wait to be buried in your cunt."

She stared in his eyes as he pulled one pant leg down. He was in too much of a hurry to get the other one down. With his free hand, he reached in his pocket for a condom. Finally. She would be a woman in only a few more minutes. "One more confession before we do this, Tommy."

"I'm going to need both hands for this. Don't you fucking move."

He pulled out his cock and she nearly pissed herself. She definitely needed to tell him. That shit was going to hurt. "Wait. I really should tell you—"

He paused in the middle of putting the condom on and slapped her. "Told you not to move."

She was stunned. And hot. She blinked then deliberately started trying to get away from him so that he would force her back into position and punish her. He slapped her again. The thrill vibrated throughout her whole body.

Once the condom sheathed him, Tommy held both of her arms down and focused on positioning himself at her entrance. "I'd normally lick and finger you first to warm you up, maybe even make you orgasm a few times first. But if you want it rough, I'll fuck you cock-first and with my tongue afterwards."

That was all fine and dandy but... "Just one thing."

His eyes bore a hole into hers. "You're not HIV positive are you?" He paused. "With two condoms, I suppose we can still—"

"No. Not that."

"You're obviously not a chick with a dick...though technically, that wouldn't be a deal break—"

"Will you give me a chance to get it out? I'm a virgin, Tommy. That's my confession. Big secret revealed."

He just stared at her, and not in his seduce-everything-not-bolted-to-the-floor way. He looked like he had seen his dead grandmother's ghost in the place of Capri's face. He shook his head. "No. That's not possible. You said—"

"I said a lot of things, none of which actually admitted to having had intercourse before."

"Jesus Christ. Jesus. Fucking. Christ." He covered his mouth with his hand. "I can't. I can't do it then. I won't be your first."

Wait. What? She'd just expected him to slow down at the moment of initial penetration, not back out completely. "What do you mean? Why?"

"It should be with someone who loves you and you love him. Someone you can connect with on a spiritual level. Someone who wants to have a relationship with you. I'm the wrong guy. I'd just sully you up. You deserve better than me." He dismounted and pulled his pants back up while she watched in frustration.

Capri spent the next hour trying to convince Tommy she was ready and could handle it. He wouldn't budge, and she didn't have it in her heart to look at his refusal as honorable.

"Trust me. I'm the one suffering here. I'm going to have a horrible case of blue balls." He smacked her ass as she stood to put her leg back in the pants correctly.

"You fucking suck, Tommy."

"Look, we can dick around and have a laugh, but I can't be the first man you open your legs for."

"Too late."

"I've actually gotten to know and like you. I couldn't do that to you." He stuck his hand out for her to shake it. "Mates then?"

And so it was. Hanging out with and getting to know Tommy had come to bite her in the ass all right. Just not in the way she'd expected. She'd grown attached to him, but the real humdinger was that he'd grown attached to her. Bonding with her sexually and breaking her heart wasn't the way he'd hurt her. He'd spent so much time getting to know and becoming invested in her until he actually felt the need to protect her from himself.

Goddamn.

It sounded even more absurd when she explained it all to Sasha. How did the one guy she wanted to have sex with, and fucked off time to make it happen, not want to be her first?

"Fuck Tommy." Capri's lust had turned to frustration. Her frustration had turned to disappointment. Now, finally, Capri had arrived at the angry stage.

Sasha couldn't stop laughing. "So y'all are just friends, right?"

"Just friends."

"So…uh…" Sasha swiveled in her desk chair to face Capri. "You wouldn't mind if I hollered at him then?"

Capri glared at Sasha while images of Capri thrashing Sasha's head into the desk crossed her mind. Once rationality resurfaced, Capri realized she had no claim to Tommy. They were friends. He could be with anyone he wanted. "Guess not."

Despite all the time Capri and Tommy spent maintaining their friendly routine for the next two weeks, those were the two words that sealed their fate. *Guess not.* With it being out there in the universe, it didn't take long for Capri to leave class early one day and walk in to Sasha on her knees in front of Tommy giving him a blowjob.

Capri didn't immediately leave the scene. Sure, she was disgusted and hurt, but the rapturous look on his face drew her in. The way his lean body tensed and coiled as he felt the pleasure Sasha's mouth provided, turned Capri on at the same time. He was so caught up in sensation; he didn't notice Capri standing there. Or perhaps he did. Either way, he didn't open his eyes. He gripped Sasha's hair and pumped his hips and moaned instead. Capri recovered her sanity and left before he finished.

She wanted to kill them both for making her feel conflicted about the whole situation. Technically, they weren't doing anything wrong. Capri decided against the killing spree. She'd already killed once, and that had been the most tumultuous moment of her life. Something she would never get over. Gathering herself, Capri did what she had become good at. She buried the emotions deep. The jealousy. The longing. The pain. The rage. Hey, Capri and Tommy were just friends. And Capri had an education to earn. A scholarship to keep. A career to flourish in…

A few deep, calming breaths later, Capri finally entered the acceptance stage.

CHAPTER 6
THREE YEARS AND SOME CHANGE LATER

"I'm coming!" Ah, fuck. Tommy grabbed what's-her-face's hair as he shot into her mouth everything he had stored in his testicles and shaft from the past twenty-four hours. At the same time, the back of his head hit the headrest, his eyes squeezed shut, and his mouth hung open. He enjoyed total bliss for about seven seconds before he could come back to reality and form any coherent thoughts.

Jesus. That was fucking nice. Nothing like blowing a load in a chick's mouth.

He zipped up his jeans while she wiped her mouth and applied more lipstick.

Now came the part he dreaded. There was never an easy way to say goodnight to these girls after they put their hearts and souls into pleasing him. In his defense, he'd told her he wasn't up for hanging out tonight after performing in the sweltering heat of the outdoor theater. She'd taken it upon herself to blow him anyway. He shouldn't be held responsible for her incorrect assumption that her oral skills would change his mind.

He opened the SUV door to exit. He liked nothing

more than the direct approach. "Thanks for driving me home."

She smiled big, showing deep dimples in her cheeks. "Aren't you going to invite me in?"

Why in bloody hell would I do that? "Sorry, but this isn't my house, right? I'm staying with my best mate for a while and she has to go to work early in the morning. She wouldn't appreciate me bringing company inside."

"You sure she's just your friend and not a girlfriend?"

"Two things—one, she's a girl and a friend, so that makes her a girlfriend in name. And two, I've made it clear that I'm not interested in a serious affair. I don't want a girlfriend, as you say, period, so where you're concerned, it shouldn't matter who she is to me."

"I know, I know," what's-her-face pouted. "It's just that this is our third night being together this week. I thought maybe you wouldn't mind spending more time with me. That you'd actually want to."

Tommy made a mental note to drop this chick like a hot iron right now. No matter how sloppy wet she gave a good BJ, it wasn't worth it. Oh and…he needed to be certain he didn't spend three evenings straight with a chick again, even if she was his drive home from the gig. When would he ever learn?

Tommy leaned over from the passenger seat to hers and cupped her cheek like she was emotionally unstable, because he never knew which girls were until it was too late. He looked into her eyes and attempted sincerity. "Of course, I enjoy spending time with you…uh…love." Damn, after three nights, he still couldn't remember her name. "But it's late. I'm beat. You're beat. I have another gig tomorrow.

I'll see you there, yeah?"

"I'm going out of town tomorrow."

Yes! "Aww. Well, maybe sometime next week then?" He brought his lips to hers and suckled on them with expert finesse, just in case he wanted to fuck her again in the distant future. He did have a fondness for watching her dimples pop while his cock went in and out of her mouth. No sense in ending things on a bad note. Hurting women wasn't his style. He preferred to be upfront and honest about his impure intentions, and let them down easy when they refused to accept his emotional unavailability. Chicks just wouldn't accept candor. They took it as a challenge to work at changing him. Each girl thought she would be THE one to make him settle down. Nope. Not happening. Capri alone understood and accepted Tommy's commitment issues. She accepted him for who he was, flaws and all. Of course, his instrument of love hadn't been dipped into her pussy, so that may have had something to do with it. Sex changed things.

He'd initially just wanted to be back before Capri fell asleep to wish her well on tomorrow's milestone. When he finally managed to break away from what's-her-face, he really did feel tired. Keeping girls level-headed when they wanted to cling proved to be a draining art.

His shoulders slumped when he realized he was already too late. All the lights were turned off inside the flat, denoting Capri had already gone to bed like she'd warned if he strolled in after midnight. By the looks of it, her roommate, Sasha, wasn't in. Sasha hardly stayed in the flat a'tall, but when she did, Tommy could get a good laugh or two in before bed even when Capri made like an old lady and turned in early.

Yes, however surprising, Capri and Sasha were still roomies. Not much had changed in that regard. The main difference being that Sasha was still in undergrad, bollocking her way through, while Capri had graduated early, and was now working on her advanced degree.

Tommy didn't have room to talk though. He'd given up on university altogether. Degrees may have been the gateway to what Capri wanted in life, but they wouldn't help him get to where he wanted. College took time away from his jealous bitch, music. To keep his first love happy, he took lots of unpaid gigs instead, and prayed one of them led to the band's big break.

Oh, well, Tommy sighed. He would have to set an alarm and hope he could get up early enough to see Capri off on her big day.

He tip-toed in Capri's room and began undressing, dropping everything on the floor by the bed just to give her something to rant about in the morning. As an official houseguest, he was supposed to sleep on the couch, but he hadn't done that one day since he'd moved in. He always slept in Capri's bed. In fact, they hadn't missed many nights as bedmates since that first time she'd slept on his futon, tucked in his arms and legs.

Once he got down to his underpants, a garment he made sure to wear nowadays, Tommy pulled back the covers of her bed and got in to cuddle up to his per usual snuggle buddy.

"You smell like dirty bitch perfume." Capri rolled on her side away from Tommy. "You promised me you'd at least take a shower when you came in from fucking those hoes."

He rolled toward her and put his arm around her waist. "I didn't fuck anyone tonight."

"Bullshit." She pushed her arse, covered with short pajama bottoms, into his groin and wiggled. "You're not hard, which means you're empty."

"I am well-sated, yes." He buried his head in Capri's hair, loving its soft, coarse texture and the scent of her strawberry shampoo. "She had the most amazing mouth. And she swallowed."

"She made you see stars, and I bet you can't even remember her name." Capri bumped him extra hard with her booty. "But seriously. If she was all up on you like that, you need a shower. I don't want my bed smelling like cheap bitch." She bumped him again. "Shower. Now."

After only two bumps against him, he already felt the stirrings of blood racing to his cock. Shit. He gripped her waist and held her snug to him. "Don't you fucking move like that again or we'll both need showers."

"Move like what?" Capri pushed back against him and her hips undulated.

Great balls of shite. He tried to hold it in but groaned anyway.

She laughed. "Tommy, you are the horniest motherfucker around."

"Cock tease." He rolled away from her and stared at the ceiling. They may have had more room in her full bed than they used to have in her twin or his futon, but they still stayed close, primarily in the center.

"Only because I know how much you enjoy being

teased."

Although true, Tommy never should have told her that. Now, she tortured him beyond any man's limit. "It's only because we've never shagged. I hear the wild siren call of your cunt more often than anyone else's. It fucks with me because I can't have it."

"You certainly cannot. You had your chance buster. Now go jerk it off in the shower."

He got up, cock standing at attention in his underpants, and cursed all the way to the lavvy. He cursed all the way through his shower. And he cursed when his seed finally washed down the drain. His shower wank wasn't nearly as good as the head he got earlier. And despite the hot water, it didn't warm him quite like lying next to Capri and rubbing up against her.

She wouldn't find the teasing as amusing if he went in there, held her down, and took her the way he knew *she* fancied.

He started throbbing again at the idea of pinning her facedown while he pumped inside her tight, wet hole.

Fucking shit. Capri tempted him so much sometimes he could scream, but he knew better than to go there. He went back into the lavvy to have another wank.

Surely, she'd be asleep now.

He slowly climbed back into bed so as not to wake her.

"Feel better?" she asked.

"Much. Thank you for your concern. Next time, just blow me. Or give me a firm hand job. Either one will suffice."

"Ha. In your dreams." She grabbed his hand and

wrapped it around her waist as they got comfortable for sleep. "How did it go tonight? Your performance, I mean. Wish I could have been there."

"Craicing. Multitudes of people showed up. We made fifty quid...um, dollars. Enough for a few pints. At this rate, I'll have my own place by the end of the century."

She laughed. "You never know. It could happen fast, especially if you increase your online presence. Either way, you can stay here as long as you want."

"Thank you, sweetheart." Tommy closed his eyes and started drifting.

A few minutes later, Capri spoke. "So which songs did you play? How were the other bands? I would have gone if I had finished my report sooner."

He knew that, and he knew she knew he knew that. She'd been at most of their shows. Sometimes, she'd been the only one to come. Other times, she'd paid people out of her own pocket to sit in the audience and cheer his band on. He also knew she had to get up at five thirty. "No, no. No more talking. Go to sleep. You're not going to blame me for being sleepy on the first day as your favorite professor's assistant. Hell no."

"I'm so nervous about it. I can't sleep."

"You'll be fine. When are you going to get over these anxiety issues? No one could possibly do a better job than you. I'm sure you're over-prepared."

Silence.

Tommy felt proud of himself for diffusing her insecurities so quickly. He started drifting again until he felt her body rattle next to him from sobbing. "Heeeey. What's wrong? Tell Godd all about it, baby."

"I told you I was never calling you that. I don't care if it is your stage name."

"Well, talk to me anyway. What's going on?" The sound of his voice must have unraveled her because she opened up about her feelings of inadequacy, which he found astonishing. She didn't have any inadequacies as far as he was concerned.

"Confession: I feel like I'm not good enough. What if I fuck up? I have a lot riding on this. His recommendation would mean everything. Then again, if he doesn't like me, I'm screwed. And if—"

"Whoa. Hold on. Your fear of fucking up is the reason I know you won't." He rubbed her back to help her calm down. "You've really got to get some sleep though."

She sniffed once then nodded her head. "I just…I just don't want…"

"Don't want to what?"

"I just don't want to let my mom down."

"And you won't. I'm sure she's proud of you." And Tommy left it at that. He knew not to probe further about Capri's mum. When Capri made vague references about her, she closed up in a clamshell immediately afterwards. His questions were never answered, and he respected Capri's decision to withhold that part of herself. She was the one studying psychology, but he knew enough about madness to know forcing someone to open up about something they weren't ready to share had dire consequences. "Confession: I think you are the brightest, most beautiful person I know. He's lucky to have you, just like I'm lucky to have you in my life." He kissed her cheek. "And if he treats you otherwise, I'll go up to his office and kick his arse. Well… I'll take Spirit with me so he can kick his arse." He expected Capri to laugh or at least have a witty response to an Irishman talking about luck. When she didn't, he searched her face and found that she was asleep.

Her innocent face made him smile. His sleeping angel.

He kissed her cheek again then laid his head down to sleep.

Tommy awakened to the sun shining on his face from Capri's bedroom window. His arms that had been wrapped tight like a burrito around her were now empty, unless he counted the inked note she wrote on both arms. His left arm read: DIDN'T WANT TO WAKE YOU. OFF TO NEW JOB. SEE YOU TONIGHT AT THE SHOW. LOVE, CAPRI. His right arm read: PS. LUNCH IS IN THE MICROWAVE AND YOU NEED TO PICK YOUR SHIT UP OFF THE FLOOR!

Ah, dammit. He'd missed her leaving. By a long shot.

Looking over at the clock on the wall, he knew he had to get moving. It was already nearly one in the afternoon. He was supposed to meet Spirit at two.

Tommy slipped on his clothes and headed for the toilet then the kitchen for lunch and tea.

"Good morning, sunshine." Sasha's greeting made him jump a mile out of his skin.

"What the fuck are you doing here?"

She waved her hand to encompass her surroundings. "I live here, remember? In fact, between the two of us, only one name is on the lease," she pointed to her chest, just above her ample cleavage, "and that's mine."

"Oh, I see." Tommy sat on a barstool at the counter. "You finally peeled yourself off the alley pavement and found your way home. Welcome back."

She smiled. "That was uncalled for Mr. Colin Farrell wanna-be. I was going to offer you a ride. Now I think I'll just be on my merry way without you. Toodles." She lifted her designer handbag and started past him toward the front door.

"Wait, wait. He grabbed her by the waist and brought her back to his lap. I didn't mean it. You know you're my favorite girl."

"Liar. Capri's your favorite girl, but I'll take it." She turned around to face him, flipping her hair off her shoulder, and stared in his eyes. "Mm mm mmm. Capri is one lucky girl." She tousled his hair. The curls reached his shoulders now, and he'd long since given up on trying to tame them. "You made any progress with her yet or is she still holding on tight to the big V?"

"You'll have to ask her that."

"Which means she's well on her way to being a forty-year-old virgin." Sasha looked him from head to toe. "My, my, my. How does she do it? Night after night in the same bed with you? She has the willpower of a robot that's been programmed to say no." She leaned in to sniff his neck, pressing their bodies groin to groin. "The offer still stands, you sexy beast. Anytime, anywhere, however you want it, it's yours."

He smiled even though her attempt at seduction had no effect on him at all. Nothing sexual had transpired between them since she'd sucked him off years ago, and it would probably stay that way.

"Thanks." He kissed her forehead. "Now about that ride. Can you take me to the studio downtown?" That would be so much better than public transportation.

They grabbed some food and his guitar and headed to the studio. In order to make sure he arrived on time, Tommy didn't take the time to scrub the ink off of his arms. He'd learned his lesson about punctuality being more important than aesthetics. Plus, he made heads turn either way. He could leave the primping to someone who needed it.

"Was Capri excited about her new job today?" Spirit didn't say, "Hello." He didn't ask, "What's up?" And he didn't ask Tommy how he was doing. He just jumped straight in to asking about Capri.

Tommy was getting ill of that. "Over the moon. She said to tell you she'd call and tell you all about it later."

"She did?!"

Tommy froze halfway down to sitting on the studio couch. There was too much fucking enthusiasm in Spirit's voice. "No, mate. I'm just fucking with you."

"Oh."

"She did say she'd be at the show tonight though." Tommy sat and held out his arm for Spirit to read.

"Cool." Spirit tried to appear aloof now, but that eager cat was already out of the bag.

The tracks they spent the next few hours putting down were the best ones they'd recorded yet. The first album had been a flop with local stations, but they wouldn't let that get them down. This second one showed real promise.

They only had time to grab sandwiches on the way to their second and final performance at the outdoor theater. While in the drive-thru, Spirit looked over from the driver's seat at Tommy all non-casual-like. Trying to look nonchalant made Spirit even more obvious.

After the fourth time Tommy caught Spirit looking at him, he asked, "You have something on your mind, man? Let's hear it."

Spirit took their food from the fast food worker and handed it over to Tommy. "Well…I'm just wondering if anything has changed between you and Capri."

Okay. Here we go. "Changed from what to what?"

"You know what I mean."

"No, I don't. Why are you being cryptic? If you have something to ask, just ask."

"I take it you haven't put a title on it yet?"

"Capri and I are mates. That's it."

"Would you be upset if I asked her out then?"

Tommy couldn't outright say yes or no. The real answer was yes. Yes, he would freak out if Spirit and Capri hooked up. Capri was *his* mate. He didn't want what little time she spent with him to be split with Spirit. Or anyone else for that matter, and that worried him. She didn't belong to him. She wasn't property. She should be able to date whomever she wanted. But was this tattooed muscle-bound drummer twat who she'd want to date? Jesus. Who was he kidding? What girl wouldn't? But what would happen if Spirit hurt her? Tommy would have to fuck him up, and that would be horrible for the band…and horrible for Tommy's face. How to answer Spirit's question… Yes or no, *should* he be upset? That was the question.

"Tommy? I didn't ask you for her hand in

marriage. I just asked if—"

"I know what you asked, dammit. I'm thinking."

"Because if it's not okay for her to date someone who would treat her right, then I think you should man-up, stop fucking around with all these skirts, and do right by her."

Tommy's eyes bucked into a killer stare. "You miss the part where I said she was my mate? She's my best mate, man. The idea of you and her poses a delicate situation. It's not a simple yes or no."

"If it's not simple, then she's not just your mate, *mate*." Spirit's emphasis on that last mate bordered on contempt.

Yet another person trying to tell him who Capri was to him. "Spirit—"

"You're just standing in the way of her having something meaningful while you string her along, fucking her and every other woman—"

That's where Spirit was wrong. "She deserves a good man. That's all. I just want her to be with someone who will love her."

They pulled up at the theater where they would perform for a few hundred people. They'd only pocket chump change, hopefully enough to cover the sandwiches they were eating, but they'd also get some adulations. Lord willing.

"What makes you think I wouldn't love her?" Spirit's voice dropped. "What makes you think I don't?"

Tommy stared at Spirit, who kept his eyes on the last bit of his sandwich before popping it in his mouth. For the first time, Tommy saw the impact of all the time Capri had spent with the band. She wasn't just Tommy's friend.

Perhaps Spirit would treat her right. Granted, he had gotten out of a lengthy relationship a few weeks ago, but at least he'd been willing to have one.

"So what's your final answer, Tommy?"

"Capri's a virgin, Spirit. I've never touched her. Well, not in that way. Uh…not in the way you're thinking, I mean. I didn't want to ruin her, and I'll be damned if I let someone else do it."

Spirit was silent, eyes focused on Tommy. Spirit's expression went from shock to confusion. Tommy watched his face as Spirit put pieces of the puzzle together. "So y'all are really just sleeping in that bed? After all this time…just sleeping?"

Tommy nodded. "Along with a few pillow fights and some movie marathons here and there."

Spirit exhaled. "Whoa, man. It's worse than I thought."

"What do you mean?"

"You motherfuckers are in love."

Tommy laughed a little until he couldn't contain himself. He threw his head back and laughed a whole lot. He couldn't stop laughing, damn near corpsing. How absurd could Spirit be? "Damn, Spirit. You don't listen well, do you? All that rock-n-roll in your ears has made you deaf." Tommy took all the trash from their meal and started combining it in one bag for disposal. "All right. All right. I shouldn't mind, and therefore, I wouldn't mind if you dated Capri. You obviously fancy her." He grabbed Spirit's arm before the smile could fully develop on Spirit's face. "But if you hurt her, you and I are done. Understood? I may not be able to beat your mountainous arse, but I don't have to talk to you."

Spirit smiled as they slapped palms and gripped

each other with affection. "I don't think you have to worry about that. I have my work cut out for me, Tommy. If my suspicions are correct, I'll be the one getting hurt here. But Capri is worth the risk."

CHAPTER 7

As Capri looked for a parking space amongst the sea of cars, she couldn't help but think of how far the band had come. They weren't making a lot of money yet, and they were one of three bands performing tonight before the headliner, but their fandom had been growing at a steady pace. Their name was getting out there as the sexiest new male rock band. Their music and swag had improved daily by leaps and bounds. Their popularity was slowly extending beyond young female admirers. Capri could see it clearly—Celestial Decadence was going to be a huge hit. Internationally huge. They would be raking in the dough soon enough. Once their second album dropped, she'd probably have to start waiting in line to get the time of day from them and paying for photo-ops.

Where would she and Tommy be then? What would she do when he had his own mansion and decided he no longer wanted to share a bed with a friend he couldn't or *wouldn't* touch? What would she do when he toured the world and met prettier, smarter, and freakier women than her? Ones willing to drop their careers to be with him. Or better yet, ones who had never aspired to have a career, so they'd gladly drop everything and put him first.

Capri and Tommy were friends, sure. She believed he valued that. But friendship would only get her so far once he became a mega hit. When he became a household name, and hungry bitches had his poster on their walls, there would be no more room for her. Or if he decided to get serious with one of his fans, Capri could just hang it up. No other woman would stand for Tommy and Capri's friendship.

What a mood killer.

She parked the car and rested her head on the steering wheel to collect herself.

She couldn't let these thoughts get her down. She'd just had a great day. One that brought early commendations from her professor turned boss. On top of that, Capri had received an A on her last class assignment. She could see light at the end of the tunnel and water in the middle of the desert, so to speak. Eventually, she'd be the therapist she'd dreamt of being, one good at helping people like her mother through their psychoses. In the same slow, steady way Tommy was in the process of achieving what he most longed for, Capri was too. In the near future, they would respectively prove anything was possible with vision, dedication and hard work. In the meantime, Capri's satisfaction could be found in balancing her roles as a student, professional, and friend. The plague on her subconscious, however, was whether, post-graduation and post-Tommy's fame, Capri would just be a professional.

Capri shook her head to clear it of such self-deprecating thoughts. She came here to have fun tonight.

As she made her way through the crowd to somewhere in the middle near the stage, she felt elated that she hadn't missed Tommy's ukulele solo. The tune rose like delicate wings of a butterfly over the dense air, falling on primed ears in great contrast to the heavy metal choruses. The contrast of such a small, gentle, childlike instrument between the song's strong head-banging chords made his solo all the more stunning. The whole song not only represented the dichotomy of their new band name, but their identity as a group: soft and hard, glamorous and masculine, melodious and sensual. They weren't punk. They weren't goth or emo or industrial. They just played tunes that rocked the audience. And they rocked hard, especially once the heavy riffs on the electric guitars resumed.

Capri's head rocked and her body swayed as she watched Tommy lose himself in the music. She hummed along as his long, expert fingers made sweet love to that sweet loving instrument. Along with the rest of the crowd, she kicked off her shoes and jumped around, beginning at the first sound of the bass. She screamed *woooo* with everything in her diaphragm when the percussion joined in. By the time their voices blended and they sang the transformative lyrics, Capri let her favorite band erase all her anxieties and frustrations. She no longer even focused on them. Instead, she let their music carry her onto harmonic waves, the ethereal planes of awareness and beauty. Even in its hardcore nature, their music transcended the genre and reminded her of another, better world. A utopia where only music and love existed.

Damn right. They were celestial, and they were destined for greatness.

The contact high Capri got from all the smoke may have had something to do with her perception. But they were still good. Damn good.

After the concert, she went backstage to hug and congratulate them on their success. Every show was a success regardless of the number of people in attendance or the amount of money they made. They would look back on these days and laugh, of course, but it was a process. Perhaps these humble beginnings would keep them humble. And yes, she had a vested interest in that humility. She didn't want to be forgotten.

For now, all she had to do was walk backstage once the show ended. There would come a time when security would—

"Hey, Capri." Spirit walked over to her and lifted her from the ground in an embrace that left her lightheaded.

Wow. Okay. "Hey, Spirit. Grrrrreat show! I'm so proud of you guys." She tugged her pencil skirt down when he set her back on her feet then wiped her hand across his forehead to absorb some of his sweat. She'd gotten used to their post-show perspiration and spike in adrenaline, but Spirit's hug was…excessive this time. If Spirit was this hyped up… She looked around for Tommy to make sure he wasn't engaged in anything destructive. When she saw Tommy with his arms around twin girls, she turned back to Spirit. Tommy's flirty behavior was within his range of normalcy. "So, what have you been up to? Sorry I couldn't make it last night. I heard it was good though."

Spirit proceeded to congratulate her on her new position and tell her about what had been going on with him. He'd be a college grad soon, and she couldn't be happier for him. After hugging Savior and Divine before they left with arm candy, she looked back at Tommy, who appeared to still be tied up. She didn't want to interrupt, so she said goodnight to Spirit and turned to leave.

"Wait. Capri…" Spirit waited for her to face him. "I was wondering if you'd like to have dinner one night next week." He tucked a lock of her hair behind her ear and made sure they had eye contact. He smiled, his eyes twinkling. "Just the two of us, I mean."

Capri laughed at his prank attempt until she realized he was serious. *Oh.* "Um… sure. Why not?"

Spirit flipped the baseball cap he wore from front to back and grinned. "Cool. I'll call you with details."

"Sure." She smiled and left, dazed, because that had been the oddest proposal ever. One, Spirit had never seemed interested in her like *that* before. He'd definitely thrown vibes that were clear tonight though. It was written all over his face—he intended to move up from the friend zone. But the oddest thing was her response. *Sure. Why not?* Well, there were a lot of reasons why not. Mainly, because this situation had the potential to get really messy. Although Capri got asked out often, she'd had no interest in accepting dates. So why now? Why Spirit, Tommy's friend and band mate, of all people?

Goddamn. When Capri did it big, she did it real big.

Later on, when Tommy stumbled into her bedroom drunk and smelling like cigarettes, she cut the tall floor lamp on and sat up in bed. She couldn't sleep anyway. They needed to talk.

"I told Spirit I'd go out with him next week."

Tommy paused in the middle of stripping his pants off. He blinked a few times before nodding. "Good. Well good. He's a good guy, that Spirit. He has spirit." Tommy laughed at his own joke. He took his pants off then fell backwards on the bed.

"So you're okay with that? Me and Spirit?"

He reached over and turned the light off. "Sure. Why not?"

"That's what I said, but I thought it was something I should run by you first."

"First? Don't you mean after the fact?"

"Before...after...whatever. Either way, it's not too late to back out if—"

"Jesus Christ. What is wrong with you two? Go out already and stop asking me a million fucking questions about it."

"What do you mean? He talked to you about asking me out?" Capri turned the lamp back on.

Tommy sighed. "Yeah, yeah. He asked me. I told him you were my best mate and you could go out with whoever you wanted. He asked you. You said yes. There. Sorted."

Flashbacks of Capri's convo with Sasha came to mind. Sometimes you had to be careful what you agreed to. It would serve Tommy right if she went out with Spirit...and ended up liking him.

He sat up on his elbows and pinned her with squinty eyes. "As a matter of fact, I've been thinking, Capri. Maybe Spirit's the one you should give your," he whistled twice, "to. You know what I mean? Let Spirit be your first. He's a good guy...and I think he has feelings for you."

Capri just stared at Tommy. He was drunk all right—slurred speech, squinty eyes, liquor breath— but he knew what he was saying. "Tommy, is this some kind of game you and Spirit have concocted?"

"What? Does that seem like something I'd do? Okay, maybe it does. But does it seem like something Spirit would do? No way." He plopped his head back down and closed his eyes. "You should give it some consideration, is all. I've heard girls say he's a good lover." Tommy started mumbling as sleep took him over. She could only make out some of it. "We've even fucked some of them at the same time DP style. He's got stamina, that man, to be able to keep up with me."

Capri gasped. Ew. That was TMFI. Too. Much. Fucking Information.

Yet, she was half fascinated and fully curious. The wheels on her brain bus started turning. While she'd never had one cock…some girls had more than one at a time. Spirit *and* Tommy? Though Capri understood the mechanics of it, she couldn't fathom the idea of handling them both at once. Not physically or emotionally.

Her first reaction to his unconscious double penetration confession, scrunching her face up and wanting to call them dirty canines, didn't last long enough to prevent the mental image from forming. Spirit in one hole, Tommy in the other? Goddamn. The more she thought about it, the more it turned her on. She had a restless sleep, to say the least.

When she mentioned it to Tommy the next day while making them lunch, he didn't remember saying it. He also couldn't deny its veracity. "You know how wild some of our parties are," he shrugged.

"Not really. You always kick me out before you really get started." It came out with more bitterness than she'd intended, especially when she knew he was trying to protect her. She softened her tone. "But it's all good. You're both young and single. You *should* be sowing your wild oats."

"You're young and single too, Capri. When are you going to let yourself have a good, wholesome time?"

"I don't have time for fun. You know that." She placed a bowl of salad down in front of him. "The closest I get to that is listening to you play."

"Awww." He pinched her cheek and shook it. "Look at you being all sentimental."

"Don't touch me," her nose crinkled. "I don't know where your hand has been."

Tommy grabbed her by the back of her head and shoved two fingers in her mouth before she could get away. Capri fought to spit out his cooties, and when that didn't work, she started biting him. The tussle continued for a good five minutes before they gave up, exhausted on the floor.

"Ow." Tommy rolled onto his back. "I'm bleeding, you twat."

"Be glad I didn't jam them in a zipper. Next time, I'll bite your nasty ass fingers off." Worn out, Capri stood and sat back on her barstool at the counter. She took a deep breath and started eating her salad. "So…what are we talking about here? You and Spirit have…?" She made a circle with one hand and poked it with the index finger on her other hand.

He sat on his stool next to her and dug in his bowl. "What…each other? Christ no." He shook his head and explained in explicit detail that he and Spirit had been with some of the same girls, sometimes one guy right after the other, sometimes via swapping, and sometimes via different holes at the same time, but never ever in a million years would they be together without a chick. "Our cocks rubbing together on the inside of a girl—that's as gay as I'll ever get. Nothing's quite like the friction of two cocks being in the same hole. Feels fucking unbelievable."

Capri and Tommy had talked in general about sex many times before, usually from Tommy's perspective since Capri could only speak in theory. Capri already knew about his escapades in random places, in latex and leather fetish garbs, and with inanimate objects thrown in to spice things up. But this revelation... For someone who'd only gotten close to having sex once years ago, Tommy and Spirit's experiences took her idea of sex and intimacy to a whole new level. She didn't know what to make of it.

Tommy swiveled her stool around so that he could look dead in her face. "I can't quite make the look on your face." He mistook it for revulsion. "If you're disgusted with me, don't hold it against Spirit. He's trying to turn over a new leaf."

Disgust may have been there, but fascination set in quickly or perhaps something more intense...like jealousy. Yes. A lot of jealousy. Whoever the bitches were that got to have Tommy and Spirit like that were the luckiest ever. While Capri worked hard to have a good, solid future based on her own merits, some girls were enjoying the best life had to offer right now. With none of their futures guaranteed, Capri could be drawing the shorter straw. She didn't like the irony of that.

"You all right, Capri?"

"Please tell me you wear condoms every time."

"Of course. Every time. And that's not easy to do with some positions or when you're in a hurry. Lots of lube. That's the key."

"I'm sure it'll get even harder the more girls throw themselves at you."

"Am I to assume that pun wasn't intended?" He smiled, ignoring her eye roll as he got up to rinse his bowl in the sink. "I just know I'm going to go mental and be so whipped the first time I go raw and let go inside a woman. I get a horn just thinking about what it would be like to let me little swimmers go to create an even bigger swimmer. A baby. Can you imagine it?" His arm and hip animation to demonstrate his baby-making technique was more comical than titillating. "It's just the idea of it, because I'd rather get AIDS than have a baby. There's just something so hot and instinctual and animalistic—"

"And dangerous and irresponsible about it."

"Exactly. Which is why I haven't done it." He bit his lip and grunted. "But I would really fancy doing it like that." He adjusted himself in his tight pants then swept his hair back with both hands. "You're blushing, Capri," he sing-songed and walked back to his stool to sit again. "I've finally made you blush."

"I don't blush. My skin's too dark for that."

"Bollocks." He started sipping his tea mug while studying her. A smile slowly took over his face. "I've finally figured out that look," he grinned from ear to ear. "You're turned on." He turned her chin towards him a second before she jerked out of his grasp. He laughed outright because he'd seen enough to confirm his suspicions. "What else makes you all hot and bothered besides the domination thing? Your turn to confess."

Capri finished her salad and put the fork down. "I wouldn't call it a 'domination thing' necessarily. That sounds too much like BDSM. I don't like pain or being tied up and beaten. I like—"

"How do you know you don't if you've never tried it?"

"Do you like Spirit's cock in your ass?"

"Point taken."

Thought so. "For me, it's about being overpowered by a guy's lust for me, not about being a submissive. I have to be attracted to him, but there's a compelling reason we shouldn't have sex, like I'm in a relationship or something. So I fight against it, and he just can't help himself."

"I feel like we've had this conversation before. That's rape."

"We're just talking about my fantasy. I don't want it to happen in real life, especially because the forbidden or illicit nature of the act would have consequences, I'm sure. I wouldn't want a stranger jumping out of a bush and assaulting me. But someone forbidden that removes the guilt from me by forcing me, I don't know. That's kinda hot."

"Yeah, until you regret it later and turn his arse in to the coppers for *rape*." He nibbled on his garlic roll. "So what else moistens your cunt? A bed of roses? A box of chocolates? A twelve-carat diamond ring?"

"Now you know better than that." She drew a deep breath, knowing this conversation served no real purpose. There were other, more important things she could be doing on this Saturday afternoon. Still, nothing could be gained or lost from talking about what they liked sexually, right? "I got out of there before you finished in Sasha's mouth, but...I must confess, I thought watching her suck your cock was really hot. I didn't think I'd enjoy watching so much, but I did. Much better than porn."

"I'm sure you can catch Sasha sucking a cock any night of the week," he laughed.

"It wasn't about watching her, you dipshit. It was about the look of ecstasy on your face. I loved seeing that. And how you sounded. It was hot...sexy."

He searched her eyes for a sign of jesting or insincerity. "I didn't know you watched porn."

"Not often. I was just curious, I guess."

He stared at her for a minute before taking another sip. "Confession...I knew you were there." His head nodded in the direction of Sasha's room. "In the room. When Sasha went down—"

"What?" Capri's brows shot to the roof. "You did?"

He nodded. "I thought about making her stop, but I don't really mind being watched. You and I were just friends—"

"And you were horny."

"Yeah, but a sick, twisted part of me wanted you to see. Honestly, I kind of like the attention. I am a performer through and through, an exhibitionist. Divine's into that voyeur shite. Savior will join in on the action with a particularly frisky girl, but Divine only watches. He even rates our performances on occasion." He poked her arm to accentuate his next point. "Spirit's ranked highest in creativity, FYI."

"And you?"

"Um..." he scratched the back of his ear, "in

deviance."

She didn't know what to say to that, except: *You're all perverts.* But then, she'd be calling herself one too in a way. She dug into her leftover lasagna and said nothing further. Statistics. She needed to work on her statistics project.

The rest of lunch was quiet. Too quiet. And after she had come back from researching at the library, and Tommy had gotten back from recording in the studio, dinner passed even quieter. Perhaps they had shared too much. If there was such a thing as oversharing between best buds, they'd accomplished it today.

He was already in bed when she climbed in around one in the morning. Truth be told, she had stalled, hoping he'd be asleep once she got in. He wasn't. His head rested on one arm as he stared at the ceiling. She couldn't miss those gorgeous green eyes in the moonlight shining through the window, though they looked a darker shade of gray at the moment.

Wearing her favorite cotton short set, she lay next to him staring at the ceiling darkness as well. "Something wrong, Tommy?"

"If you start seeing Spirit, we won't be able to continue like this. He's not looking for a happy threesome. He wants to be my replacement."

So the Spirit thing was bothering him. That's what Tommy got for giving them the go-ahead. She rolled toward Tommy and stroked his cheek. "No one can replace you."

He stared into her eyes until she felt uncomfortable, vulnerable. He grabbed her hand to make her stop rubbing his face. "If you believe that, Spirit's right. I've been selfish, doing my own thing, keeping you from true love. Keeping you from finding the right replacement. What kind of mate am I for doing that?"

She felt irritated that he and Spirit had discussed in depth what was best for her without her input. "I'm an adult capable of making my own decisions."

He looked back at the ceiling but still held her hand. "Who are we kidding anyway? Sleeping in the same bed every night, no sex? What are we doing?"

"Trying to prove how weird we are?"

"I'm a musician. 'Weird' doesn't exist in my vocabulary. Things just are or aren't. And you are a twenty-one year old virgin because of me."

There were worst things she could be. A child molester, a drug addict, a Nazi… She felt like Tommy had already started pulling away from her, and he wasn't even a big star yet. "You can sleep on the couch if it'll make you feel like a better *mate*." She thought they were happy. That refusing to conform to norms just for conformity's sake was a good thing. Capri and Tommy did what they wanted to do and that was that. They were forward thinkers. Rebels. Now he was throwing shit on it all, like their way of doing things lacked validity. "Why *are* you in here every night anyway?"

He took a deep breath and exhaled noisily. "Because this beats sleeping alone. I hate that. I like to cuddle. I'm not a lad meant to spend much time alone. If I were a four-legged creature, I'd be a pack animal."

"You can sleep next to anyone."

"Where's the craic in that? Who wants to weed through the snorers and linen-hoggers? Besides, birds confuse everything to mean you want to be with them, when I don't. I just want to fuck 'em, maybe rub one out in their mouths, and send 'em on their merry fucking ways. I stay with you because I fancy you." He brought her fingers to his mouth and kissed them. "You satisfy my need for closeness and affection without demanding anything else from me. And since my cock stays in my underpants, I don't have to worry about it ruining us. We have the perfect arrangement."

"Ah. A romantic with commitment phobia."

He looked concerned. "You get the same thing out of this, yeah?"

She supposed she did, but she didn't spend time analyzing it. "Yeah," she shrugged. She would have been just as content with things being sexual between them back when she'd offered her virginity to him on a big humiliating platter. She wouldn't have stifled him anymore than she wanted to be stifled. At least she believed she could have handled it. Now, she'd never know.

She wondered what had happened in his life to make him this way. Overly needy with a strong aversion to pair-bonding—an odd combination. She'd be willing to bet it was all part of his defense mechanism kicking in. But why? Surely, not the ol' cliché of a bad breakup. He was too young for that to imprint on his whole life, and he'd never mentioned being heartbroken before. Capri wouldn't press the issue. Not now. Not at this hour. He would be inclined to inquire about her deepest, darkest secrets if she did. She'd save this profundity for another time.

Plus, this was a better time to ask something else that had been on her mind since his confessions from earlier in the day. "So…as a bonafide deviant, which hole do you prefer?"

"Deviant or no, I prefer anything over the shitter." Tommy proceeded to explain why, in vivid detail, using some of his worst experiences as examples. By the time the story had ended, she was in tears from laughter, and not at all interested in any backdoor action. She was also very tired.

Grabbing his hand, she rolled Tommy over with her so his hand would be on her waist as they settled into their spoon position for sleep. Whatever void they filled for each other, and however long fate would allow them to fill it, she'd not take a minute of it for granted.

Capri felt Tommy scooting his lower body away. "What are you doing?"

"Trying not to poke you."

She laughed. "You poke me every night."

"Tonight's different. Too much sex talk."

"You need a cold shower?"

"No. I'll be fine. It'll go down." He gripped her waist and moved her hip away from him. "Just stop moving."

Capri held tight to his hand and backed up into him, sealing his erection to the cotton on her butt cheeks. He groaned just like she knew he would. She had no intentions of stopping this time. Deep down, she hoped alleviating some of Tommy's other needs would prolong their "perfect arrangement", especially now that he had started questioning its appropriateness. She rolled her hips, feeling him thickening and throbbing at once.

"Not tonight, Capri. No teasing tonight." He whimpered and started to pull away.

"Okay. No teasing." She gripped his hip and held

him firm while she rolled her ass on him again. "It's okay," she soothed when he made an attempt to move away again.

He rotated his hips into her and jerked. When he started panting, his mouth was so close to her ear, it sent shivers throughout her whole body. She could feel her pussy pooling with lubrication.

"Capri, please. No teasing," he whined.

She started out rocking slowly to the beat of his exhales then increased the pressure and pace. His arms tightened around her, one around her abdomen, the other tight in her hair. She didn't let up. She could do this for him. "No teasing this time, Tommy. Just a friend helping another friend get off."

"Capri," he whispered. The desperation in his voice said everything. He wouldn't stop if she didn't, provided it didn't lead to intercourse.

His shudder shook her whole body. She kept going, undulating her ass against his erection, intending to keep going until he orgasmed. She wanted to continue hearing him whisper her name and grinding himself against her.

Her. Not the twins. Not her roommate. But her.

When his hand slid down to the juncture of her thighs, she grabbed it and held on tight. She just wanted to give him pleasure and hear his surrender to it. Even though she wanted his touch badly, there was no need in him doing so since he'd remained firm against deflowering her. He'd have to settle for dry humping her ass.

He settled all right. By the time his breath caught in his throat, and his mouth clamped down on her neck, she'd bitten her lip to keep from begging for his touch. She wanted those same thrusts deep in her core, where it oozed, pulsed and ached to be filled. She wanted the hands digging into her hair and hip to be on each breast as he pumped toward an orgasm. Just as she was about to test his willpower under these heated circumstances, she knew it was too late. His moment had arrived. One strong grunt later, and a tight squeeze of his arms around her, she felt his cock jerk.

"Ah, shit. Ah, shiiiiiit." Tommy groaned as his cock continued to spasm. His leg came down on top of hers and pinned her tight as he came.

Though he had many, and certainly better sexual experiences to compare it to, it had been the hottest moment of her life. The only thing that could have made it more perfect was if she could have seen his face at his moment of release.

She let him go and sighed. He detangled himself from her and sighed.

Then, silence. The quiet after the hormone storm. That moment after all the tension had built and released, and he had messy underwear to clean, and she had the dilemma of whether to feel ashamed or empowered.

"That's one lethal arse you got there, love," he said as his body shuddered one last time. "Makes me glad I didn't go sleep on the couch tonight."

Empowered. Definitely.

She smiled in the darkness. See, nothing about this had to be awkward. She just had to figure out what to do about Spirit.

CHAPTER 8

This was Tommy's fifth time playing Andrew Latimer's "Ice" solo, and he just knew he'd have to play it again once or twice more. It had been that kind of night, even though it didn't have to be. Capri had left him the keys to her car to go wherever he bloody well pleased as long as he topped off the gas tank. What did he do instead of catching up with some fiery young thing with perky tits and a plump derriere? Sit around Capri's flat and brood because she had gone out with Spirit.

How fucked up was that?

He looked at the clock on the wall again. Three hours. They'd been out doing fuck-knows-what for three hours. In all the time he'd spent sulking in her living room with his guitar, he couldn't be certain whether he was upset that the two people he'd most want to spend time with had run off and left him to his own miserable devices, or whether he was jealous that the most amazing girl he'd ever known was out with another pretty fucking fantastic guy, who also happened to be man enough to know a good thing when he saw it.

This sucked furry balls. Not only was Tommy getting a tragic glimpse into what his future nights of loneliness would look like, he was getting a crash course in *You Snooze, You Lose*. How ironic and moronic that he had practically pushed them to be together.

He struck a chord unnecessarily hard and broke a guitar string.

Fuck this.

He pulled out his mobile phone and searched through the contact list. Nah…Asa was too spoiled. She'd expect him to take her somewhere posh, as if he'd already graced the cover of *Rolling Stones* magazine and had a shitload of money. Consuelo, too rigid. Last time, she went mental when he walked in on her using the toilet, oddly after he'd just licked her squatting arse. Darlene talked too much, and he liked to be the one running his mouth. Plus, she didn't have anything interesting to say. Who cared about how many professional ball players had hit on her? Patricia K. had a scary Rottweiler who growled whenever Tommy was on top. He even attacked once when Tommy gave her arse a loud smack. Patricia R. had already shagged his whole band, which wouldn't be a problem, if she hadn't posted photos online of them all smoking grass together. Rowena was too ghetto. She'd have him shot up in her hood for sneaking around behind her gangster father's back.

Tommy thumbed through to the end of the list. No, no, no, and no. He wasn't in the mood for any of them. Not for fucking or companionship.

So he grabbed his backup guitar and played the damn song again.

Another hour passed before he heard a key in the

front door as it opened. It wasn't Capri, but he was happy nonetheless. Being alone was killing him.

"Sasha, baby. I'm so glad you're home. I'm so bored, I was about to start counting my scrotum lint. I've been—" Tommy stopped short on his way to the front door to greet her when he saw the man standing behind her.

"Tommy, this is my boyfriend Rob. Rob, Tommy." She closed the door behind them and addressed Rob. "He's a gifted guitarist who goes by the name of Godd in his rock band."

"Nice to meet you, Tommy. I'm more of a country music fan myself."

Tommy nodded and shook hands with the fella then looked at Sasha with unbridled skepticism. *Boyfriend? Country music? What is the world coming to?* "How long you two been going out?" So he'd know how much longer it would be before he saw unicorns and zombies walking about.

"A few weeks. We met at a strip club after a bachelorette party. It was love at first sight," she grinned at Rob.

Love? Ha! Tommy gave them a few more weeks max. There would be world peace before Sasha maintained peace with this tool. Rob was too…tamed for Sasha. Tommy could tell by the way Rob buttoned his shirt all the way to the top and parted his hair on the side. And were those trainers freshly polished on his feet? Perhaps they only had another week.

"I'm just coming by to get some clothes. Where's Capri?" Sasha gestured for Rob to sit on the couch, and he did, crossing his arms and legs.

Tool. "Out with Spirit."

She froze in route to her bedroom. "What do you

mean *out*?"

"They went out to dinner."

"Uh huh." She started walking again. "Why aren't you out with them?"

"Two's company. Three's a crowd. You know the saying." Tommy stood in her doorway as she opened drawers and threw clothes everywhere on top of clothes that were already thrown everywhere. He picked up a pair of her knickers and sniffed them.

She snatched them back. "That's why she's out with him and not you, you know. Don't you ever get your head out of the gutter?"

What? "Spirit's been just as bad as I've been." And what had this uptight chick done with Sasha?

"Been. Past tense. People change, Tommy. Everybody but you."

"You mean to tell me…" he lowered his voice and stepped close to her, "you no longer want me anytime, anyplace, any way I want? Sponge Bob Square Pants in there is doing it like that for you now, is he?"

"You're a walking, breathing poster boy for misery loves company," she said without stepping back. With reverence, she rubbed his chest through the t-shirt he wore. "I once thought of you as a fucking god in the flesh." She dropped her hand and stepped back. "But Capri and I talked the other morning while you were still getting your beauty rest. She didn't come out and say it, but I got the feeling something happened between you. Something she wanted to continue." Sasha had an accusation on her face.

"We didn't shag, if that's what you're getting at."

"Maybe not. Still. Something happened to make the idea of you serving her up on a platter and handing her off to your friend a punk move. You should have grown a pair and been who she needed you to be."

See…that's why he and Sasha would never work. Too volatile. Too batshit mental. "Capri is happy with the way things are." Why was he explaining anything to Sasha? "You think because you've had a friendly boy for five whole minutes that you met on the strip circuit, you can turn your nose up at me?"

She opened her closet door and turned to face him, flipping her hair as she did. "I'm not turning my nose up at you. Someone needs to punch you in the nose, but I'm a lady." She flipped her hair again. "You don't get it, do you? You really think Capri should be out with him right now instead of you?" She threw up a dismissive hand and turned back to her closet. "You don't deserve the name Godd. Not with the way you're fucking up, Tom Tom."

He picked up her dildo off the dresser and waved it around. "I don't need relationship advice, roomie. If you got the hookup on a record deal, I'm all ears."

"No, you don't," she laughed. "'Cause you won't have a relationship with Capri if you keep this up."

The word relationship made him twitch. "Keep what up? We're just mates." Tommy tossed the toy on her bed and left her room. He'd heard enough. Perhaps being alone wasn't so bad.

Sasha wasn't done. She followed him to the kitchen. "You want to know why Capri and I are still friends even after she saw us together? Because we're ride or die. I got her back. She got mine. We wouldn't let anything or anyone come between us. What about you?"

He was about to say he would actually die for

Capri and challenge Sasha to beat that, but movement from the center of the living room drew their attention. Tommy and Sasha noticed Capri and Spirit standing there next to where Rob, the twat, sat on the couch.

"Well, this is awkward," Tommy said.

More awkward conversation ensued until Sasha and Rob left, taking all her words of fine wisdom with them. Tommy didn't know how much of Sasha's past she had divulged to Rob, but Tommy suspected the ride to wherever they were going would be an interesting one. Tommy was more concerned with how Spirit would take Sasha's perception of him "coming between" Tommy and Capri.

Spirit didn't bat an eyelash. Perhaps he'd already adjusted to however awkward the situation would get. He certainly didn't look uncomfortable giving Capri a chaste kiss on the cheek that just so happened to make Tommy's guts rumble. Spirit did that only after Capri mentioned she had work to do early Saturday morning, *and* because she agreed to go out with him again that night after it was done.

So they were going to make a habit of this, eh? Cool. Peachy.

Tommy turned on his side away from Capri once they got in bed. For the first time he could remember, he didn't feel like cuddling. He also didn't feel like leaving her side and going to sleep on the couch. He listened to her talk about how she and Spirit went bowling and ice-skating. She talked about Spirit's real name being Gary, and how his band name had been a blessing in disguise. And she talked about the significance of Spirit's tattoos. How they each told a story about a scary period in his life as a reminder of how far he'd come. None of the bits about Spirit was news to Tommy. He felt miffed about not knowing Capri had an interest in bowling and ice-skating. He could have taken her to do either of those things at any time if he had known.

When Tommy had heard more than enough about her date, he went to sleep, leaving Capri to yap about Gary Fucking Spirit to herself in the darkness.

Tommy didn't fare any better the next night, except he played "While My Guitar Gently Weeps" by the Beatles. And it didn't take as long for Capri and Spirit to come back. Two hours, to be exact. They came in, sat with him on the couch for a while, and watched *Chappelle's Show* on the telly. This improved Tommy's mood greatly. Not only was the episode hilarious, but things must not have gone well on their second date. Tommy had never thought of himself as a petty man, but the idea of Capri and Spirit not working out warmed his heart. Tommy's competition for Capri's limited free time had been eliminated without a fight or harsh word on his part.

His victory was short-lived, however. By the time Tommy came back from popping popcorn, Capri and Tommy were making their way to Capri's bedroom.

What just happened?

Tommy grabbed Spirit's arm in reflex as Spirit walked by him. Spirit froze, and thus began their standoff. It took Tommy a second to breathe deeply and realize he didn't need to be confused or angry or possessive or combative. He just needed to give Spirit a final warning. Tommy just needed to remind Spirit that Capri would need tenderness, patience and lots of foreplay. At that moment, nothing came out of his mouth.

Spirit shook Tommy's arm off, reached in his jeans pocket, and handed Tommy the keys to his car. "Go take a drive, man." Then he went to Capri's room and shut the door.

Tommy stared at that door for ten minutes straight before deciding he had no right to bitch about anything. No right to interfere or instruct Spirit on the art of penetrating Capri's delicate walls when he hadn't had the courage to do it himself. As Sasha had pointed out, he had not grown a pair and been what Capri needed him to be. Spirit had a car, a degree, a decent part-time job, a rental house he shared, and the desire to be Capri's one and only. Tommy barely kept a job for more than a few weeks at a time, and he owned nothing but his instruments of love…and lust. Things were as they should have been—with Tommy outside the door while another man went inside and took care of Capri. *His* Capri.

For the first time since he'd handed Capri that concert flyer years ago, Tommy grabbed a blanket from the bathroom linen closet and slept on the couch.

The punch on his shoulder that woke him came as a surprise, and not just because it had been hard enough to wake him from a deep slumber. Spirit didn't have the look of jubilation on his face Tommy had expected. In fact, he looked disappointed. Tommy sat up. "What happened? What did you do? You knew you had to be gentle, you fucking shit-face-looking rat. Where is she?"

"Calm down. She's fine." Spirit brushed off Tommy's insults and held out his hand. "Where are my keys?"

Tommy's eyes narrowed. "Uh uh. I'm not giving

them to you so you can be *that* guy."

"She doesn't want me to stay, Tommy."

"Why not?" Tommy reached in his pocket and handed over Spirit's keys. "Are you sure she's okay?"

Spirit nodded. "I'm sure. Go check on her. She should be out of the shower now. Probably waiting for you." He headed to the door. "Oh—we have a meeting with a club promoter and possible band manager at three. I'll call you later."

Tommy rose from the couch, dazed in his half-sleep state and because he didn't understand why Spirit was leaving. "Spirit, what happened? Did you fuck her?"

With his hand on the door to leave, Spirit stopped, but he didn't turn to face Tommy. "No. I tried to make love to her. But that's not what she wanted. She didn't want me to kiss her or hold her. She just wanted sex. No attachments. No intimacy. I can't do that. Not with her." Spirit turned suddenly. He cocked his head to the side as if he'd had an epiphany and smirked. "And you can't either, can you? That's what all this shit is about. You're afraid she's going to have you by the balls."

"I don't want a serious relationship, period."

"So you keep saying. But you're kind of in one, aren't you? Just without the sex."

Aye. Whatever. It occurred to Tommy that Spirit's feelings may have been hurt. "Are you okay then?"

"Yeah, man. Listen though. Before either of you bring someone else into your twisted world of love and denial—don't. Work out your personal issues instead."

"Huh?"

Spirit left without another word.

Tommy had no idea what Spirit had gone on about. After all that cryptic talk about making love, Tommy couldn't be certain Spirit and Capri had even shagged. Tommy headed to Capri's room to make sure she wasn't hemorrhaging on the floor, just in case. Spirit was not a little fella.

Capri was changing the bed linen when he walked around to the side of the bed opposite her so he could help. That's when he put the pieces of Spirit's disjointed story together. Spirit had definitely been inside Capri. Tommy's Capri. The bloody sheet on the floor confirmed there had been penetration. Tommy hadn't realized he'd been hoping it hadn't happened until the evidence stared him in the face. So there it was. Spirit knew what it felt like to be inside her. To have her arms wrapped around his back, her legs around the backs of his thighs. To know the look on her face as her body expanded to accommodate a cock for the first time, one of substantial girth, at that. To hear her moans of pleasure and pain while he took only pleasure. Tommy should have been relieved that the responsibility did not fall on him, but he wasn't.

Jesus Christ. He had too many conflicting feelings when he didn't want to feel anything.

He swallowed the lump in his throat. The imagery would make him mental if he didn't stop it. "Spirit didn't look too happy with your performance. Did you get his cock stuck in his zipper too?"

"Haha. Funny. Like you care that I sent him home. You like the couch that much?"

"No, I do not fancy the couch, but Spirit's my mate. He's your mate too. You didn't have to be so cold about it. I told you he had feelings for you." Which was why it never paid to feel like that for anyone. Falling hard meant landing in the pits of H-E-L-L. People took your heart and smashed it on the floor once they knew they had the power to do so. That's what being seriously involved with someone was all about. No, thanks on that. "You've had sex one time, and straightaway, you're already a fem fatale. One day you're going to have to confess why you're like that."

"You first. Tell me why you whore around and avoid catching feelings at all costs."

"That's where you're wrong. I feel lots...especially when I hold a girl's face while I'm fucking her mouth. The ones with no gag reflex let me go deep enough to feel their tonsils."

"Deflection. That's what I thought." She took the soiled sheets to the kitchen trashcan and came back. She put the pillows back on the bed and climbed in. "Guess we're even now. I hooked up with your friend, you hooked up with mine."

He picked up the comforter from the floor and put it at the foot of the bed. "Yeah, but I never had sex with Sasha. Blowjobs don't count any more than what you and I did last week."

Capri's eyes widened. "All this time I thought you had."

Not that knowing details would have changed the outcome, but he shook his head. "You thought wrong. She sucked me off just the once. That's it. Now she's blowing Rob, the love of her life."

They had a laugh at that, knowing Sasha's current situation wouldn't last long.

Capri's face changed to guilt. "I feel like I used Spirit."

"That depends. Did he come?"

121

"Oh, yes."

"He'll be fine then." Tommy climbed in bed next to Capri, turned off the lamp, and spooned behind her. "You're fucked up, you know that?"

"Yeah. So are you." She pulled out her mobile phone and started dialing.

"What are you doing?"

"Texting a random number to tell them I'm pregnant and the baby's theirs."

Tommy laughed. "My, have you come a long way, Ben Stein."

They texted a few unsuspecting folks who didn't bother responding with anything more exciting than "wrong number" before they gave up on what should have been an epic prank.

Capri jumped out of the bed and ran to the kitchen. She came back with a bottle, no glasses. She climbed back in bed. "Let's toast to me finally entering womanhood."

"Took you long enough." He managed to duck her elbow aimed at his ribs. "All right." He raised the bottle and said, "Sláinte," before taking the first sip.

He caught himself staring at her moonlit lips too long as they took turns sipping. But he was getting as good a stare back as he was giving. After a few rounds, he held his hand up to stave off his next turn at the bottle. He rested his head back on the pillow and redirected his eyes to the dark ceiling.

"It should have been you, Tommy."

He almost retorted with something witty and totally unrelated. Her pensive tone of voice made him change his mind and address the elephant in the room. "I know. I'm sorry." What else could he say? She knew it. He knew it. Sasha and Spirit knew it too.

Everybody knew it, including every girl he met who wanted a piece of his heart, and couldn't get close to having it. They all knew one other irrefutable fact as well: sex changed things. He didn't want things to change between him and Capri. In the end, that had been the prevailing desire. He wanted her to remain in his life…as his best mate. "It should have been us out there ice-skating and bowling too. Why didn't you tell me you wanted to do that instead of always going on about how much work you have to do?"

"I never thought about it until Spirit mentioned it." She started running her fingers through his hair. "What about Six Flags? I've never been there. The tickets are probably too—"

"Don't worry about it. I'll make it happen. I'll take you to Six Flags." He pulled her head down to rest on his chest. "We'll go. Soon. It won't be a date though."

"Oh, I know. Of course not."

Another minute passed before he had to ask it. "Was it all that you imagined? Sex, I mean? Would you do it again?"

He felt her jaw move into a smile. "Definitely. As often as I can."

Sweet. Tommy closed his eyes and pretended he'd never asked her the question.

CHAPTER 9
FOUR YEARS LATER

Capri looked over on her desk at the framed picture of her hoisted on Tommy's shoulders and smiled. Seeing it and remembering when it was taken always brought a smile to her face. She had that one and only photo in her office as a psychological, visual reminder for the workaholic in her that there were more important things in life than work and accolades. One day the message would finally sink in.

It had been a hot and sunny day, one perfect for being adventurous with friends. They'd gone to the water park at Six Flags and rode on everything they could, ate everything they could, and laughed as hard as they could, until they'd passed out later from exhaustion. Prior to that day, she couldn't think of any other time she'd devoted a full day to just having fun. Even though she and Tommy had looked like a happy, committed Hallmark couple, it hadn't been a date, of course. Sasha and Rob had gone with them and made it their first double non-date. Capri didn't find out until much later that Tommy had paid for the trip by pawning his favorite guitar. His sacrifice had made the day and its memory even more special.

Though he'd never said it aloud, she knew it had been a defining moment for them. He'd basically shown that she and her happiness meant more to him than anything else. His platonic love for her was deeper than either of them had realized up until that point.

She'd wanted to make an equally demonstrative statement, except she had no valuable personal possessions. As much as she loved him as her BFF, she couldn't give up what she treasured most for him: work. One of the benefits of being a friend and not a formal girlfriend meant she didn't have to. Two years later, she'd bought Tommy an even better guitar to celebrate the release of album number two, but the gesture had seemed vapid compared to his. It hadn't shown much sacrifice or imagination on her part since she'd had the money. At that point, he'd had the money too.

When her former professor/mentor turned boss offered her a permanent, salaried position in his mental health clinic, where she could assist with treating many of his longstanding patients, she took it with no hesitation. That meant she couldn't go on tour with Tommy to select cities nationwide to promote his second album. "Angels with Stubby Wings" was comically light, and the album became a huge hit, however, her job was a coveted, hard-to-come-by start in the professional world. It was a great way to gain on-the-job experience under the supervision of a well-respected licensed therapist while she established her own name in the field. She couldn't get that experience on the road with Tommy. His band couldn't rise to stardom with him hiding in the safety of her apartment.

A dreaded separation had been imminent.

For two people who shied away from attachments, their first split had felt like an amicable breakup. Hard to do, but with no hard feelings. Whether out of habit or codependency, they managed to speak daily throughout that looong year. When he'd come back to record in the studio and perform at local spots, it had been a utopian-style reunion. She'd hoped he'd always stay tucked away in her corner of the world. But that's not how success worked. That's not what Tommy was destined for.

While Capri had continued working towards her doctorate, winning several awards for her research analyses and published journal articles, Celestial Decadence's darker, more hardcore third album, "Slurp, Slurp: Angel Blood", had been even more well-received, resulting in platinum status. The song, "Creepy Cold Vixen", written by Spirit about his short fling with Capri, had catapulted the band to stardom across the country and internationally. Though it had only been six months ago that the band had gone on their first worldwide tour, this second separation between Capri and Tommy felt like a lifetime.

She and Tommy no longer talked on the phone daily, though they did try to remain connected via email, text, Skype, Facebook…whatever technology they had available with easiest access. With him overseas, and both of them busy, staying in touch had proven a more difficult task this time around. He'd asked her to join him several times, even sent a plane ticket once. Other than being overjoyed that Tommy's dreams were being realized, Capri didn't give her role in the tour a second thought. He had his dreams; she had hers. She had to be supportive from afar. Yes, it would have been nice to see Europe, especially with him, but she couldn't put her career aside for that, no matter how devastating the distance between them seemed. She couldn't take a leave from her patients and studies. Not when she was [this] close to achieving everything she had worked toward. Her mother would be back one day. Capri would need to give an account for the time, opportunity, and second chance she'd been given. Staying the course was the right thing to do. It was what a responsible person would do.

But she missed the band terribly.

Okay. She missed Tommy. Terribly. His absence was like a hole in her chest that couldn't be filled no matter how many random trysts she—

"Hello? Ms. Jackson?" said the man sitting on the patterned couch in front of her. He waved his hand at her again. "I asked if you thought I did the right thing."

Capri tore her eyes from the photo and looked at her patient, mister uh… She looked down at the manila folder in her hand and read the name. "Yes, of course, Mr. Langston. You did the best you could, given the situation. More importantly, how do *you* feel about what you did?" Langston never followed her advice. He just liked coming in every week for an hour to talk about all the reasons he couldn't follow her advice. He really just wanted a verbal affirmation that he was sane. As long as he didn't harm himself or others, and he remained on his medication, Capri could give him a few attaboys.

"Yes. I did my best," he nodded.

"Good." She peeked at her watched discreetly. "I think that's all the time we have for today. Be sure to follow the breathing techniques we discussed. Okay?" She gave him her warmest smile and intense gaze. "I'll see you again next week." She stood to walk him out.

As soon as she escorted him to the front desk, Capri walked briskly back to her office and locked her door. She couldn't wait until later. After listening to four back-to-back patients talk about problems that were so miniscule, she didn't understand why they were "problems", Capri needed some relief. Some major relief. Of the sexual variety.

After closing the blinds, she hiked up her skirt to her waist, plopped down in her desk chair, and threw one leg on top of her desk. She spread her legs to gain access to the throbbing bud at her center. Sliding her hand inside her panties, she intended to tease herself a little and gradually build it up. That intent didn't last. She threw her head back at the first touch and bit her lip. Damn, she needed this release right away, no delay. But after she flicked and rubbed and thrust and massaged for so long, she still couldn't arrive at the climax she desperately wanted. It all made her tenser and more frustrated than when she'd first began. Fuck!

She kicked off her pumps and pulled off her blazer to get more comfortable. This orgasm had to happen now. She pulled the Magic Wand out of her bottom left drawer, leaned further back in the chair and applied it right where she needed it, right on her aching clit. Where it would work at the right pressure and pace to get her off. Except the fast pace numbed her after a while, and she was even further from coming. Fuck it to fucking hell!

She needed a minute to collect herself, so she lay back in the chair and closed her eyes. She took deep breaths to still her body and mind. She looked over at their photo, the thing that always grounded her when she felt frustrated. In that one moment frozen in time, she saw happiness, love, peace, and contentment. It was all there along with so much more. Talent. Passion. Beauty. Olive green eyes. Wild curly hair. Smooth taut skin. A perfect smile. A really sexy, blood-pressure-raising accent… Capri grabbed the wand again and put it on a lower setting. She rocked her hips into waves of pleasure, gradually increasing the tempo until she shot straight to the stars. In her final moment before exploding in the chair, she glided two fingers inside and stroked to maximize the sensations. She kept her eyes on the picture. On his smile. When her release came, it was urgent and intense…and confusing as hell.

Nooo.

This was a dangerous path to go down. And not the kind of danger she enjoyed.

She turned the frame face-down and stared at the back of it while she collected herself. Once her breathing returned to normal, she got up and cleaned herself off with baby wipes she kept stashed in her drawer.

Once cleaned, she drummed her manicured nails on the desk. She really could stand another round. But not by herself this time. She pushed a button on her desk phone. "Excuse me, Sierra, but do I have any meetings scheduled for this afternoon?"

"No, ma'am. No appointments. No meetings. Your next one is with Mr. Harper tomorrow at ten."

"Okay, thank you. I'm going to run an errand. You can reach me on my cell, if need be." Capri grabbed her purse and her briefcase and headed to the nearest bar.

Masturbating while looking at a pic of her and Tommy was bad enough—horrendous—but now sitting at the bar…scoping a lookalike…that was horrendous to the tenth power. Still, she scanned the room. Nothing unusual about that. She scoped out a fuckbuddy in this same bar a few times a week. You might call this a routine of sorts. Looking for a tall man with a lean body and a head full of messy curly hair was not. After a thorough search, she discovered there were lots of good-looking, well-dressed men here. None of which were as captivating as her Irishman.

Two seats down at the bar, Capri saw a guy that fit the description except he had ginger hair. No, that wouldn't work. The hair needed to be dark brown at least. She'd be flexible with eye color, since she didn't intend to stare in them, but not the color of his hair.

She shunned three or four men interested in keeping her company, one of which she'd already picked up in the same bar before. Eventually, she went back and took him up on the offer. If memory served correctly, he'd been a pretty impressive fuck the first time around, and she really needed a good fucking. She ignored him when he asked for her name. He didn't seem too offended. Skipping the pleasantries, he allowed her to lead him by his tie to somewhere less crowded.

They didn't go far. Capri didn't need much privacy. Where was the fun in that?

Stepping her feet on the toilet rim, she tore off her panties while he put on a condom. When he was ready and sheathed, she slid down on his cock as he gripped her ass. She let him pound her hard against the bathroom wall, avoiding his lips every time he tried to kiss her. He banged her over and over. Bang, bang. Bang, bang. It sounded like John Witherspoon narrating from the adjoining stall. His rhythm felt good, intense enough to drive the demons inside her head away and replace the emptiness with ecstasy. But she couldn't reach her elusive orgasm. It just wouldn't happen.

"Come with me!" he growled.

"What the fuck you think I'm trying to do? Finger paint?"

He lasted another thirty seconds before she felt his first shudder. When he'd finally relieved himself, she stood back on the toilet and flicked herself off while he buttoned his pants. He smiled at the show, even tried to hold her and help her out. She used the heel of her shoe to push him back to the stall door. *Just watch* her eyes said to him. He did until she climaxed.

"You are so hot, woman." He pulled her toward him. "So. You gonna give me the digits this time or what? Don't make me come back in here every day hoping for a chance meeting."

How cute. Too bad she preferred anonymity. "You're not getting my number," she smirked. "See ya when I see ya." She righted her clothes and squeezed by him to exit the stall. Feeling better, she went back to the office to work. Turned out it was better not to fuck a knock-off version of Tommy. That would have been like fucking Michael Pitt and envisioning Leonardo DiCaprio. What the hell had she been thinking? Never mind the fact that it was *Tommy* she was thinking of here. Her *friend*.

Capri was getting out of control, the result of

letting dormant issues go untreated. Clinically speaking, Capri knew she was using sex as a distraction from dealing with her real issues. Some things just couldn't be ignored by working herself to death. Besides, she really liked fucking.

Men came in so many different sizes and shapes. So many different fucking styles and techniques. Each guy brought a different personality to his fucking, a different level of intensity and emotion. Above all that, there was nothing like watching one orgasm. The look on his face at the moment nothing else mattered but what he felt flowing from his cock. The sound of his breathing as he focused on getting to that moment. The rise and fall of his chest, the throbbing of his shaft glans, the indenture of his abs, the way sweat rolled down his temples... Fucking was an art, each male an artist. Capri just wanted to sample and enjoy as many different artists as possible until she discovered which combination of touches, sounds, tastes, smells, and personalities were best suited for her. And then maybe she'd still continue to fuck random strangers just for the hell of it. Why not? Virginity, abstinence, chastity, purity, celibacy, monogamy, all those restrictive nouns were so overrated. It was so much better to fuck and have orgasms. Verbs—those made life worth living.

What of the Tommy thing? She hadn't worked through the details of that yet. Given a guess, she'd wager that she had transferred her general lust to him because of his forbidden fruit status.

Then again, inserting Tommy into one of her fantasies could have been a fluke. As in, something that just happened by chance because his photo happened to be there. Purely coincidental. Even if it hadn't been an accident, fantasizing about him wasn't anything to be ashamed of. She'd broken no laws. It was natural, considering he was just another gorgeous man she hadn't experienced sexually. While it wasn't the most becoming thing for a best friend to do, she wouldn't lose sleep over it. There were plenty of other hunks to keep her occupied. Most likely any one of them would be better in the sack than Tommy anyway, since the fantasy was always better than the real thing.

Hopefully, he'd be able to make it in time for Sasha's wedding this weekend. It would serve him right to eat crow too as Capri did her maid of honor duties. Sasha, Capri's roommate of many years and reformed, self-proclaimed whore, was marrying the man of her dreams. The fact that Tommy and Capri had scoffed and betted against their relationship, had made Rob and Sasha's impending nuptials even more enthralling. Outside of Rob's awful southern twang and poor taste in music, he wasn't too bad a guy. Who knew?

As Capri drove up to her apartment, she started yawning. She'd gone in at five a.m., and it was now after ten. Time to shower and crash, as usual, and follow the same routine tomo—

She almost leapt out of the car before it had come to a complete stop. She screamed, throwing the car in park as she straddled between two parking spaces and ran into Tommy's awaiting arms. "When did you get here? How long will you be? Why didn't you call me?"

"Wait. Slow down." He spun her around in his arms, grinning. "I arrived about an hour ago. I can't stay longer than the weekend. And…duh. I wanted to

133

surprise you. If I would have called, you may not have jumped on me like this."

"So you like me jumping on you, huh?"

He shrugged. "Yeah. It's nice to get a hearty Golden Retriever welcome sometimes without having to endure fleas and mutt breath."

She slapped his arm. "Well, the joke's on you. I could have been here an hour ago. I worked later because I had no one to come home to."

"As if that would have made a difference. You worked late because it's what you do."

"I would have come home early to see you."

He looked as if he didn't believe her.

"I would have! I would have even picked you up from the airport."

"It's okay. The limo driver dropped me off first before taking Spirit to his girl's house." He set her back down on her feet and looked around as if something had just dawned on him. "Wait. I'm not imposing am I?" He flattened his hand on his chest. "Is there a significant other I should get approval from to stay at yours? I just assumed… I mean you never mentioned—"

"Don't be ridiculous. Of course, you can stay. I would be offended otherwise." She grabbed one of his bags and put it on the shoulder she didn't have her purse on. "And hell naw, there isn't a significant other. What do I need with one of those? Come on. I'll make you some tea." She held up his t-shirt to expose his lean belly. "And some food. Damn boy, you been eating?"

"Tins of beans, mostly. After suffering through food poisoning, I don't trust fast food. I rather eat beans and sardines right out of a tin."

"I have just the thing to put some meat on your bones." As she walked up the steps to her two bedroom apartment, the thought crossed her mind that she didn't know whether he'd sleep in her guestroom or with her. She'd made the second bedroom her home office, but it could easily be a place of rest and privacy for a guest who wanted it.

Tommy seemed a bit uncertain where to go next once he walked in the living room as well. He'd never been to this place since she'd moved only a few months ago after Sasha moved in with Rob. Capri had needed something within her own budget. Seeing him put his stuff down in the living room by the couch felt strange and familiar at the same time. He had the same travel gear she remembered. He was still her Tommy even without the bouffant hair. Seeing his belongings dumped and bundled in her spotless front room without being organized in her closet and drawers, however, looked more like an alien invasion. It didn't feel like he'd actually come back to where he belonged.

It had been six months since she'd seen him in person. Maybe they should play the sleeping arrangements by ear. Maybe *he* had a significant other he hadn't told her about.

She set her things down on the counter, dropped his bag with the rest of his pile, and got busy putting two mugs of water in the microwave. "I'm so glad you could make it. I feel like I can make it through the whole fiasco now. Why someone would want to commit to one person for the rest of their lives, I'll never understand. Did Divine and Savior come also?" She noticed he was still standing in the middle of the room with his hands in his pockets, checking out her wall painting. "Come sit down." She patted a seat at the kitchen table. He looked like he didn't feel welcomed. "Don't get brand new. You're at home here."

"I was just thinking of how this feels more like coming home than when I went to Ireland a few weeks ago." He gave a melancholy smile. "And no. Savior and Divine stayed in Prague. They send their love."

"Surely, your parents were happy to see you and proud of the musician you've become."

"Not like you. No one ran and jumped into my arms. My mamó would have, but she's gone. She would have jumped across the Red Sea to welcome and congratulate me. My brother just used me to pick up chicks. Guess I've missed you more than I thought." Their eyes met, and it was awkward. Charged with something...nostalgia? "I should take a load off," he laughed nervously, walked in the kitchen and sat.

As cocky as he carried himself, Capri wasn't surprised by his need to have his ego stroked. She'd never known him to be nervous though. "Well, I'll have to channel your grandmother and have enough pride and giddiness for both of us. I'm so proud of you, Thomas Allen Delaney." Capri walked over and hugged him to her bosom. "I've missed you too. Very much. Things aren't the same without you."

"So come back with me." His piercing eyes looking up at her nearly stunned her off her feet.

"You know I can't." She escaped to the microwave to get their mugs and her emotions under control. Emotions, libido...she honestly couldn't be sure which energy he stirred up most.

BEST FRIENDS, FANTASY LOVERS

He nodded. "I had to try again anyway." He leaned his head left and right as if to crack his neck.

She placed his mug and the honey jar in front of him then reached out to finger his hair. "I see you have a new do." He'd grown a light mustache and chin hair also that didn't connect to a goatee. It was just enough to remind her he was a man, not just some guy she liked to kick it with. "The facial hair is all well and good, but I thought it was understood that you would never, ever cut your beautiful hair." His mass of curls had shortened to smaller, more defined ones. His do was shaped like a man toying with the idea of being less artsy, less androgynous, and displaying a more heartthrob-ish, masculine persona. She liked *and* disliked it. She loved how the shorter hair drew more attention to his eyes and eyebrows. Olive green popped out of his head like beacons to Sexyville. She didn't like having less to run her fingers through. And she didn't much like being reminded that he was a red-blooded, heterosexual male with a thick, uncut cock that she knew exactly how to handle now.

"Time to try something new. You know my hair grows like a weed. In two weeks, it'll be out to here." He held his arms out wide.

She looked in his eyes and thumbed his bushy eyebrows down in a smoother arch. "You're beautiful either way. Just flawless." Boy, had she laid that ego-boost on heavy. Although she'd meant every word, when his eyes met hers, she wished she'd used a more playful tone. They were getting it all wrong this evening. The sexual undercurrent was too strong to deny, yet too wrong to acknowledge.

He held her gaze and spoke low. "I'm sure there

are health benefits to drinking hot water, but in order to have tea, I need a teabag, love."

Drats. Maybe it was just her that couldn't get it together tonight. After working all day, it was understandable. She'd blame it on fatigue.

She procured herbal teabags from the cabinet and dipped one in both of their mugs. Feeling his eyes on her the whole time, she filled two plates with pot roast and potatoes from the slow cooker she'd left on all day. Sitting in a chair next to him, they ate in the uncomfortable silence of reunited, sexually aroused friends.

"That was scrumptious, Capri. Thank you. Best thing I've had since I left." He patted his belly then stretched. "You know we're up for a Grammy, yeah?"

"Yeah. For that ol' fucked up song Spirit wrote about me." Capri rolled her eyes. "I should have a cut of the profits...and his balls hanging from my rearview mirror."

Tommy spit out his tea as he laughed. "I will buy you whatever you want: a house, car, yacht, island... And I'll double it all if you manage to get his balls away from his girl."

That put the conversation back on the right track. They talked about everything and nothing and caught up like friends should. After rinsing their dishes and loading the dishwasher, they moved to the couch. There, they talked about how establishing the band as industrial rock had been the best thing for it. They talked about how Capri saved a ton of money on work suits by shopping at secondhand designer shops. They were on their second cup of tea by the time Tommy mentioned how much he loved touring, with emphasis on how tiring it was.

"You're young and vivacious. This is everything you wanted," Capri said.

"Yes, but… Okay, confession—and I never thought I'd say this, but—I'm tired of having random sexual encounters."

Her brows shot up. "Wow. I never thought I'd *hear* you say that. 'Excess pussy comes with being a rock star', you used to say all the time. You looked forward to it."

"Well, it's gotten boring. The same old thing happens every night after a concert. A hot girl, several, in fact, will be waiting for me. Sisters, friends, cousins, married women, it doesn't matter. They just want to be fucked. That's it. It's no longer thrilling. There's no chase. No teasing. I have no doubt whether one will turn me down. She won't. I don't even have to ask for it. It's like they just want to be able to say they fucked Godd. They don't care who I am on the inside. They don't care what I like or dislike…unless it involves a kinky position. I've finally gotten the groupies, more than I can stand, and I don't want it. I don't want chicks who don't even know me and who I don't know. I could be any Joe Schmoe with a guitar and they'd still want to shag me. It's all rubbish. I don't want that kind of attention. The last few times I've had sex, I didn't even finish."

She studied his face to see if he was being sincere, and saw that he was. Whoa. "First off, you're not giving yourself enough credit. You are worth all the attention. There're plenty of them who would actually like you, but you don't give them the opportunity to because you're lumping them all in the same groupie boat. Secondly, you've probably done too much, Tommy. You had girls calling you Godd before the fame. I imagine it's all a bit underwhelming now. All the orgies. All the public, spontaneous places. All the different girls… You probably should give yourself a break. Try abstinence."

He nodded and toyed with one of the silver medallions around his neck. "This weekend. This is my break," he smirked. "Next week, it'll be back to the rock-n-roll lifestyle. I do have a deity reputation to maintain. I can't deprive the ladies of a good story to tell their mates." He held up his pinky and index finger to flash the universal rock sign. "What about you? Still not thinking of settling down with your own personalized ball and chain?"

"I see no reason to. I have no desire to be a quote unquote honest woman." She tucked her feet underneath her ass. "Unlike you, I'm enjoying all the random sex. The more cocks, the better."

"Peachy." Only, Tommy didn't sound peached. "Are you at least being safe?"

"Of course. And you got a head-start on me, so don't go getting all puritanical on me now that I'm enjoying all the wild oats."

He looked away. "You don't have to play catch-up, you know."

"I know. Not that I ever could, whore." But it was too much fun attempting to do so.

"You know, out of all the drugs I've tried, nothing is better than good sex. I miss being enthused about it. You better pace yourself before you get bored with the high too."

She smiled coyly. "Confession…" She waited until he looked up. "I never have an orgasm during intercourse. I get close, but it just doesn't happen. My favorite part is watching them come. That's my high.

I like hearing them at that moment and feeling their energy soar. Don't get me wrong—I love getting off too, and I do on my own immediately after because watching them turns me on so much. There's something so otherworldly about watching a man achieve the ultimate pleasure. Being there at that moment, being the cause of it… Believe me, I'm a long way from boredom."

Tommy frowned. "All this sex you're having and claim to be enjoying and you never orgasm *with* them?"

She shook her head. "Not with them inside me. Doesn't mean I don't enjoy everything else." Capri had long gotten over feeling like she had a physical deficiency. More than likely, the issue had mental roots…something she didn't care to look at too closely. "Anyway…I need a shower," she said, patting his shoulder. "After that, what do you say we indulge in a good ol' prank for old time's sake?"

He shrugged. "What did you have in mind?"

"I don't know. Something that's not too elaborate. Think about it. I'll be back in a jiffy."

When she came out of the shower, he took a turn in. Not long thereafter, they were clean and dressed in t-shirts and underwear, heading out into the parking lot. That's where they asked random drivers where the complex's security guard was because they needed emergency help. Being half-dressed helped their ruse. When asked what kind of help they needed because there was no security guard, Tommy and Capri mooned the Good Samaritans and ran off. Things took an interesting turn when a guy recognized Tommy, took a picture of Tommy's ass, and asked for an autograph. Perhaps pranking needed to be more elaborate, and from a distance, now that he had a face that could easily be seen on television. Tommy signed the guy's t-shirt and had a drink with him in exchange for having the picture deleted.

After enjoying a laugh with Tommy's fan but losing the pranking mood altogether, Capri and Tommy went back to her apartment and fell out on the living room couch. Things worked themselves out when it came to where they would sleep. Within minutes, Tommy spooned Capri like the good old days. All was right with the world.

Until she woke up.

Saturday morning brought an erection so hard, Capri thought Tommy would cut through her t-shirt that had ridden up her thighs during the night. It was the first thing she noticed as her brain surfaced to consciousness. The arm thrown across her hip and the other hand shoved in her hair served as reminders that her one and only bed buddy had actually come home. The evening hadn't been a dream. The part of his body standing at attention in his sleep, told her his appetite for all things salacious had not disappeared or lessened with age...or stardom, as he'd have her believe.

She needed to slip out of his grasp and start getting ready for work. A S A P.

In spite of her innocent intentions, she took a moment to marvel Tommy's size. She'd seen and felt enough cocks to know his was surprisingly nice, especially for such a lean man. She considered how it would feel entering her from his position behind her. How powerful his thrusts would be. How wet she'd be for him. The thought made her pussy clench violently, and she knew she had to get up. If at all possible, she needed to do so without waking him. At this point, waking him would be better than the alternative. Getting away from the manly part of him calling her attention and awakening her lust was the priority.

When she tried to get up without disturbing him, he gripped her tighter to his body and murmured in his sleep. She tried to get up again.

"What are you doing? Stop moving," he groaned.

"I have to go to work. I'll be back early so we can hang out before the bachelor/bachelorette party."

"Why are you whispering?"

"Because I don't want to wake you."

"I'm awake."

"I'll slip off the couch, and you can go back to sleep." She tried to get up again, which caused her to rock into him.

He groaned again and held on tighter, burying his face in her hair. "I haven't been to sleep yet."

Oh. If he'd been hard like this all night, poor baby must have been in serious pain.

She stayed still, feeling him throb against the thin cotton of her panties. "I see you're still a horny fucker."

"I'm sorry. I've gotten out of the habit of sleeping next to a woman. I didn't mean—"

"Don't worry about it." She rotated her butt cheeks before he could tell her not to. "Let me help." As her gyrations continued, she loved the feel of him straining to get tighter to her. Loved the way his breath caught and came out ragged. And then…she decided this time wouldn't be all about him. She wanted to orgasm too, dammit. He felt so good wrapped around her. He sounded so good in her ear.

He smelled so delicious. She couldn't take the torture. She didn't have to. She grabbed his hand and pulled it from her waist down to the rim of her panties. He took the hint from there, thank God, bypassing the thin material until he got to her throbbing clit. Her hips bucked on contact. Regardless of how long it had been taking her to come with other partners, this time with Tommy would not be like that.

"I see *you're* a horny little fucker," he whispered in her ear.

The way he never pronounced his T's, made his accented way of saying "little" burn her insides.

She didn't respond, unless you consider her draping the heel of her foot behind his leg. It spread her open further, allowing his fingers more access. She reached around behind her and stuck her hand in the opening of his boxers so she could stroke him and ease his painful erection. Judging by his labored breathing pattern, he wouldn't last any longer than her. They'd come together. It would be beautiful and—

Aggressive beating at the front door brought them out of the fantasy where what they were doing didn't have consequences. They both jerked as if they'd been caught doing something wrong. The beating began again.

"Capri! I know you're in there. Your car's outside. Open up!"

Sasha. At Capri's door at…the clock on the wall said quarter after seven. What in the world?

Capri removed her hand from Tommy's boxers and got up. She pulled her t-shirt down, but it wasn't enough to hide all the moisture on her thighs. "Just a minute!" she shouted. After she wiped with a hand towel, she and Tommy put on shorts to cover their indiscretions before Capri headed to the door. She paused once more before opening it to make sure Tommy was composed. He looked frustrated as hell but otherwise acceptable. He placed a throw pillow in his lap and nodded.

She opened the door for Sasha.

"Took you long enough. What the fuck?" Sasha barged in. "I went by your office first. I just knew you'd be there. Anyway—I can't. I can't do it. What was I thinking? I can't marry Rob tomorrow." She took one look at Tommy on the couch and screamed. She rushed over to him and hugged him. After mentioning how good it was to see him, and thanking him for coming back for her wedding, her tone dropped. She stepped back, narrowing her eyes as she looked back and forth between Tommy and Capri. "Did I interrupt something?" They both shook their heads as if TSA had asked if they were carrying explosives aboard a plane.

Before Sasha could think about it further and ask more questions, Capri led her to the kitchen. "What the fuck you mean you can't marry Rob tomorrow? You love him. You guys are great together. Tommy and Spirit came all this way to see it happen." In the kitchen, away from a flushed Tommy, Capri could talk about men, love, marriage and commitment. Yeah, because Capri knew all about those things and subscribed to the ideology of monogamy. Well, maybe not. But she did know a lot of money had been spent on Sasha's wedding. Tommy and Sprit *had* left their tour for it. And Sasha really had met the love of her life all those years ago.

Capri was out of her element here. Element or

no, she knew she had to say something to warm Sasha's last minute cold feet. With any luck, perhaps Capri could learn to take her own advice. Ha! Yeah, right. At the very least, Capri needed to say the right thing to get Sasha out of the apartment so Capri could resume her activities already in progress.

Because that shit with Tommy had been scorching hot. Hot enough to make her go back for seconds, maybe even thirds, if she wasn't careful. Even if it meant crossing a line never meant to be crossed between friends. She and Tommy made the rules for their friendship anyway. Couldn't they eliminate their one prohibition...at least temporarily?

CHAPTER 10

Tommy hadn't heard one syllable Capri and Sasha spoke in the kitchen, but he could probably sketch out an exact replica of what he'd been fixated on since Sasha interrupted the hottest moment he'd had in ages—Capri's luscious arse. He wanted in there badly. From the back, from the front, sideways, upside down…

Jesus Christ.

Tommy needed to shag someone else…and fast, or else all hope at preserving the most important relationship he had would be lost. His cock had always gotten him in trouble. Always. Not being sexual with Capri was the one time he'd gotten it right. The one time he'd kept his cock to himself no matter how perfect her breasts were. No matter how many times she'd teased him and let it be known all he had to do was take it and she wouldn't stop him. He'd been a good little lad with her, for the most part. And now he was about to fuck it up royally. For what? An orgasm? He could get that anywhere.

What he couldn't get anywhere was the girl who had put up with him being so broke she had to feed him, and loan him her car, and give him a place to stay. Or the girl who opened her arms to him every night without wondering how weird he was for needing to spend that time in her arms, without her pressuring him for more. The girl who rented crowds of cheering and adoring fake fans so that his struggling band didn't perform to empty rooms. The one who'd always believed in him. The one who'd known he'd be right where he was today. She, who worked so hard to be the best at what she did, and still managed to make him feel like the luckiest man alive. She, who knew all…well, most of his secrets and faults, and loved him anyway. He couldn't get that everywhere.

What idiot would fuck that up?

Tommy went to the lavvy and beat his meat until it was proper empty, holding a bottle of Capri's perfume up to his nose as he let the last of his pent up lust go. He could have done without that reminder of the woman he wanted to be inside of more than anything. Nevertheless, he hadn't been inside her. He'd shown his cock who was boss. He was the master of his flesh and wicked desires. He would not let either ruin a good thing, which happened to be the healthiest relationship he'd ever had. After a cold shower, he felt loads better.

That lasted until Capri had calmed down her raging mate, if you could call it "calming down". Sasha had gone from wanting to call off the wedding and run away to the Himalayans to being ready to elope in Vegas with Elvis giving Rob permission to kiss his bride. A little more fine-tuning later and Sasha decided she could wait until the already scheduled ceremony took place.

Eek. *Ya think?* What was it about weddings that made bitches become rabid beasts?

Once Sasha left, Tommy and Capri stood in the living room staring at each other.

Talk about tension…

"I don't want you to think—" he said at the same time she said, "I'm sorry if I—"

They tried again. "I know that we shouldn't—" he said as she said, "We should probably—"

They laughed.

Tommy sat on the couch. "You go first."

Capri opened her mouth a few times then lost her nerve. "I should get ready for work."

Aye. Work. The perfect escape from what was going on between them. But Tommy wasn't ready for her to leave him yet, not even for an hour. He knew it was a long shot, next to impossible, but he had nothing to lose by asking. "Can't you call in today? I'll only be here the weekend. I don't know how long it'll be before we see each other again." He'd never known her to take a sick day or go on holiday. He just had to—

"I guess I could work from home for a few hours. Then I'm all yours." She smiled then skipped off to her bedroom, leaving his jaw on the floor.

He rubbed his hands across his face roughly. Keeping his cock to himself would be a challenge because he wanted to be inside her…like right now. She'd just put him before her work…sort of. And that was major. Grandiose. Merging their bodies, making sweet, slow love, as they'd finally had a profound meeting of the minds would be the ultimate—

Disaster. Fuck. What was he thinking?

He needed to find something else to occupy his time while she did what she needed to do. He thumbed through the contacts on his smartphone, because some*thing* meant some*one* else, of course.

No, no, no, and no to each of the chicks on his contact list. Same old story, different day.

How 'bout sleep? He could use some of that now that her arse wasn't igniting a flame in his loins. *Fabulous idea, Tommy.* He stretched out on the couch and slept.

He woke up with a blanket thrown casually over him.

"You must have been tired," Capri said from the couch where she held his feet in her lap.

"Guess so," he yawned. "How long have you been sitting there?"

"Long enough to remember some of the fun we've had over the years. Remember the night we met?"

"How could I forget? We had to run out of the pub like fugitives." They laughed. "You know Mr. Steely's been calling on us to do another show at his pub?"

"No. Really?"

"Begging us to return." Tommy sat up until he was shoulder-to-shoulder with Capri. "Spirit told him to fuck off. The rest of us said we should do it. I mean, we did fuck up the man's business that night. It's the least we could do, innit?"

"Yeah, you did," Capri laughed. "I think back on that night and laugh all the time. You falling from the stage has got to be the funniest thing ever."

"I didn't fall. I dived. Those sons of bitches just didn't catch me. Funny how everyone and their mum wants to put their hands on me when I surf the crowd now. You'd think just one touch would cure them of disease and inoculate them from future illness." He told the story of his last dive and why he didn't do them anymore. Security had to get him back to the stage after excited fans had touched him inappropriately and taken off everything but his underpants. He still loved telling her stories that made her laugh. "So what time is this bachelor/bachelorette thingamajig and is there any way we can get out of it?" Having a coed party at the same spot where Sasha and Rob had met was cool…if you liked torturing your mates to death. Tommy would rather eat a bullet.

"In a few hours and no. *She* would be my best friend if you weren't so good at cuddling." She snuggled in to his shoulder. "I have to go, so you have to go."

Tommy growled with feigned discontent. He'd go anywhere with Capri. "Sorry I slept most of the day away after asking you to take it off. I've gotten used to going to sleep around six in the morning."

"It's okay. I had a teleconference at ten without even leaving my house. Saved gas and time that way. It was nice to work from here. I should do it more often."

He felt her forehead with the back of his hand. "You must have a fever. One brought on by sudden head trauma or terminal illness."

"No, silly. You just always help me put things in perspective. It's been engrained in me to work, work, work. No one's going to give me anything. I have to work for it. Hard. I have to pour my heart and soul into it. But when I die, what will I have to show for that?"

"So you *are* dying?"

"No more than anyone else. It's just that…it's that… Well, I allowed my mother to get in my head, is all, and I'm trying to deprogram myself from making my life about work and achievement. You've been instrumental in helping me see there's more to it than that."

"'Bout damn time. But how and why did your mum get in your head like that?" He wondered if Capri would actually go into it for once.

A minute passed before she spoke. "Because I owe her."

"Why?" he whispered out of fear of spooking her. He wanted to know Capri's secrets, and he didn't want to scare her away from sharing them.

Another minute passed. It was obviously a difficult thing for her to discuss. In fact, she always clammed up and changed the subject whenever he brought up her family. "Because she went to prison for me."

Prison? What the fuck? He was the one spooked, yet he kept the same tone. "Why?"

She exhaled a deep breath. "You're going to hate me."

"Not possible." He lifted her chin until she had her eyes on his. She just needed some prompting, and he was not above using The Stare, as she'd dubbed it. "Tell me. Confess. It's good for the soul."

"What soul?" Her eyes watered as she took a deep breath. "I killed someone, Tommy, and my mom took the blame because she had a history of mental illness. She thought she'd be able to get off because of her bipolar disorder, but they rejected the insanity plea and threw the book at her. I was a juvenile and she didn't want it to ruin my life, so she never said a word. She sat there in the courtroom day in and day out and let them talk about how horrible she was for committing the crime, then she took her twenty-year sentence like it was nothing. But it was for nothing she did. She made me promise to never visit her in prison, to never write, to never think about her but to excel in school, to excel in my career, and to be the best I could be. She said that would be repayment enough. That it would have all been worth it, if I did that for her."

Tommy wiped under her eye with his thumb. He couldn't remember seeing her cry since that night she was anxious about her first day as a grad assistant. She'd come close to shedding tears that time she got a B+ on an oral presentation, but chocolate had helped to stabilize her mood. He'd also never heard her go into detail about her mum or about…*killing* someone. Jesus, that was heavy. He suddenly felt like the worst mate in the world for letting her carry this burden all this time. He should have pressed for answers long ago whenever she clammed up instead of trying to keep things light between them.

And now that she'd unleashed her haunting secret, he was dumfounded. How did one prepare for a response to this revelation? This went beyond his mid-grade jokes and pranks. He felt inept in a discussion of this magnitude. Perhaps it would have been better if he hadn't peeled back the scab to look in.

"But when does it end? How long must I focus on being the best? At what point have I repaid my debt to her?" she sniffed. "If I keep at this rate, the life she tried to save, mine, would have been lost that day too." She regained some of her composure. "Don't get me wrong. I enjoy what I do. I just wish there was no guilt attached to it. My mom said that remaining focused would be therapeutic for me, that I'd be too busy to feel guilt. That wasn't true."

"Being busy is no substitute for therapy, Capri. Did you ever get help? I'm pretty sure killing someone is a traumatic event."

"I've never spoken to anyone about it until now. She made me promise not to. She was afraid it would be used as exculpatory evidence to set her free and imprison me. I can't believe I've broken my promise, but…I just wanted to…talk. Today, staying home made me feel like a person, not a machine. I *should* take time off every now and then."

"Maybe you should go see her. You need to relieve yourself of the guilt based on a choice she made to take your place at sentencing. Let her release you and herself. During the past few years, she may have regretted some of what she told you to do. You said she was mentally ill. Perhaps she wasn't thinking clearly."

"I promised I wouldn't see her. She begged me not to. She swore to come see me the minute she got out."

"At what expense? You've been in a prison of your own making ever since." He just needed to offer his support. She'd see the error of her ways. "I can go with you."

"Thanks but no. That's why I didn't want to tell you. I knew you'd judge the decision I've made to follow her wishes. I knew you wouldn't understand."

"Bollocks. That's bollocks, and you know it. I stand by you no matter what. I just think it would be better for both of you if you didn't continue holding yourself to a promise you both made when you were a juvenile and she may have been off her meds. She did what she thought was right, but that doesn't mean it was. By the way, I'm really going to hate myself for asking this, but why did you kill someone? Is there something I should be worried about?"

"No. I'd never hurt you," she blushed. "It's too embarrassing to say."

"Confess." Tommy tensed, thinking it better not have anything to do with her being molested by her mum's boytoy or Tommy was going to fucking lose it and go find her mum himself.

"It's your turn to bare your soul. And I don't mean your latest sexcapade gone bad. Something about your family, Tommy. There's something weird going on there with you and them."

"Um…" He'd stumbled right into that hornet's nest. Just because she felt like being chatty today, didn't mean he did. "My brother and I grew up with my mamó."

"And?"

"And she really loved us."

She sighed. "I'm not telling you shit until you give up some details."

"Fine. Keep your secrets." He stood and went to the kitchen.

She went after him. "I just told you I killed someone, that my mom is in prison for it, and that I haven't talked about it with anyone else. Ever. You think whatever you got is worse than that?" She stood with her arms folded as he made two teas. "Give me something, Tommy."

He continued facing the counter away from her. "When my mamó became ill in the final stages of her disease, she refused treatments. She asked my brother and I to tell her jokes every day to keep her jovial. We did. Every day. When I told you she died after my brother and I did a prank, I wasn't taking the piss. That wasn't a lie."

"What was the prank?"

"We jumped out of her birthday cake wearing speedos and danced around with the residents at her nursing home. She laughed so hard her lungs collapsed, her spleen ruptured, and she had a heart attack. She died a few days later." He turned to face her. "Thing is, she died happy, which was what she wanted. My brother and I were happy she left this world with a smile on her face. Sorry to see her go, but happy she got her wish."

"So we're killers, you and I."

"Except my parents blame us for her death. Yours do not. Was the person you killed your father?" About the only thing he knew about Capri's origins was that her mum was black and her absentee father was Italian. Now he wondered if Capri's pop lacked presence in her life as a result of Capri's actions.

"No."

Phew. Maybe he was off the hook now. "Have I shared enough?"

"I know there's more to your story, but yes. For now, you have." She went back to the couch with her cup. "I thought the man—the one I shot—was raping my mother, but he wasn't. He had her bound with rope while he fucked her from behind and he was choking her and...well, it was consensual. She enjoyed it. She loved him. He'd never abused her. Ever. She explained to me how she enjoyed rough sex. I was fifteen. I didn't understand what I saw then. I do now. I just wish I hadn't left practice early that night. I never would have seen what I couldn't understand then."

Ooooh. Shite. So much more about Capri made sense now. He sat on the couch next to her. She looked like she was in the kind of deep thought that made you spiral into depression. He couldn't have that. "You think Rob will let me take a crack at Sasha one time before they say I do tomorrow? It'll be good for Sasha to have one last hoorah, and I've been dying to even the score between us, since you fucked Spirit and all."

She rewarded his effort to draw her from a funk with a laugh. "I'm pretty sure he keeps a Smith & Weston tucked in his belt. I wouldn't try it if I were you."

"Bummer. I did get even with Spirit though. His girl? I shagged her in a pub bathroom."

"You're a dick, Tommy. A d-i-c-k."

"Hey, I hit it first. If he had a problem with it, he should have steered clear. I can't help it if he always wants what's mine." He knew he shouldn't have said it the moment it left his lips.

If she noticed his unintentional possessiveness, she ignored it. "Yesterday, I got smashed against a bathroom wall at a bar down the street from the clinic."

"You dirty whore. Tell me more."

They passed the afternoon swapping wild sex stories, eating, and watching a movie. When it was time for them to dress for the pre-funeral...uh, bachelor/bachelorette party, they had to do so in a hurry due to all the time they'd spent procrastinating. Good thing they didn't have to do much to make themselves presentable.

"Limo's here. Ready, love?" Tommy had donned a buttoned-down red shirt with black buttons and skintight black leather pants for the occasion. Sasha better have a friend or two to blow him tonight for all the effort.

Capri stepped out of the bedroom looking finer than the rarest gem on the planet. "Have you seen my keys?"

His eyes narrowed to take her all in. She wore a low, loooow cut blouse. In fact, he was pretty sure she couldn't possibly have a bra on with how low it dipped. The material didn't even connect in the front. Both sides covering her nipples sloped down into a slim waistband and skintight mini skirt.

Jesus. Christ. That arse. Those boobs. "Look, I know you're embracing this new liberated sexuality thing where you can fuck on office desks and kitchen counters with every man from popes and congressmen to drug dealers and felons, but sweetheart, you are not going out of the flat with me looking like that."

She looked up from where she was moving pillows around on the couch. "Aha." She lifted her keys from the cushion and turned toward him. "What?" Her eyes took him in with undisguised interest.

"I said I forbid you to wear that dress. Go to your closet and find the other half of it immediately."

She held her stomach and laughed. In his face. "Yes, I'm ready. You look great too. Let's go." She grabbed his hand and headed out the door.

To what had to be the most boring party ever, bachelor, bachelorette, or otherwise.

Tommy looked around at the girls in Sasha's party.

They weren't nearly drunk enough to enjoy the one male stripper attempting to entertain all fourteen of them. Poor little fella. Tommy supposed the average woman would find the nearly nude man aesthetically attractive, but even in the club's dim red lighting, the stripper looked like he was about twenty years too old to be dancing around like a buffoon. Tommy had taken to sitting a few tables back from the stage, which happened to be the perfect location to watch Capri watch the stripper.

As the stripper shook his thonged cock in front of all the females' faces circling the stage, Tommy wondered again what sort of narcotics Sasha and Rob had to be on to subject their wedding party to this. Just because this was where they met all those years ago, did not mean it held sentimental value to anyone else. Tommy wasn't opposed to the honest work of exotic dancing, and he was all for the teasing, he just didn't understand why someone who had found the one they wanted to spend the rest of their life with needed to celebrate it by doing embarrassing things the night before they became husband and wife. Not to mention the whole husband and wife thing was antiquated and ridiculous. One woman, one man, vowing to be together forever…until they hit a rough patch and decided to get a divorce. Bollocks. All of it.

He would rather be back at Capri's, sipping her bottled wine and waffling on about nothing important or listening to her confess more secrets. He'd rather be doing anything but this. Maybe Tommy was just jealous that her eyes stayed on Mr. Buffoon. And they perked up when Mr. Buffoon number two came onstage.

Shoot me now!

Someone bumped his arm with a cold beer bottle, startling him from his reverie.

"Aren't you that cool rocker dude from that cool rock band?" Spirit said in falsetto, mimicking a chick trying to get Tommy's attention.

"Twat!" Tommy said as he wiped the condensation from the bottle off his arm. "Don't sneak up on me like that. I almost shat myself."

Spirit sat in a chair next to Tommy. "You going to sit back here and stare at her all night?"

"Stare at whom? I don't know what the fuck you're talking about, mate." Tommy chugged the rest of his whiskey and held the glass up to get the barmaid's attention. "In case you haven't noticed, there are two dicks on the stage. Hardly my type. It'll take more to win me over than shaving your legs."

"Or maybe they need curlier hair and darker eyes."

Tommy thanked the waiter for bringing over another full glass. He ignored Spirit.

"And maybe their names should begin with a C."

"We're not in high school, Spirit. You got something to say, just spit it out."

"I know you think your silly sunglasses are hiding your eyes, but...let's just say, I'm surprised Capri hasn't fallen out from the hole you're staring in the back of her head."

"If you can see my eyes so bloody well, or knew anything about me, you'd know I wouldn't be staring at the back of her head. My eyes would be glued to that fat arse in that short, tight dress."

"Lord Almighty. Her ass in that dress." Spirit smacked his lips. "But no. You wouldn't be focusing on an ass you're so familiar with. Besides, you see ass every day. Everywhere. It's the woman with the ass.

The one onstage being used as a prop by the handsome stripper."

At that moment, Mr. Buffoon flipped Capri out of the chair, where she sat onstage, onto his face with her legs straddling him. Tommy felt like visiting the toilet. He stood and chugged back his glass. "I'll be back."

"Yeah, all right, man," Spirit laughed. "Or…you could go snatch your woman off that stage and tell her how you feel."

Whatever. "You're high, and I'm not high enough for this rubbish."

He signed an autograph on the way to the toilet, then stood at the urinal for sixty seconds or so before actually taking a whizz. He rocked his head from side-to-side to work through some kinks and emptied his bladder. Capri stunned him when she hopped up on the sink counter next to him as he washed his hands. "Stripperman done licking your cunt?"

"Asshole," she laughed. "I asked Spirit where you'd gone. His girlfriend's cute. Want some?" She held out a joint.

He shook his head then changed his mind. He dried his hands and held one out for a turn at the joint. "Sure. Why not?"

She lit it, inhaled and passed. "We have to do something to liven this shithole up."

"Thought you were enjoying yourself."

"I'm trying to make sure Sasha enjoys herself. None of this is for us. It's for the bride and groom."

Good point. He puffed and passed, leaning against the sink. She inhaled deeply and leaned toward his mouth to shotgun him. He caressed the side of her cheek and tilted toward her mouth. Their lips didn't touch, but he sucked in all the smoke into his lungs as if he were sucking sweet nectar from her tongue. The boner couldn't be helped. It would go away. He leaned away and braced himself against the wall. She grabbed the lapels of his shirt and brought him back in her line of vision. She inhaled and brought her lips close to his to share her exhale. He sucked it all in again, staring into the eyes of the girl he was going to fuck tonight.

They both knew the inevitable was going to happen.

Shite.

He bit his lip and pulled her face close to his. He had to have her. Fuck that other bullshite.

She resisted the pull all the way to his lips and put the joint between hers again. When she spoke, smoke blew in his face. "Confession…"

He waited, staring at her lips. He needed to suck them.

"I think we should just do it. Just once. Just to say we did it. Go ahead and get it out of the way, you know? It doesn't have to change anything, if we don't let it."

He could pretend he didn't know what *it* was or… "Confession…"

Her eyebrows rose.

"More than anything, I really want to know what it feels like to be inside you."

She gulped. She puffed. She exhaled. She smiled. "Confession… I'd really love to see your cumface." She slid over to the edge of the sink, letting her skirt rise.

He stared at what she exposed then moved to stand between her legs, slowly, inching closer to the warmth at the apex of her thighs. Holding onto her hips and angling them downwards toward his erection, he pulled her until she fit snugly. It nearly undid him. Her breathing became just as arduous as his. He found solace in heading towards destruction along with her so neither could blame the other.

"You like shagging near toilets, apparently," he whispered because he didn't trust his voice.

"I've never fucked in a limo."

"I haven't fucked in *this* limo," he smirked. "Let's go."

They told Sasha and Spirit they were going out for some fresh air and headed to the limo. The driver accepted Tommy's monetary tip to turn on something mellow and get lost. Soft rock set the mood for them as they stepped in behind dark tinted windows and locked the doors.

He was so conflicted about what he was about to do. There was something so right about it and so wrong at the same time. How was that possible? Right was right. Wrong was wrong. There couldn't be this many shades of gray between them. But he did want to fuck her. Badly. No denying that fact. A big source of hesitation came from knowing it would be more than fucking. That was equally good and bad. He wanted the deeper connection. Needed it. He hadn't felt connected to anyone enough. He wanted to get lost in her, to forget who they were and just feel how much they meant to each other and how good they made each other feel.

But what would happen once he did? He'd be connected, just to put the distance between them again when it was done?

As soon as they got inside, Capri's own conflicts

surfaced. "We shouldn't do this, should we?"

"It's a bad idea, innit?"

She sat next to him on the leather seat, the pink fluorescent light along the floorboard illuminating her eyes and teeth. "It doesn't have to be. It could be a good thing. Sex will ease some of the tension between us. I know you feel it too."

"Afterwards, we can go back to being just mates, yeah?"

"Yeah."

He reached over for her hand and held it. Skin-to-skin contact, you couldn't beat that connection. Being inside the person he cared about most, he couldn't wait to know what that connection would be like.

She lifted his hand to her breast and squeezed his hand around it. "I know you like these. You're always staring at them."

Yes, he did. Very much.

Moving the material of her dress over one inch, bared the mouth-watering breast he'd spent way too much time staring at. He slowly dipped his head until the nipple slipped between his teeth. She fisted his hair and gripped him closer. He made a vow to himself then to let his hair grow out so she'd have more to grip. He couldn't think of much else. He just wanted to suck on that one nipple for the rest of the night, but he couldn't leave the other one hanging.

Christ, he wanted to be inside her so badly. His cock jumped in excitement, knowing he didn't want to wait another second. Maybe he could snuggle in closer to her. Rub on her a little to ease his ache. "Lie back," he whispered. The only light in the limo came from the floorboards. Not much, but enough light to see that her eyes were closed. "How are you going to watch my cumface with your eyes closed?"

She opened one lid at a time.

He saw lust in them, but mostly apprehension. She may have been enjoying his mouth, but she was also worried about what crossing this line would do to them. She didn't let that worry keep her from lying back and lifting her skirt as she did.

They couldn't stop now. They wouldn't.

For a moment, his eyes roamed her outstretched body, her open invitation to be ravished. He moved in until he could fit his body right where he wanted...no needed, it most. Damn. Right. There. Instantly, upon contact, they started panting like they had run a marathon. He raised her legs around him so that she could cradle him tight. He felt like exploding already and his clothes were still on.

He went back to sucking and massaging her breasts, the perfect twin mounds that they were. She became impatient, digging her heels in the backsides of his legs, pressing his erection tighter to her. They shared a moan, harmonizing as only two people can do when they are impassioned. She started pulling his pants down by the waistband, reaching underneath to undo his buckle.

Oh, hell no. That would be the only thing to break his concentration on her breasts at the moment. Even though he admired her enthusiasm, there was no way in hell he'd let her unzip his pants. "Let me do that," he said in a deep, husky voice as he slid his zipper down.

She smiled, and he realized he couldn't see enough of her face, which meant she wouldn't be able to see her favorite part, his cumface. He didn't want her to miss that any more than he wanted to miss coming.

He reached up to turn the interior light on.

Seeing her lying there fully surrendered to him touched him more than it should have. Instead of going back to his previous position, he went down lower and planted kisses on the inside of her thighs. He planted kisses on her mound, dripping with juices that said she was more than ready for him. Then he pulled her panties to the side and feasted like she was a Thanksgiving meal served by the American natives. Smelling and tasting delicious, he couldn't think of anything he'd rather do for the rest of his life.

Wait a minute—

"My turn," she whispered, grabbing onto his hair as best she could. That was no easy task given its length. She started pulling him up. He was still collecting his thoughts when she sat up, rose to her knees, and sheathed him with her wet, hot mouth. As much as he loved blowjobs, and as well as she sucked, he felt driven by connection and possession more so than pleasure. Sure, it felt a million and one ways good, but he needed to take her body. He needed to take a dive in her depths and stay until they were both sated.

He shifted positions, which threw her off balance, and before he knew it, they'd hit the floor.

This would have been a good breaking point. As in—you've had your craic, now get back to being mates and put this sex mess behind you.

But nooo. They were too gone for that. She sat up next to him and slid her blouse straps down her arms. She kept sliding them until she got to her waist, then she slid the lower half down her hips, knickers and all.

Holy fuck. He'd caught glimpses of her fully naked, but never like this. He'd seen many a naked woman, but none had affected him in this way because none had been his mate Capri. He was going to wear her arse out.

Staring down at her while he unbuttoned his shirt, all the different positions he wanted to do with her crossed his mind. He'd have to shag her face-to-face at first. Letting her see what she did to him was most important. After that, he had to hit that arse from the back so he could smack it and rub it down. He rushed to get his shirt and pants off.

Oh, fucking raggedy ass bollocks. "I don't have any condoms."

"What do you mean?"

"It's not like I thought we were going to get busy in the limo. I'm supposed to be taking an abstinence break, if you recall."

She let out a frustrated breath. Moments passed before she sat up and cupped his jaw with one hand. "We can… I mean, you will pull out, right? We can do something neither of us has done before."

His cock twitched and his eyes narrowed. In that moment, he would have served a prison sentence for her too. He wanted to do it raw with her so badly, his testicles tightened at the mere thought. But would he pull out in time? Did he even want to?

No. Truthfully, he did not. However, she trusted him, so he would do what needed to be done.

She lay back, pulling him with her. Like a moth to a flame, as they say…

He positioned himself and started to ease in. He would take this really slow. He would savor every minute as if it were their last. It could be. Should be.

But damn if that didn't feel like a slice of heaven. A whole lot of heaven. He knew he should look away.

There would be less intimacy than staring into her eyes as he took over her body. As her breathing and his combined and sounded like the beginning of a thunderstorm. The way she squeezed and gripped him. How slick she was. How they both had a surprise look on their faces, like they couldn't believe they were actually doing this...or that something as simple as penetration could feel so fucking good. Her mouth was shaped like an O just as his was. He shouldn't focus on that. On those lips. That tongue. He grunted long and low when he finally hit her base. It was such a snug fit. A natural fit.

She licked her lips. "That feels..." her voice caught, "really...fucking...amazing."

He rested his arms on the sides of her head, prepared to fuck her nice and slow for the next hour. He didn't have anything better or more desirable to do. She turned away when he leaned in to capture those parted lips. "How dare you," he whispered. He bit her bottom lip gently and forced her to turn her head back around toward him. With his coerced access to her mouth, he went in rubbing his tongue to hers. Rubbing, massaging, twirling, tasting pot, and loving the texture and thickness of her lips.

She seized up, suddenly, her pussy squeezing and teasing and massaging, and pulsating.

He rocked into her deeper, watching her face for signs of discomfort. He got an opposite reaction, and it drove him near the edge. "If you keep squeezing me like that, I'm going to come."

"I'm not doing anything."

"You are. You're...pulsating."

"I mean, I'm not doing anything on purpose. It's an involuntary reaction to..."

He shifted his knee to get in a better position to extricate when the need arose, and it was arising sooner than expected.

"Damn that feels good, Tommy." She lifted her hips up, rocking her pussy on him without moving much else a'tall. It was enough for him to feel every strong pulse. "You're going to make me… Oh, shit," she moaned.

Just the mere thought that she was going to come with him inside her after she said she'd never orgasmed like this before, made him too excited. Like too bloody excited. His orgasm began its progression from way down low. He hadn't even done anything more than enter her. It was too soon.

"Wait. Don't move," he panted, doing everything he could to ignore her body's quakes and quivers. "It's too soon. You're going to take me with you."

She reached with both hands and pulled him back down to her face and kissed him like she meant it, sucking his lips, massaging his tongue. He couldn't stay still. The need for more friction arose like hunger and thirst in the desert. He pulled back until he was nearly out of her and started his hellishly slow decent again.

"Oh, oh…"

"Say it." With all her trembles, and the look in her eyes, he knew what was on the tip of her tongue, but she was holding back. "Say it."

"Oh, Godd! I'm going to come."

He felt her doing just that. And it was too much to take. She'd not only said Godd while she did it, but she seized around him again, and he felt her whole body convulse. He lost it then. The grip of her pussy started milking him harder and faster than anything he'd ever known before. He started withdrawing.

"No, no. Not yet." Her head swung from left to right as he felt her body trembling and pulsating. "Oh, Godd."

Whether she meant a deity in the heavens or that Tommy felt like a god, didn't matter. He couldn't hold on any longer. He withdrew completely, replacing his unprotected cock with the safety of his hand. He rammed two fingers inside her and used the heel of his hand to stimulate her clit. He put pressure on both and stroked fast to stretch out her orgasm. Without touching himself, his seed spewed all over her trembling abs as she continued to experience the bliss only Tommy had been able to provide her.

Oh, shickle pinickle. What had they done?

He was still too hard to think harder about that. Too much blood still flowing to his lower half. He wiped the tip of his cock with his thumb then entered her again. Dammit. He was not going to be able to last long the second time either.

He didn't.

Third time's the charm, yeah? Wrong. He wiped and entered her a third time, but her orgasm pulses were so strong, they threw him into another wave quickly. This time when he withdrew, he pumped his cock with his hand. He needed a complete release this time in order to keep from coming so quickly the next time. He pumped and pumped until he'd emptied himself and started softening.

When their mini earthquakes stopped, Tommy crashed on the floor next to her, her juices drying on his cock. They both stared at the limo ceiling.

Please don't let this be awkward.

She was so quiet. What was she thinking?

"Wow, Tommy. That's some cumface you got there, buddy. But what I want to know is, what happened to all that stamina bullshit you've been talking?"

Haha. He'd noticed a difference too. "Your pussy just does something to me."

"Oh, that's right. Your first time with no barrier."

"It always takes me awhile, even when I have a wank."

Silence.

He wished he hadn't said that, because now they were stuck with the implications that his mind-blowing experience in the limousine directly related to his connection with Capri. "Yeah well, what happened to all that talk about having to come on your own? Thought you couldn't do it during coitus."

She hesitated before replying, which was more telling than her actual words. "Guess your cock does something to me too."

Yet another implication he didn't want to face—sex with him, someone she had a deep connection with already, did something particular for her that random hookups could not. Yeah, they had finally fucked. More so than that—they had really fucked *up* big-time. How did their friendship come back from this?

CHAPTER 11

Sex with Tommy had been so overwhelmingly good, Capri had every intention of fucking him again right away then decided against it. She'd prided herself on being rational and cool, free-thinking and radical, a nonconformist, who could keep her emotions out of everything…until now. She couldn't rightly say with any shred of conviction that she could handle another round with Tommy without becoming an emotional wreck. The first time had been too intense, too intimate, and too damn good. It was best to leave it at that.

She placed a hand on his chest, stopping him mid-hover as he rose from beside her to get closer to her lips. She looked where her hand touched. His skin so smooth, unmarked, unblemished… She turned her head away from his intended kiss, from the longing in his eyes that matched hers. Though she felt disappointment rattle through him, he asked no questions about her rejection. He made no demands that she acquiescence to his advances.

Good thing, too, because she would have been powerless, a state she rarely found herself in given how much she hated feeling weak and incapable. Fact was, she felt too sensitive to his touch, too wide open to his charm. She would have opened her mouth and legs and received what she'd just enjoyed merely minutes prior. And it would have been a mind-fuck. She was too invested in the situation. In him. Too deeply entangled with the man who made her laugh, the man who played music that lifted her soul, and the man who made her come at the same time she gave him climatic pleasure. She'd never felt more alive, more womanly, or more vulnerable. Tommy held all the cards in his hands.

She needed some time and space to collect her deck before she lost herself in the game completely and indefinitely. "I don't want to be a cliché."

He didn't ask what she meant. He sat up and leaned forward, his naked back to her. "Are you okay?"

"Yes." She started gathering her clothes and something to clean herself with. "Have you seen my—"

Tommy lifted his foot off her panties and handed them to her. She reached for them without looking at him. She just couldn't right now. Not without thinking of how she'd spent so many nights next to a man who looked and sounded like that when he came, and she'd lain there without a clue as to what she'd been missing.

Her pussy spasmed at the recent embedded memory.

Goddamn it. She needed to think about something else. That convenience store across the street from her apartment complex that got robbed last week… Anything.

She refused to be the girl who couldn't separate good sex from love. She wouldn't allow them to be the pair of friends who couldn't remain friend-zoned after a heated, long-time-coming romp on the limo floor. Wasn't that the trite, overly-used plot device found in hundreds of romance novels and movies? Well, close enough. All she had to do was switch the limo for a barn...or Tommy's guitar for a paintbrush...or their reason for not having sex all these years for trying to appease over-bearing parents from opposite sides of the tracks. She would have no part of that cliché in any form.

In the end, all those romances came down to the same thing: *a talented, misunderstood boy meets the most beautiful girl in the world and they want to hump, but they deny their animal attraction to each other and decide to just be friends because of XYZ bullshit conflict, until that one fateful day when the stars align and they have sex. Then their feelings spring from thin air like poof! They realize how they were always meant to be together so they vow that no one and nothing will keep them apart. They say to hell with all the obstacles in their way, conquer the world, and fall in love, 'cause what else are they going to do after sex like that with someone they already cared about? Duh. During the final act, they run off into the sunset together with big cheesy grins and unrealistic expectations to live happily ever after. They never look at another man or woman. They never have an argument that isn't followed by steamy make-up sex. They never get bored with their daily routines. Blah, blah, blah.*

No, thanks. Capri wouldn't be that girl, the one who dreamt of this Disney malarkey or the one who attempted to live it. She knew better. What the romances neglected to include in an Epilogue, was that several years down the road, after a few obnoxious children and living above their means, said romantic couple of the century, got bored with each other and divorced. That sweet, conventional Harlequin romance became Stephen King's latest horror thriller with more blood and less affirmations of love.

Capri and Tommy dressed in silence...which was eerie as hell because they were hardly ever quiet around each other. *That's* what happened in reality. Awkwardness, uncertainty, regret—the staples of lapses in judgment that resulted in friendly rumbles in the jungles. Maybe not regret in this case…because it had been stellar fucking, but definitely the other nouns.

Tommy exited the limo first, pulling Capri in a tight embrace as she followed him. He leaned his back against the vehicle and held onto her while she squirmed and tensed. His affection after the silence and coldness they suffered through while dressing had caught her off guard.

Neither of them had ever had an issue with PDA, but this felt weird, like they were putting their recent transgressions out in the open for everyone to see and scrutinize. For no good reason at all, she felt exposed, embarrassed. What if someone they knew saw them? How would she be able to explain that she'd just had the best sex of her life with her best friend? Because anyone could take one look at her flushed skin and messy hair next to his disheveled look and know they'd just done the wild thang. And why the hell did she care what anyone thought?

He held onto both sides of her face, forcing her to look in his eyes and stop fidgeting. "You promised me sex wouldn't change anything. But here we are, instead of post-coital bliss, we're awkward and scared to look at or touch each other. You feel distant. Why are you pulling away from me?"

She met his stare head-on in a challenge. "Isn't that what you want? For me to remain detached? For us to continue on like nothing's happened? I'm holding up my end of the bargain. I refuse to be one of your groupies, pining after you with unrequited feelings."

He looked confused. "I'd never think of you as a groupie, or I'd never have gone in you without a condom." He rubbed a hand up and down his face. "As far as detachment goes, I think we both dropped the ball on that years ago. I just want you to be you. Just be my Capri. The one you've always been, not this hard, Elvira version of you."

"*Your* Capri? I belong to no one. I don't know how you folks do it in Ireland, but we're free here." She tucked her stray curls behind her ears. "Elvira though? Really?"

"I call it like I see it. But eh—you're right. Let's rewind," his index fingers twirled backwards, "tonight's dirty event and pretend it never happened. What do you say?" He gave a winning smile.

She liked his use of the word *dirty*. That made her smile. "As if I could ever forget your cumface."

He licked his lips and lowered his voice, dipping his head so that their foreheads touched. "Or the way your internal muscles squeezed my cock." He shivered then palmed her ass, pressing her tighter to his fresh arousal.

"My, God. I don't think there's a hornier man alive." Or woman, because Capri had become aroused the moment she'd thought of his cumface.

"You keep calling me Godd and I'll show you how horny I am."

"I wasn't...I..." *Oh, forget it.* "Tommy, neither of us wants things to change but neither of us can deny the sex was pretty fucking amazing. Chances are we're going to do it again. Soooo how do we balance these competing interests?"

His lips disappeared behind his teeth as he thought about it. "We have to keep seeing other people."

Continue having random encounters with people they didn't care about to keep from falling for the one they did? It could work. "All right. Plus, we can't have any more expectations of each other than we've had already. You can't expect me to tour with you. I can't expect you to stay here."

"And we have to keep constant communication open." His arms rested around her waist.

She settled into his chest, looking up into his face. "And be completely honest. Confessing our thoughts and feelings and baring our souls."

"Without judgment."

"Or negative consequences."

They smiled, giving the equivalent of a handshake. All awkwardness had vanished. Tommy leaned in to—

"And no kissing," Capri mentioned her last stipulation in a hurry. She enjoyed tasting him too much.

Tommy stood up straighter on a noisy exhale, tension returning to their negotiations. "Wait. No. I don't agree to that. I like kissing you," he cajoled.

"We can still cuddle."

"Okay, fine. But I need to wear rubbers. I didn't want to pull out a'tall."

Capri reflected back on his fantasy about making a baby. Yikes. That was definitely not something she wanted. "Okay, fine."

They disengaged and turned at the sound of shouting coming from the entrance of the strip club. Damn. She'd forgotten all about why they were really here tonight. She was supposed to be making Sasha's night special, not her own. Sasha was going to kill her, rightfully so.

"I saw you, Gary!"

"What did I tell you about calling me that?" Spirit took long strides behind his girlfriend as she clonked rapidly in her heels to get away from him. Mike Myers chasing his prey came to Capri's mind.

"Fuck you, Gary! Go back to your 'ho and leave me alone. Your shit will be outside in the garbage by the time you get home."

"Home? All you've done is complain the whole time I've been here. That's not my home."

Capri and Tommy watched quietly from the side of the limo as Spirit and his girlfriend had a shouting match outside in the parking lot. After shouting back and forth, the girlfriend got into the back of an awaiting cab. She threw something at Spirit before riding off. He squatted on the pavement until he found what she'd thrown then put it in his pocket.

"You're not going to be the bigger man and run after her?" Tommy chided.

Spirit looked up, surprised Capri and Tommy had witnessed the whole ordeal. He walked toward them. "Naw. She'll just find something else to fuss about later. She can burn all my stuff for all I care. I knew better than to leave anything valuable over there. She's fucking nuts."

"What did you do to upset her?" Capri asked, knowing women didn't typically fly off the handle for no reason.

"This time?" Spirit rubbed the back of his neck. "She got pissed because the stripper gave me a lap dance."

"It's half bachelor party," Tommy said. "What did she expect?"

"Yeah, but I used to bang this particular one, and Irene knew it. She asked if that's how Kinky J. used to ride me naked, and I said yes."

Tommy laughed.

"Ohhh." Capri understood now. "What did she throw at you?"

He pulled the small object out of his pocket and held it up. The diamond ring sparkled under the streetlight.

Capri whistled. "Wow. That's one hell of an engagement ring."

"When were you going to tell me you were getting married?" Tommy didn't seem pleased at all.

"Um…never. Not that it matters now. I'll just exchange it with the jeweler tomorrow. Get me some huge diamond stud earrings, maybe a new watch."

Capri found it interesting that he'd wanted to marry his girlfriend one minute and was ready to let her go the next. "Orrrr…you can give her some time to calm down then give it back to her." Romance was fickle as hell.

"Not this time. We're over. She's too jealous. I thought it was cute at first, that she cared that much about me, but it's not cute. It's craziness. I've been faithful to her, but all she can dwell on is my past. I don't worry about her previous lovers. She shouldn't worry about mine. Our marriage would have never lasted."

Capri may not have been a full-fledged subscription member of romantic ideologies, but she knew that wasn't how love was supposed to work. "Do you love her? If you loved her, wouldn't the relationship be worth fighting for? Wouldn't you do whatever it took to make it work?"

He looked back and forth between Capri and Tommy. "I don't know. You tell me." He looked pointedly at Tommy. "Let's say there's someone you love with all your heart, but you're too used to being a prick to admit it. If given the opportunity, would you do whatever it took to be with them?"

Tommy spoke in a clipped tone. "Gee, I don't know, Spirit. But I know I wouldn't be at a strip club getting a dance from a former flame in front of a fiancée I already know is mad jealous over me."

Capri didn't like the way Spirit and Tommy were squaring off with each other. She needed to get the conversation back on Spirit and his recent breakup and away from the obvious innuendos about her and Tommy. That elephant always stepped front and center of the room whenever the three of them got together. "You must have loved her enough to want to marry her. That's enough to want to fight for her, right?"

"Actually, I asked her to marry me because I thought it was the right thing to do since she had my son."

Capri knew Spirit had a two-year-old child with his girlfriend, but she'd never met the woman until tonight, and she'd never seen the boy. Capri was certain his jealous girlfriend wouldn't have welcomed her in their midst given Capri's history with Spirit. "Do you need a place to stay for the rest of the weekend?"

"No, I can go stay with my cousin." He looked down at his watch and saw the late hour. "Or a hotel."

"Nonsense. You're welcome to stay with me," she glanced at Tommy, "I mean us. It's not the French Riviera you boys have grown accustomed to, but I have a guestroom slash office with a pullout couch."

"Sounds perfect. Thanks."

"Shouldn't they be wrapping this party up by now?" Tommy didn't hide his annoyance with having to be at the party, period.

Capri didn't know what he had to be upset about. It wasn't like he'd spent the whole time inside. She didn't say anything, though, because it got worse. "Yes. The party at this location should be coming to an end. There's one last stop to make on Sasha's itinerary for tonight. She wants to go down to the beach and release some doves. She has a violinist and cellist scheduled to be there as well.

Tommy and Spirit both gagged and hacked and growled as if they'd been selected for jury duty in a capital murder trial. Capri couldn't blame them.

Later on after the doves and sand, the three amigos went back to Capri's place to crash for the night. Only she didn't feel like crashing once they got there. A devious plan had come to mind while they rode in the limo back to her apartment. She took a shower and pondered on it some more until determination took over the plan and all reason. Nothing to it but to do it.

She waited until Tommy got out of the shower

and Spirit went in before approaching Tommy. She needed to talk to Mr. #1 in Deviance alone first. "You know how earlier we set the terms for our arrangement?"

He looked mischievous. "Aye. I'm ready for round two whenever, wherever you are." He popped her ass once.

She sucked on her bottom lip. They were already starting off on different pages of the same book. "Okay. It sort of is round two, but...you know how you told me about you and Spirit doing double penetration on girls?"

His countenance darkened and his index finger went to his bottom lip. "Aye."

"Well...? I mean...?"

"You mean," he pointed to himself, her, and the bathroom door where Spirit had gone, "the three of us?"

She nodded and grinned.

He looked uncomfortable. "I can be chill about you shagging other lads but—"

"Prove it."

"Really? Spirit? The guy you gave your virginity to? You want the two of us to fuck you? Like right now?"

She nodded again, resisting the urge to remind him he'd done it before countless times. This should be no different. "That better not be judgment I'm hearing in your voice, Thomas Delaney. Besides, I wouldn't trust any two guys more."

Tommy deliberated on it a minute before looking resolved. "I'll go talk to him. He just broke up with his girl, his fiancée tonight. He may not be up for it." Tommy went in the bathroom where he and Spirit started mumbling.

Capri could hear some of the discussion through the door.

Spirit did not immediately jump onboard as she'd thought he would. "I haven't done anything like that in years," he said.

Hell, he'd written a song about her. She had left her mark on him, or so she thought. The mark had turned out to be more like a wrinkle. She hadn't expected a love connection, but damn. Repeat sex...after she had matured more physically? And after his girl had thrown his ring back in his face? What did he have to pass up? It should have been a no-brainer.

Capri crossed her arms with impatience as she stood in the hallway awaiting their decision. It had to be unanimous.

"I know," Tommy said.

"Man, I've left that life behind."

"I know."

"She wouldn't even let me kiss her back then."

"I know."

"What about your feelings in all this? On second thought—tell her no. I'm not getting in the middle of you two again."

What? The first guy she'd ever allowed into her body had just rejected her? Fuck that. He'd have to tell her to her face.

And technically, *she*'d be in the middle.

The innocent girl Spirit had broken in was but a shadow of the sex queen she'd become. She stormed into the bathroom, surprising Spirit, who stood with his arms folded across his damp, bare chest and a towel tied around his waist. Frightening tattoos with bold colors covered nearly his whole muscled chest, even more than she'd known him to have. Through his buzzed black hair, a third eye tat appeared on the side of his head, forcing her attention to his dark, boyish eyes. She cupped both sides of his face, brought it down to her lips and kissed him. She hated that tat on his head, but she loved his lips.

Tommy didn't miss a beat. He stepped in behind her and raised her t-shirt over her head. Next, her panties dropped to the floor. She couldn't be sure which man had pulled them down, and she didn't care. Hands were everywhere. Apparently, having a ménage à trois met right up there with riding a bike. After some prompting and a kiss, you could get back into the swing of things easy.

This was better. This made her feel empowered. She could handle Tommy if he stayed behind her. She reached behind her to grip a handful of his hair and felt disappointed that there wasn't more on his head. She didn't have long to contemplate that. The bottom half of her torso lifted until it was at Spirit's face level. He started a sweet assault on her pussy lips that rivaled Tommy's oral skills from earlier. Speaking of Tommy, that sexy as fire devil, reached around and cupped her breasts, plucking the nipples in rhythm to the motion of Spirit's head as he continued to devour her. She lost track of what Tommy was doing as she boiled over and out of her skin with a searing orgasm from the very first man to have given her one with his mouth years ago. He hadn't lost his touch, and his fiancée was an idiot.

Capri's legs had turned to mush in the process. Not a problem. Spirit wrapped her legs around his waist, her arms around his neck and walked to her bedroom. He went back to kissing her and she let him. Things were as they'd always been with Spirit—safe.

She lay on the bed, where she watched Tommy drop his underwear to the floor and Spirit drop his towel.

Goooooddamn. Was she really going to do this?

You bet your sweet fat baby's ass, she was. Any woman who claimed she would be able to resist them was a liar.

Tommy reached in her drawer and pulled out condoms, tossing one to Spirit. They both stared at her naked body on the bed as they sheathed themselves. When they approached, however, all her nerve went out the window.

She raised her hands to stave them off— "Wait. I'm not sure I can handle both of you." She covered her face with the sheet. "Sorry. I don't know what I was thinking."

Tommy sank down on the bed next to her first. "Just relax. We'll take care of you." He eased her down, positioning her on her back. "You don't have to do anything but enjoy it." He leaned in to kiss her neck while tracing circles with his blunt nails on her abdomen.

The bed dipped as Spirit crawled on the other side of her. He put a hand on her shoulder and tilted her away from him to face Tommy.

Capri was about to protest the turn in Tommy's direction, when her train of thought was interrupted by Spirit's arm snaking around to the front of her. His fingers were still as expert on her anatomy as she remembered. Her lids started to close.

"Has your arse been fucked before?" Tommy whispered as he thumbed her cheek.

She nodded, looking through half-open eyes.

"Good. Well good. Where's your lube?"

"Same drawer."

Tommy's eyes flicked to Spirit's behind her.

Capri closed her eyes as Spirit went to the drawer. Tommy's hand took over where Spirit's had left off. She just wanted to feel, not see, not think.

"Open your eyes. I'll abide by your rule against me tasting those sweet lips, if you at least keep your eyes on mine."

Had Tommy already forgotten the purpose of avoiding a kiss with him? Staring in his eyes would defeat that whole purpose. But she lay defenseless against those green orbs and long fingers as they stroked and stretched her, teased and readied her. They transported her to a sea of pleasure, where only her core existed.

When Tommy entered that core, it wasn't slow like earlier. It was deliberate and efficient. Familiar. He threw her leg over his and pushed into her as they lay face to face, eying each other for signs of ecstasy and discomfort. For total emotional connection and mental penetration.

Tommy closed his eyes momentarily and let out a deep breath once he filled her completely. He squeezed her thigh with one hand, her hair with the other, before beginning a punishing rhythm.

Capri's breath escaped in a wave of shock and awe. The bond between them had not been a fluke before. He definitely touched something deep on the inside of her that no one else did, and it wasn't just her pussy. It was higher up in her chest. She linked her arm under his and gripped the back of his shoulder to hold steady for his strokes. They were deep and languid and hard and rough—

"Um...maybe I should go." Spirit's voice crashed through her mental fog as he made a move to leave.

Capri had forgotten he was there.

Tommy broke his rhythm and eye hypnosis to grab Spirit's arm. "Stay, mate. It's what she wants."

Spirit settled in behind her, closer this time. His meaty chest provided a sense of warmth and support that made the third body worth it already. She felt a slick fingertip go in her rear first then gradually more of the finger. By the time three fingers—if her count was accurate—had opened her up, Spirit's cock took their place.

Wowser.

And holy shit.

She'd only *thought* she'd been filled completely before. She had never known fullness until Tommy had filled one orifice, Spirit the other. She was overcome with sensation and fullness...but nowhere near the extent of sensation she felt when they began to move together. As one of them massaged her clit, Tommy pushed in as Spirit pulled out. They did it languidly at first until the frenzy grew and the fever seared and the passion awakened. All she had to do was hold on for the ride as they took her to new heights and pleasure came crashing down on all their heads at once.

"This is what you want? To be fucked like a whore?" Spirit whispered in her ear.

She nodded.

"No, say it."

"Yes."

"Say I want to be fucked with two cocks because I love being a whore."

"I want...to be f-f-fucked with two cocks because...I'm a dirty whore and I love it."

"Good, girl." Spirit rewarded her by picking up the pace. "I can't hold out as long as you, Tommy," he groaned.

Tommy gripped her jaw and squeezed, forcing her eyes open again. "You want two cocks to come inside you?"

"Yes," she breathed.

"Are you going to give me what I want?"

"Yes."

"You're going to come with my cock in you again, yes?"

"Yes, Godd yesssss."

Tommy lifted her knee and rolled onto Capri at the same time Spirit rolled onto his back. They were in sync, managing to stay inside her and intensify the depth of penetration. Tommy grabbed the headboard and pumped hard and fast while Spirit held still. "Come with me," Tommy moaned. "Come with us, Capri."

"Aw, fuck!" Spirit hissed.

Capri squeezed her eyes shut and shouted something unintelligible when her climax erupted from everywhere. Her clit, her cervix, her anus... Shit, maybe from her toes. She didn't even mind when Tommy broke her rule and clamped his mouth on hers to absorb the energy she released and share all the energy he had to give. Spirit bit into her shoulder and she felt them both kick more than a few times inside of her.

With her body trembling and feeling like a pile of mush, she considered how this had been her second orgasm via penetration, and both times Tommy had been there. He'd been the facilitator. All up in her face. All up in her body. In her mind. Her heart. She was too exhausted to ponder it for long. She was too tired to do anything. Once both men withdrew, she fell into what felt like a drugged sleep upon a pillow of endorphins. After one time with Tommy and one time with both of them, she felt worn out.

She also felt like the luckiest bitch to ever walk the earth.

CHAPTER 12

When Capri woke up, both men were gone from her bed.

Great. She'd fucked up not one, but two friendships in a matter of hours. In a fury, she threw one of her pillows across the room and knocked some books off the dresser.

Tommy rushed in. "Top of the morning to you. Is everything okay?"

She smiled at her foolish premature conclusions. "Everything's better than okay." She stretched like a content feline. "You're up early. Where's Spirit?"

"Actually, it's afternoon. You're up late," he said, pointing a spatula at her. "He left a little while ago. Said he'll see you at the wedding later."

She plopped back down on the bed. "Shit. The wedding." She looked over at her clock. "She had to be at the church in an hour. "Why did you let me sleep so late?"

"You looked like you needed the rest. You were snoring and everything." He made a horrible face to demonstrate how horribly she had looked.

"Was not."

"Was too. Go get prettied up. I have lunch ready."

Capri stared at the door long after he left it. Lunch? What in the holy hell had gotten into him?

Fuck getting dressed. They needed to talk. She got up and covered her naked, well-used body with her robe and followed him into the kitchen. "Are you okay?"

"Aye." He looked up from the sink where he stood rinsing his dishes. "Why wouldn't I be?"

"I mean, last night happened. You were there."

"I was."

"And I was there. And Spirit was there."

"Nothing wrong with my memory, love. I know who was there."

"And you're all right with all of that?"

"Jesus." He slammed his mug down. "Here you and Spirit go with this shite again. I'm fine. It was just sex…something I've had plenty of, as a matter of fact. I've been ramming my cock in twats long before you'd ever seen a cock. I'm sure yours won't be the last pussy I ram or even the last one I share with Spirit. Happy?"

"Thrilled." She threw up her hands and walked to the bathroom.

Yeah, he seemed fine, all right.

Once they were dressed, they rode to the wedding in heart-breaking silence. The previous sexual tension between them was much better than this bitter, angst-laden tension any day of the week. Sex she understood. Not being able to communicate with him, she didn't. This strain in their friendship was unchartered, unfamiliar territory, and it was in direct violation of the terms of their agreement.

Like she'd ever thought for one minute they would

abide by it.

The damage to their relationship had been done the moment they'd stepped in the limo and took off their clothes. This same limo that served as a reminder of their wanton behavior. Their lack of self-control.

Tommy took his frustrations out in his typical way by flirting with every woman at the wedding and reception. Such a predictable attention whore. Capri rolled her eyes. If he thought she was going to watch him push up on bimbos all evening, he had another thing coming.

Capri faked a smile at the reception so that she wouldn't ruin Sasha's perfect day, when she felt the least like smiling. She did brighten up when she spotted Spirit a few tables down. She headed in his direction and stopped midway when she noticed his girlfriend, Irene, hanging tight to his arm. A boy who looked just like Spirit, except without all the ink, held her hand. Nice. They must have kissed and made up.

Idiots.

Sasha approached Capri with the subtlety of a four-alarm fire. "Tommy sure looks like he's having a good time. What's eating you, hon?"

Yuck. Sasha had even started sounded like a country bumpkin.

Capri plastered a smile to her face. "Nothing at all. I'm just—"

"Cut the bullshit, and save it for someone who doesn't know you."

Capri dropped the façade. She pulled Sasha by the arm to a spot by the open bar. Talking about what was on her mind might improve her mood. If not, she'd try a strong drink. "I fucked Tommy."

Sasha's eyes grew to the size of stereo speakers. "OMG. It's about damn time. It was that morning I showed up at your apartment, wasn't it? I knew it! How was it?"

"No, but…it was unbelievable."

"Okaaaay. So what's wrong? You should be bouncing off the walls."

"Everything."

"You two have been friends for too long to let something like this interfere—"

"And last night I fucked Spirit *and* Tommy. At the same time."

Sasha blinked. "OMG. OMG. You lucky beotch." She shook her head. "No. You cruel beotch. To tell me this after I'm married. After I've committed my life to fucking only one man."

"You're much better off. Trust me."

Sasha twisted her lips. "Like you really believe that."

"Yeah, you're right. I don't." Capri held her stomach while she laughed. "I just said it because it's your wedding day. Seriously though—they made me see stars. The whole galaxy."

They snickered.

Sasha sipped her champagne. "If everyone was down at the time, what's the big deal now? You'd already had sex with both of them separately before the freaky group thing, so why would Tommy go ballistic? It's not like he's even remotely related to the Virgin Mary."

"Well…it's still sex. And you know how that changes things."

"Girl, please. You two have been close friends longer than some folks have been married. Nothing has to change." Sasha broke away to hug a guest then came back.

"But you know how men are. Breaking friendship parameters and having sex with them is one thing. Oh, they'll just call that Friends With Benefits. Getting with their friend in front of them is another story. He'll always have visuals now."

"Men, yes. Rock stars? No. They live by a different code. Actually, I'm pretty sure they're codeless. They just do whatever feels good, and if the world's lucky, a new song will come of it. Rock god aside, Tommy doesn't strike me as the type to have double standards."

Capri didn't think so either, but...he cooked earlier. He snapped when she asked if he was okay. And he didn't say two words to her on the way over to the country club. "Dammit, Sasha. Why didn't he just fuck you when he had the chance? We'd be even."

"I'm sure Tommy has done stuff to make your threesome seem like a nursery rhyme. But you've bypassed me on the freaky deaky side by leaps and bounds. I've never done a threesome, 'ho. We are not even."

"Hip hip hooray." Capri raised her arms in Rocky Balboa fashion. "I feel so victorious, like I just won the slutty competition." Light humor hid the pain in her chest, the anxiety she felt over being at odds with Tommy, but only for a second. "Maybe I'm reading more into his behavior than I should."

They looked across the room to where Tommy had thrown one of Sasha's bridesmaids over his shoulder and headed to the restroom.

Sasha shrugged. "That's not really unusual for him.

But he's going to have to hold off on his little sex romp. He promised me a performance. It's almost time."

"He's performing?" Capri didn't know that. "You still want him to perform after that toast he gave?" Capri had cringed all the way through it and apologized to Sasha and Rob afterward.

"Meh. I thought the same thing before I met Rob. Men who go to strip clubs to pick up horny overflow chicks after a male revue *are* lame-os." She laughed. "Like Tommy said, when you aren't cool, you have to be smart and creative to get chicks. I'm thankful Rob was lame, because that meant he had to be smart too." She looked to where Tommy had exited her reception. "Tommy is a real piece of work. You two are perfect for each other. You just have to find a way to work through this hot mess you've created until you're both mature enough to be in a real relationship. In the meantime, go tell him to bring his ass back here and deliver my wedding gift. Stat."

A real relationship would never happen with Tommy or anyone else, for that matter, but Capri didn't bother telling Sasha that. It was her wedding day for Christ's sake. Sasha was entitled to be wrong today. Capri assured Sasha she'd have Tommy on the stage in no time.

When she got to the hallway where the men and women restrooms were located, Capri took an educated guess that they had gone into the women's room. You might find a clogged toilet or two, but all in all, women's stalls were always cleaner than men's. Capri should know.

She heard slurping as soon as she rounded the corner inside the toilet area and knew what she would find. Sure enough, the bridesmaid had ripped her long, tight gown to kneel in front of Tommy and suck him in her mouth. They hadn't even bothered to go into a stall. He just stood there in all his hedonistic glory inviting anyone to watch him get head. Tommy's head, the one with the brain, was thrown back on the wall. With his eyes closed, he looked like he was miles away from what the bridesmaid was putting all her effort into.

No wonder he was so bored with groupie sex. It had taken what, ten minutes, to get her on her knees? At Capri's pace, how long would it take her to get bored with her own promiscuous behavior? How many men would she have to screw to get tired of it? It had taken Tommy years to get to this point.

Tommy's hands gripped the back of the bridesmaid's head as he moved her down and up on him faster. He was a vision to behold with his black shirt unbuttoned all the way, and his black suit pants opened for service. It was his recklessness that bothered Capri. That was the biggest indicator that his mind wasn't where it should be.

Perhaps Capri should let him finish. Then again, how long were we talking here? Thirty minutes? An hour? Capri could save the girl some jaw and knee pain by interrupting now.

Just then, he opened his eyes and brought his face forward until his eyes locked with Capri's. Had he sensed her there or was it coincidental? She noticed a change in him immediately. He wouldn't be much longer, not if he continued to watch her watch him. He liked being watched. More notably, he liked her watching. He liked her eyes on him, his eyes on her. She'd bet money he didn't enjoy Divine's eyes on him as much as he enjoyed knowing he was turning Capri on. And he was.

She leaned against the wall near the paper towel dispenser and lifted her long gown with care. She wouldn't rip hers in a rush like the woman on her knees did. Capri would take her time getting to her sweet spot. It would make the show better for Tommy as well. He removed his hands from the girl's head and slapped them against the wall next to his hips, throwing his head back but keeping his eyes on Capri.

Capri's hand finally reached its destination, where she rubbed the outside of her panties and licked her lips. She would have loved to come with him, but she was just getting started and Tommy was too far gone, exploding in that moment. "Holy fu—!" He grabbed the woman's head as she tried to back away from him and rammed himself in her mouth.

Capri felt sorry for her, but his act of brutality at worst, selfishness at best, pleased Capri. She liked knowing she had that effect on him. If Capri was honest with herself, she also liked that he didn't give a fuck about the woman on the floor. He was heartless with everyone but Capri. Bored with everyone but her.

The woman stood to her feet, ripping her dress even more before she slapped Tommy across his face. "You fucking brute!" she said as she turned and looked at Capri with disgust then stormed out.

Tommy and Capri, never taking their eyes from each other, laughed.

Capri looked at his limp cock. "I would have let you gag me with it and choke me until I swallowed."

"Would you now?" His bushy eyebrows rose. "I'll

keep that in mind."

She pulled her gown down and went to the sink to wash her hands. Cleanliness ranked higher on her list of importance than modesty. "You didn't tell me you were performing at the reception."

He smiled. "I didn't tell you I wasn't."

"Cute." She handed him some wet paper towels. "Clean up. You're up next."

They said nothing more. Capri left to rejoin Sasha.

When Tommy stepped onstage, pride swelled in Capri's chest. She couldn't be sure whether it was because her best friend was also a big star now or if it was because her best friend was now her hottest, most compatible lover ever. Either way, as she sat next to Sasha, and they turned their attention to the stage, it took everything in her to hide the feelings that surfaced as Tommy got comfortable behind the piano. Yes, the piano.

Rob, of all people, stepped to the microphone, where he talked about his love for Sasha. It would have been a lovely speech for anyone into sappy speeches. "Without further ado, I give you Godd. He's all the way here from the Republic of Ireland, by way of his Celestial Decadence tour in Europe, to celebrate with us today. And we're so grateful to have him here." Everyone stood to give a standing ovation. Tommy stood from the piano bench, raising a shot glass in salute then tossed it back. He followed that shot with two more before sitting again.

"We love you, Godd!" Someone shouted from a table by the door. Apparently, that someone didn't get the memo that this was a wedding reception, not a rock concert.

Once Rob left the stage, Tommy acknowledged

Spirit's presence in the crowd. Though Spirit would not be playing during the selection, he stood from where he sat next to his family and received applause and whistles as well.

The next sounds that emerged from the speakers struck her in the gut with an invisible spear. Hard. To the point she thought she would cry right there, and that was unacceptable. Tommy had told her he played piano, but she'd never heard him play. He'd never mentioned having the skill of a prodigy. She didn't know the song, but she felt the emotions emanating from the chords. They blew her away. He didn't express his feelings through words. Words, to him, were meant for cracking jokes. He used instruments to convey his deep down, subconscious thoughts. That's where he released his burdens, his demons.

How much of himself did he keep from her, bottled up until he picked up his guitar or sat at a piano? As much or more than she'd kept from him? She had opened up yesterday. It was his turn to unleash everything on her. She could handle all of him. She'd do whatever it took to make him feel safe enough to divulge his inner self, whatever still laid hidden behind that jovial exterior. There was obviously so much more to the man than what met the eye. She wanted every little piece of him with nothing held back.

There was a standing ovation at the end, and not a dry eye in the reception hall. Sasha started for the stage with a napkin in her hand to dry her eyes.

Capri stayed where she was, on her feet, a safe distance from Tommy. She wasn't sure if she wouldn't embarrass herself if she got close to him right now. She loved that he made her feel things through his music, with his smile, even whilst he was being an ass. She hated that he made her feel things she didn't want to feel. Joyful, beautiful, tranquil...yes. Dependent, vulnerable, hopelessly in love...NO. Doomed to certain heartbreak...no. Behaving contrary to everything she believed about romance and relationships...no, no, no.

He stood up from the piano, knocking over the bench and tripping off the stage after he took a bow. If that weren't enough, when Sasha went to help him up from the floor, he embraced her and tried to kiss her. Spirit and Capri rushed to get him off the newly wed before Rob or one of his groomsmen did.

"Get him out of here," Sasha said to Capri, trying to hide her amusement. "We kept the media out, but I can't promise someone won't sell their personal photos or videos to TMZ."

Capri nodded, hiding her own need to laugh. She grabbed Tommy under one arm. Spirit grabbed the other. She looked at Tommy's drunk self as he smiled and waved to guests on his way out the door. She shook her head. He was absolute perfection. A mess and a half. A perfect mess.

She really loved him. *Really* loved him.

Well, damn.

She knew right then and there she could never have sex with him again. She loved him too much to do it to herself and him. He could do no wrong. Not even kissing her other bestie on her wedding day could diminish Capri's high opinion of him. She would forever remember him playing that beautiful piano piece more than anything else from today's event. If there was any chance at salvaging her scrambled brain and smitten heart, that part of their relationship had to end immediately. That would be best for them both.

He needed to go back to his tour and boring groupie sex, while she went back to fucking men she didn't even like enough to tell them her name, let alone get her off. Though the idea of doing it with Tommy one more time before he left Sunday night had definite appeal, she just couldn't risk it. Sex with him made her too susceptible to everything she'd made a habit of fighting.

She asked the limo driver to turn up Marilyn Manson's "Pistol Whipped" and put it on repeat while she and Tommy rode back to her house. The song felt so appropriate given her current mood.

"You're a mess, Tommy."

"Yeah…well… This is a new revelation because…what?"

"Never mind." She turned her head to look out the tinted window. Probably best not to talk to him while he was in this state. Perhaps she should ask the driver to turn on Manson's "Heart-shaped Glasses", a song about getting too deep with someone and begging them not to break your heart, instead.

"I know you think I was upset over what happened between the three of us last night, but that's not the case. I fancied it. It turned me on to see you enjoying him, both of us. I've often fantasized about that. You, enjoying other men. I listen to all your stories, and I fancy them. I don't want to fancy them, but I do."

She just looked at him without responding. *You're a little pistol and I'm fucking pistol whipped.* Yep. Manson must have had a Tommy in his life at the time of writing that song. Tommy was beating her, killing her softly.

She felt the pull towards him. Tommy that is, not Manson. She slid over as if he'd called her and hiked up her gown. It ripped all the way up the side seam. Fucker was too long anyway, and fuchsia was so not her color. Tommy pulled her across his lap, helping her rip the rest of the dress off. In seconds, she straddled his thighs, opening wide to him. He touched her core softly over her panties and rubbed until they were drenched. He held her gaze the whole time, soaking in each breath she exhaled. When his fingers found the inside of her panties, she cried out. His other hand pushed her ass in rhythm to his fingers, urging her to ride them. She was almost ready to peak, when he cupped the side of her face and moved in toward her lips.

She jerked her head back, not to avoid his kiss, but to issue a warning. "This is the last time, Tommy. Last time."

He stared into her eyes a moment before easing ever so slowly to her mouth. She opened it to him, and he took her lips carefully. Too carefully. Did he know she meant this was the last time for everything? Kissing, fucking, eye fucking, fucking without a condom... All of it stopped after this. Maybe even the cuddling. They would be like normal friends who talked on the phone, emailed, texted, and slept in separate beds.

"We should make it memorable then," Tommy said suddenly. Next, he told the driver to pull into a car park. After some back and forth and translation issues, Capri and the driver understood Tommy wanted to go to a parking garage. "I've never done it in a garage. You?"

She shook her head.

"You game?"

She nodded. She didn't trust herself to speak. She just might say something she'd regret forever, like how much she really cared for him. She already regretted feeling that way.

He smiled and kissed her again. That had almost been all it took. Only thing that stopped her was that he opened the limo door and got out, pulling her with him. He took his shirt off and gave it to her to put on over her underclothes. "Come on." He held her hand as they ran to the opposite end of the nearly full car lot. When they got to a corner cradled by a white van and a navy SUV, he pinned her up against the block wall. The vehicles gave them a little covering, not much.

She tried to ignore the cool, hard wall or the possibility people could catch them, and concentrate on the man she was with. That wasn't hard to do. She gripped his face and kept the kiss firm and delicious. He lifted her leg to the bumper of the van and unzipped his pants. He didn't remove her panties, just pushed them to the side and slid himself into her with a strong thrust of his hips. She threw her head back to absorb the shock of his forceful entry. He pinned her arms next to her head on the wall and took out his frustrations, anger, passion…she couldn't be sure which she was experiencing at the time, but she loved the power of it. Just like she loved him. Maybe he just wanted to get them to climax quickly given they couldn't hang out all day in the garage, fucking or otherwise.

He picked up the pace once she shuddered. Using one hand, he grabbed her throat and squeezed. She realized she'd given him the greenlight to choke her, and that's exactly what he was doing. Just when she didn't think she could take another moment, he let go and pumped with excruciating ferocity, taking her to climax as she struggled to catch her breath. He withdrew and followed her to bliss a moment later, rubbing his cock against her thigh as it released whatever he'd accumulated in the last hour.

He backed away from her to admire his art work on her skin. She slid to the floor, unable to face him. Unable to conceive of all the different things she wanted from him, to give to him, and to do with him. She really just needed to get away from him. "I really think I hate you."

He picked her up from the ground and buttoned his shirt on her. "There's a thin line between love and hate, I'm told. So hate's good." He took her hand and walked back down to the limo, zipping himself as he went.

She rested her head on his shoulder the whole ride to her apartment. They weren't completely distant, but they were silent. Maybe silence was good. Especially, if she would be less prone to saying dumb shit like *I really think I hate you.* What the fuck?

Tommy exited the limo first. She collected her things and followed him to her apartment.

"I'm just coming in to get my things. I'll be out of your hair in a moment."

"What? What do you mean? Where are you going?" She ran behind him.

"To Spirit's. Actually, no. That boy of his makes too much damn noise too early in the morning. Don't worry. I have plenty of other places to lay my head."

"Tommy. Tommy, wait. Stop, dammit." She ran to

get in front of him. He finally stopped. "I didn't really mean I hate you."

He studied her face. "I know you didn't. You meant you loved me. You're falling for me just like…well, we both know that's not good. We've started something we can't stop if we stay around each other. Shagging other people is not going to derail this train. We have to stop it, just like you said. That was the last time. We need space. We need to get our heads together before you really do start to hate me."

"I could never hate you. In a world where being judgmental, uptight and hypocritical is the norm, not the exception, you are the brightest shining star."

"That's a lovely thought, but I'm toxic for you. I'm definitely no one you should love in *that* way."

Deny, deny, deny. That's what she should do, say she felt nothing. She'd omitted information before, but never lied to him. Should she start now? Would lying about her feelings make them go away? Probably not. On the other hand, Tommy had a point. That kind of love between them was a no-no. Acknowledging any feelings put them on the wrong path to destruction. "Do I need to slap the other side of your face? I love you as a friend, Tommy. Nothing more." Half-truths weren't technically lies. She could make herself believe her feelings were pure friendly love.

He looked at her with blatant skepticism.

"Look—you're leaving tomorrow anyway. You'll be miles away from me. We should at least spend as much time as we can together now."

"You understand the temptation will be there for us to repeat what we've done?"

The way he looked at her lips just now made her cheeks flush. "Resisting temptations can be just as fun as succumbing to them," she smiled. *Yeah, right.*

Naw, Tommy didn't buy it either, but at least he waved the limo driver on. She didn't know where the driver was going, but at least he left without Tommy.

"So what's your story? Why would you call yourself toxic?" Capri wanted to take a peek at those demons Tommy allowed to escape his soul while he played instruments.

Tommy turned to walk toward the apartment. She grabbed his arm and stopped him.

He sighed. "Typical family drama. My mum cheated on me da. He caught her. I mean, in the act. He forgave her. She did it again. He forgave her then he found out my brother wasn't his son. All hell broke loose. I swear, all I heard him say over and over again like a broken record—'Don't ever fall in love, son. Never. It was the worst mistake of my life. Use the bitches for what you need, but that's it.' Their madness messed my head up. Chick I was seeing at the time—we were in high school—she was a virgin, gorgeous, saving herself for marriage. I sure as hell wasn't marrying her, not after what happened between my parents. I just didn't tell her that. I seduced her then fucked her best friend the next day. She cried and she threatened to kill herself and me. I was too numb to care. And what's so bad about it, she was one of the only people to give me the time of day in school. I used to get beat up and bullied every day. She was really popular and sort of validated me. All the beatings stopped once she made it cool to be seen with me. Then I shat all over her.

"So what did she do? She got me back. She turned

around and fucked me da. I swear it was like something out of a psychological thriller, minus the stovetop rabbit. Both of them had an axe to grind and they stabbed me and me mum. They made sure me mum and I were there to catch them." He laughed. "Madness, yeah? You know what's proper madness? Me mum and da are still together making their unconventional relationship work. Both are needy, affectionate people, who just can't replace each other. Guess they have an open marriage now or some mental shite like that. I don't even see the point of them being married."

Though she'd been paying close attention, Capri couldn't help but notice how thick his accent had gotten during his monologue about his past. She also didn't understand why he'd kept this to himself. It wasn't like he'd killed someone. It did explain his stance on things though.

"That's why you're so messed up." Capri's offhand remark held more truth than the humor she'd wanted to convey. It also made her feel less alone in her own family dysfunction.

He shrugged. "Everyone's messed up. This is why I'm messed up in the particular way that I am. I will never be a solid partner for anyone to depend on."

"Good thing I don't want that from you then, Tommy."

"Excuse me. Do either of you know where the security guard is on duty? I've been in an accident and need help." The speaker that walked up to Capri and Tommy resembled a hobo wearing a long trench coat.

Tommy and Capri looked at each other and laughed.

Tommy turned his back to the hobo. "Good try,

but you're looking at the two people who started that prank in the neighborhood, fella. Go flash your arse somewhere else."

"Hey, aren't you that guitar player guy?"

Tommy nodded but didn't turn around.

The hair on the back of Capri's neck rose. Something about the motion underneath the guy's coat made her nervous. She was just about to tell Tommy to step aside, when it was too late. The guy opened his coat, raising a wooden bat in the air. "Then you have money, motherfucker, so empty your pockets!"

Capri sprang into action, pushing Tommy out of the way, which kept his head from getting bashed, but did nothing to protect his shoulder. She ran into the attacker's midsection, bowling him over into the concrete walkway before he had a chance to raise the bat again. She kneed him in the balls and scrammed for the bat before he got a chance to. She'd never thought Tommy would be much of a fighter. She also hadn't expected him to get blindsided from the back. That just wasn't fair at all.

She stood to her feet and raised the bat to bring it down on their attacker's head.

"Please don't hurt me. Please don't. I'm sorry. I just need money for my sick baby. I don't have insurance, and the hospital bill and prescription drugs are outrageous."

"Capri!" Tommy held his shoulder, wincing in pain. "Wait."

Capri didn't drop the bat, but she didn't bring it down in the manner she'd intended either. She waited to see how things would play out.

Tommy reached in his pocket and tossed the

cowering punk a stack of rolled up bills. "I'm a bloody leprechaun, and it's your lucky day. I've just turned over a new leaf from practical joking to paying it forward with random acts of kindness. Now get the fuck out of here, twat."

The would-be thief collected his charity and took off running.

"You sure about that? He tried to *rob* you." Capri finally lowered the bat. She'd keep it now. Finders keepers. "How do you know he's not just going to snort it up and really hurt someone over his next high tomorrow?"

"I don't. But I gave him enough to overdose if he does spend it on drugs," Tommy winced.

"Let's get you to the ER." She waved off his protest. "I'm not trying to hear it, Tommy. I know there's no blood, but you're right-handed, and that's your right shoulder he used as target practice. What if there are internal injuries? You're going."

"Fine. Let's go to the hospital for me to get treated for simple bruising, why don't we?" Tommy got in the passenger seat of her car. "Just so we're clear, I'm moving you from this neighborhood first thing in the morning."

"I just moved here...like three months ago."

"Too bad. Me…my mate, won't live somewhere without a security guard on duty at all times. And gates. You need gates."

She tried not to think too hard about his usage of the word mate. It had always meant friend to him. Nothing more. But what word *would* he use if he meant an actual mate?

And this was why you didn't fuck friends. Things got really confusing. Of course, he only meant friend.

Duh.

Tommy called his manager and explained what had happened. He wouldn't get off the phone until it was agreed that his flight plans would be delayed for one more day. He'd asked for another week, but his next concert was Tuesday night. "Tomorrow, we'll find a house for you. I'll buy it. You'll live in it. And a car. You have to have a new one, something more fitting."

"More fitting for what?"

"More dependable. This one's raggedy, something to be used in a circus act with clowns. I can't trust that it won't break down on you."

Nothing was wrong with her car. She looked at him through narrowed eyes. Was he treating her like a mate or a *mate*? There was no way she would accept those things from him, but she'd wait until after a doctor examined him to argue about it.

CHAPTER 13

Tommy awakened to a thunderous noise coming from the lavvy that caused him to sit up on the couch. He heard Capri whisper *shit!* in response. The small ray of light peeking from under the lavvy door indicated she was in there. He groggily went to the door and opened it. He watched her arse as it straightened from where she had bent down to pick up a container of hair accessories. "Where are you going?"

She was decked out in a gray suit and cream blouse. "To work. Sorry I woke you."

"What? Why? It's Sunday."

"And your point is?"

Okay. Here we go. "The point, my love, is that you should rest. Go to work tomorrow. Enjoy the rest of the weekend."

"I took off Friday, which you slept through by the way, and I took off yesterday for the wedding. I have bills and responsibilities. We all can't live the capricious life you do."

He heard bitterness in her voice. "Capri, the non-capricious… Ah, the irony. Not my fault you choose to be as boring as Ben Stein." He shook his head and left the doorway to grab a wad of hundred dollar bills out of his luggage case. "Here. How many of your Sunday hours can I buy with that?" He didn't mean for it to seem so sleazy when he threw them at her, but…well, it was done now.

"You switching over to rap now? Practicing how to make it rain?" She watched the money fall all around her. "None. You can't buy me at all."

He looked perturbed, rubbing his shoulder where it was bruised but thankfully, not broken or fractured. "Is this because I almost left last night? Did that make you feel insecure? Or is it because I offered to buy you a better place to live and a better car? Maybe I offered too much security and you can't use the whole 'nobody's going to give me anything, I have to work my fingers to the bone' edict anymore. I've completely debunked your safety net, your excuses for burying yourself in work and away from anyone who gives a damn about you."

"I already told you my motivation for success. Devoting myself to work has never been about money for me, though providing for myself is a welcomed perk," Capri said.

"Bollocks. Not even the guilt you've been holding on to can be your crutch. Not when you willfully allow past mistakes to be the thing that keeps you from living your most fulfilling life. You can't blame your mum or even that lad's death for how you've purposely chosen to live your life. You're out of justifications, Capri." He stepped toward her and grabbed her arms. "I can't help it any more than you can that there's more between us than dogging in public and being best mates. Messy shit happens.

212

Work does not have to start being your escape from me too."

"You're one to talk about living your most fulfilling life. How's that working out for you with the groupies? As far as there being more between us, Tommy…" She shrugged his hands off and put her flat iron down on the counter. "I can't handle this. I thought I could, and I can't. It was supposed to happen only once between us. Sex was supposed to eliminate the mystery and relieve tension. Things got out of hand. Then you were only supposed to be here one more day. Now look at the mess we're in. Look at who we've become." She pulled down her blouse collar to show the hickies he'd put all over her neck.

Oh. Those…

He'd had the overwhelming urge to brand her, so he did. "Um…that's temporary."

"Yeah, but my feelings are not. And you're playing with them."

Tommy couldn't say he was proud of his actions from last night. He'd definitely gotten carried away. It had felt well good being inside her, glued to her body all night, sweating through her bed sheets. He'd felt possessive and obsessive, knowing no other man had or would please her in the way he did. No one else could pleasure her mind, body, and soul simultaneously. But delivering and receiving that pleasure meant he hadn't been a man of his word. He'd been a caveman.

Outside the flat, they had agreed to not have sex anymore. She'd practically begged him not to touch her and it had made him want to even more. He knew her reasoning derived from how he turned her on more than anything else, and that had made all the difference in the world. He'd given her The Stare. He'd touched her knickers gently. He'd bitten her lips, tongued her ears, and licked her arse. Her "please don't" became an invitation to "please do" because of how lustful she'd said it. She enjoyed being with him too much to not want to take him inside herself over and over again. And unlike a best mate, he'd exploited that.

Just like when Capri had said she hated him and meant she loved him, when she'd told him not to touch her...well, he knew her. He didn't have to guess what she really wanted. She wanted orgasms. With him inside her. Problem was, she didn't want to want them. It would have been better for them both if they had never opened Pandora's Box, but the damage had been done. If they had been less attracted to each other, this wouldn't have been a problem. But the sexual chemistry was there. Every time they touched. So he kept touching her. He kept using his sexual power over her, realizing she lost pieces of her soul to him every time he took her. He'd seen it in that bird's eyes that shagged his da. He'd known he was touching a part of their souls meant only for one ready to make her his lifelong soul mate. That look wasn't meant for a lad just wanting to have a good craic. Tommy had been that lad back then in high school, and he'd been that lad last night.

Capri's legs, mouth, eyes, arms...her whole body had opened to him as if Capri had no control over them. The control belonged with Tommy and he reveled in it. He would have stayed like that all night and woken up inside Capri if she hadn't put her foot down and said enough was enough. Just like he knew when she didn't mean it, he knew when she did. They couldn't even cuddle at that point. No spooning privileges for the horny toad who couldn't behave himself. He had been relegated to the couch.

"I'm not playing with your feelings. I'm playing with that pretty cunt, giving you the best sex of your life with the hottest guy in your life," he grinned and wagged his brows.

"Go fuck yourself," she said as she tried to storm past him.

He blocked her exit from the lavvy. "Okay. Okay." Making light of the situation would not fly today. "I don't blame you for being cross with me. You're scared. You're worried. You feel like you're alone in this. I get that. You ever thought I might be scared too? But you know what? I'm more afraid of returning to my capricious life without you than I am of what's developing between us." He waited until her face softened before he leaned his head down, aiming for her mouth. Just one kiss and she'd forget about work.

"I should have let you leave with your limo last night."

Ow. That was a harsh blow. Maybe a well-deserved one. He dropped the thoughts toward seduction and wrapped his arms around her. It was just a hug. For comfort. Something to say he was sorry for being one raging hormone after another around her. Just holding her made him want to knock everything off the lavvy counter and fuck her on it. Practicing restraint with her had been a challenge ever since he'd finally sampled her goods and decided he'd rather have her than anything else. Almost anything else. He still needed music like he needed water to live.

"I'm sorry. I've never been in a situation like this. I don't know what I'm doing. I don't know how to fix this," Tommy said.

"I hate to admit it, but I am in over my head in this. I'm too unfamiliar with these…feelings to understand them. I can analyze it from an impersonal, theoretical perspective. I just haven't dealt well with emotional stuff my whole life, and I'm not ready to do so now. I'm not emotionally mature enough to handle this. Avoidance and denial are my default coping mechanisms." She touched the side of his face. "I'm sorry, but you should probably stay with Spirit tonight."

He was stunned so much his stomach ached. He didn't want to leave tonight. He didn't even want to leave tomorrow. "Capri…"

It was too late. She gave him a forlorn look before walking past him, grabbing her briefcase and leaving for work.

He opened the waistband to his underpants and looked down at his instrument of lust. He thumped it hard. "Look at what you did, you stupid, stupid piece of stupid meat." Tommy plopped on the couch and went back to sleep.

When he woke up, it was at a more respectable hour, sometime in the afternoon, well after the roosters had said their howdydoodies. That ache in his stomach had not receded, and it wouldn't until he and Capri were best buds again. He'd made things worst between them even after knowing how vulnerable Capri had been. It was his responsibility to make them better. He wouldn't leave the country until he did.

For the next few hours, he did what came highly

recommended to people experiencing depression, which was exactly where he'd be if Capri shut him out of her life—retail therapy. A shopping spree, more like. It was something he spent very little time doing since he was on the road so much. But after his first few purchases, he decided shopping was something he quite liked. It was infinitely healthier than using pussy as a resolution to a problem that came about as a result of his love for pussy.

Actually, things would be much better if his issue had only been about pussy. It was more about his love for Capri and how he had jeopardized her love for him. His mood dampened at the thought of how despondent she'd looked when she'd left for work. All because of him. Her face had looked much different as she came over and over again, trembling in his arms throughout the night.

Stop it, jerk off!

He went back to her flat to wait until she got back. It didn't matter if it would be ten o'clock, midnight, or three the next morning. He'd wait up for her and explain how much he wanted their old relationship back. The one before sex complicated everything.

Good sex, that is.

The best.

He found some mediocre porn and wanked twice to make sure he could keep two clear heads whenever she arrived.

Her key turned in the door at six o'clock, surprising him from his phone conversation with Spirit.

"I have to go. She just walked in."

"Remember man, if you can't handle the responsibility of protecting her heart, you shouldn't unlock it. As cold as she seems—and no one knows her cold side better than me—she's still a human being. Everyone has a breaking point. Good luck. Ciao, man, and congrats again." Spirit hung up.

"You're still here?" Capri couldn't hide the cheerfulness on her face as much as she tried to disguise it in her voice.

Tommy took a deep breath of relief and sat up on the couch. There was hope for them yet. "I'm not going anywhere, not until my flight takes off. You're my best mate. I wouldn't dare leave things like this with you."

He got up from the couch and dangled a set of keys. "This is for you. It's a new car."

Her eyes bucked as she stood in silence with her back to the front door.

He knew it would take her a while to adjust to the idea. "It's in the car park. Top of the line. Nothing but the best for you."

"Tommy, you can't—"

"And this real estate," he held up the rent to own documents he'd gotten started and would have completed tomorrow for a spacious loft in uptown, "is for you too."

She dropped her briefcase on the floor and slid down next to it. She was still in shock. It was to be expected. "I'm not going to live in a house or drive a car you bought me. That's final."

"I bought them for me, sweetheart, and I need someone to take care of them until I return." That seemed like a reasonable explanation.

Capri's big brown eyes of hers stared at him like he'd lost his marbles. Her dimples deepened as she worked her jaw. "You're crazy."

Ah. She did think he'd gone mental. "It's no big deal. I have nothing or no one else to spend my bucks on. No one I want to anyway. What's the purpose of having all this money, if I don't spend it, yeah? You don't want me blowing it on a bunch of fair weather gold diggers, do you? Spirit's got a family. I've got what? You. Just you. Why can't I share my wealth with the person who's been there for me through thick and thin?" He rushed over to his luggage carrier. "I had bought you another, smaller gift that I've been meaning to give to you since I got here, but well…it's uh…" He pulled out matching BFF bracelets and handed them to her. The chains were platinum, one with a charm shaped like a chocolate chip cookie, the other with a charm shaped like a glass of milk. "The engraving is sort of non-applicable now."

Despite her frustrations, it brought a smile to her face. "Is this supposed to represent you being white and me being black?"

"Actually the cookie's mine. You need to keep your figure. I could stand to gain an inch or two."

She read the inscription on the back of the milk charm. "To the only girl I love enough not to shag." Her laughter came out weak. "Guess you don't love me as much as you thought you did."

"I don't. I love you more. I need to get it updated to read: To the only girl I love enough not to shag again until we're both ready to devote our hearts and souls to one another." He smiled until he saw her eyes water.

"It's beautiful."

He squatted in front of her on the floor. "I know I fucked up. We fucked up. We ruined a good thing. But maybe something better can come out of it."

Tommy took her hands but he didn't force her to look up at him. "Confession…" She looked at him then, encouraging him to spill his guts. "I do love you, Capri. Don't ever doubt that. I love you enough not to run away from what we had in the past, what we have now, and what we could have in the future. I love you enough to do some really strange things too. Like…go on a real date."

She started shaking her head and pulling her hands back.

He held firm and kept talking. "Tonight, I'll sleep on the couch. Tomorrow, we can finish with the real property transaction. Then we'll have a date. No sex. And just see how it goes. Assess where we are in life and see what needs to be done to salvage our relationship." He ignored her shaking head of disapproval. He'd given this some thought all day. He'd never even tried to have a relationship since the one he shatted on in high school. Maybe it was time to give it a real try since part of why he hadn't felt a burning need to have one was because of his relationship with Capri. She had most of his needs covered before there was ever any sex involved. "We'll put our heads together instead of our genitals…and who knows, maybe we can figure out how to be a real couple. I can be open to that. With you." Now that they'd explored the sexual side of their relationship and knew they were compatible, maybe she could be open to being a real couple too.

"A real couple?" She laughed like he was doing standup at Comedy Central. "Then what? You'll cancel the rest of your tour, move back here with me permanently, and we'll run off into the sunset together and let them write a movie about our romance? The one where we two-timed our friend, Spirit, and my home girl sucked your cock? The same girl you tried to kiss on the day of her wedding?"

"I was thinking more like a song. Maybe even a rap. But sure, a movie will work too."

She twisted her lips in disbelief. "What drugs are you on today, Tommy? I mean, seriously."

"Point is. I'm willing to do whatever it takes to see where this goes with us. If it doesn't work, if we say hell no, fine. Our times together, even without the sex, have been the best days of my life."

"Well, when you put it like that…" She reluctantly agreed…to everything except the house and car because she said, "Those gifts are too extravagant, and I'm nobody's mistress."

He'd make her come around. He'd consider it his good deed for the day.

They talked for the rest of the evening and night, and when the morning came, she called in sick. It had been her first time ever. She didn't plan to work from home. She didn't plan to take any work calls. She was all his.

He was a proud man, excited about their date.

As they sat down at the ritziest restaurant table he could find, he felt giddy. There was no telling where this would go for them. He was on an actual date with the youngest recipient of the mental health services award in excellence at the clinic where she worked. She also happened to be hot as lava, perfect for those cameras snapping footage of Godd, the lead guitarist for Celestial Decadence, out on the town. It was hard to forget that was who everyone saw when they saw him. But when blinding bright light interrupted his conversation with Capri every thirty seconds or another fan came up and asked for his autograph, he began to realize Capri wasn't on a date with Tommy. By the time two waitresses asked him to sign the inside of their thighs, he could see the frustration on her face. He was happy to be with her. She had had enough.

She didn't want to ruin it for him though. He could tell, because she kept fake smiling. He did his best to give her his undivided attention, since she was giving him hers. But he would never be rude to his fans, especially when cameras were rolling.

"I'm so sorry," he said again.

"Please stop apologizing. You had to have known your sunglasses and kango wouldn't really hide your face. You have that magnetizing effect on people. You draw them in whether you're trying to or not. That's one of the special things I like about you and would never want to change."

He leaned forward and whispered, "But we're sitting in the back."

"But you're famous now, Tommy. Things will never be the same."

He wiped his mouth and threw his napkin down on the plate. "I don't want to be famous anymore."

"It doesn't really work like that, does it?" She sipped her wine. "It was a lovely thought though. Thank you for the date. The food is delicious."

"We can go, if you want. To somewhere more private."

"Like home, you mean? 'Cause that's the only place we can be without distractions."

He'd wanted today to be perfect for her. For them. "Defeats the purpose of going on a date, doesn't it?"

She looked as if she had accepted defeat.

"Exactly."

Just then a group of goth teens came over, squealing for his attention. He looked at her with an apology written on his face.

She smiled and waved him toward his fans. "Go. It's okay. This is your life now. Who knows…maybe we'll be together in your next one."

Their smiles were full of sadness because they both knew a real relationship would never work.

"Go. You were born to be a star. Now go shine brightly." She waved him toward the group again.

She sat alone while he stood and talked to them. He kept looking back at her where she sat at the table watching him, and he knew he was one hundred percent in love with her. There had never been a feeling in his chest like the one he felt right now. It wasn't lust. He wasn't even hard. It wasn't just friendly love. He'd felt that for her a long time and it had never been this all-encompassing energy. No, this was different. And it made him sad.

As much as he was in love with her, and he knew without a doubt she was in love with him, a normal relationship just wasn't in the cards for them. It was a cool fantasy, one never meant to be their reality. Maybe in a decade or two, they'd have it all together. For now, it just wasn't meant to be. The one time in his life when he had it all, including a once in a lifetime kind of love that he was ready to accept for what it was, it just wasn't possible. He found that to be horribly sad.

CHAPTER 14
FIVE YEARS LATER

An incessant buzzing noise slowly penetrated Tommy's stream of unconsciousness. He rolled over onto a sea of warmth and softness in order to escape it. Consciousness was for corporate monkeys and the elderly.

Buzzzz.

"Nooo. Go away."

There were stirrings next to him, or underneath him, or on top on him...he couldn't be sure, but a moment later, his phone found its way to his palm.

"Answer it, Godd," a soft voice said from somewhere close to his ear. "It's Spirit. He's been calling for the past few hours."

Spirit? Oh, no. It must have been serious. Tommy hoped Spirit's calls didn't mean...

Tommy rolled back over to his back, peeling arms and legs and the tangle of sheets off himself. He threw a robe over his naked body and took the buzzing phone to the balcony. By the time he'd closed himself off from the bedroom and was ready to talk, the buzzing had stopped. Since Spirit had called twenty-six times, Tommy immediately hit redial.

After one ring, Spirit answered. Sniff, sniff. "They're saying she's not going to make it, Tommy. What am I going to do? She's not going to make it," Spirit wailed.

Tommy rubbed sleep from his eyes. "How long does she have?"

"I don't know, man." Sniff, sniff. "I don't know. Not long."

"I'm catching the next flight out of here. Text me the hospital info."

"Okay."

"And Spirit? Hang in there, mate. I'll call Divine and Savior. We'll all be there with you."

Nothing but sniffing now. Tragedy had a way of breaking even the strongest down to puddles of tears and mucus.

Tommy wished he was already there to help bear some of Spirit's overwhelming burden, but the band hadn't been together in over a year. Everyone had been off doing his own thing. Tommy had done three Hollywood movies, and had just wrapped up his first appearance on a popular Irish drama. He'd spent last night doing an RTE interview then partying at his house with folks he didn't know.

Divine and Savior had formed a second band and spent most of their time on that. They appealed to a young, hipster crowd. They hadn't split from Celestial Decadence; they'd just been exploring other interests. If and when the band ever decided to drop another album or do another tour, they'd be there, cocks in one hand, instruments in the other.

Spirit, he'd been the one to have it all—the wife he loved, the two sons and daughter he loved, the production company he loved. Some of the songs he'd written had gone platinum and won various awards. In fact, his office was loaded with awards. He'd been the envy of all the other band members, because he'd had the most normal life. His happiness and fulfillment had only been dreams and fantasies for the other lads. But Spirit had lived it…until life had gone and thrown in a disaster. The universe just couldn't accept love without pain, happiness without despair, or life without death. And did it care how those most affected would manage after irreparable damage was done? No. The universe would create other moments to bring fleeting moments of pleasure, illusions of fulfillment, and simulated happiness until everything turned upside and the other side dropped it all on its head. The cycle of life sucked: Spirit's wife dying after being hit by a drunk driver, Exhibit A.

"Godd, is everything all right?"

"No. No, it isn't." He turned away from the beautiful countryside and cool morning air of his home of origins to look at a voluptuous brunette standing naked in the balcony doorway. "I have to go."

"Is there anything I can do?"

"You can get yourself a cab. There's money on the dresser." He turned back to look at the sunny sky one last time. "Oh and…you can stop calling me that. My name is Tommy." He was certainly no god. He'd fix Spirit's wife so she could be there for their children, if he was.

He called Divine and Savior as he'd promised. They were on their way and would probably get there before him since they were already in the states. Next, he called his manager to handle his flight arrangements, scheduling and such. Then he stared at his phone. Capri. Should he call her? They barely spoke anymore, his biggest, most regrettable heartbreak in life. If he could go back and change…well, there wasn't anything he'd do differently. How could he? Every moment with her had been good. He would have had to change himself in order to change the course of how their lives intersected and divided, and she wouldn't have wanted that. If he had been any other person, he wouldn't have been able to get close to her in the manner he had. He probably would have been able to hold on to her though.

What am I going to do? Spirit's miserable voice echoed in Tommy's head. Fuck if Tommy knew.

Tommy would need help with the emotional fallout behind Spirit's wife passing when she did. Yes, he needed to call Capri.

He called twice before deciding to leave a message. He didn't know if she was avoiding him because of her relationship or if she was tied up with work. Both were plausible reasons she never answered when he called, and it always took her a week or more to call back. She'd been dating her boss, mentor, former professor for a few years now, so Tommy called sparingly anyway. He didn't want to cause problems or have a negative impact on her chance at happiness and normalcy. As far as her work went, she'd completed her PhD, opened her own counseling and therapy center, and traveled the world speaking as an expert in the mental health field. She was also a mentor to several young, aspiring professional women, something that made Tommy so proud. Maybe things would have been different for Capri if she'd had a mentor like herself rather than a prison, mentally unstable mum and male boss who'd probably been trying to get in her knickers all along.

He eased up on his crushing grip on his phone. He'd need that in case she called back.

He walked back in his bedroom, annoyed. Seeing the three bitches still partially clothed junking up his room didn't help his mood a wee bit. One was still asleep on the bed where he'd left her. One was brushing her teeth in the bathroom like she had a dental exam in an hour and would get punished for a cavity. And the one he'd told to get a cab had her skanky ass in front of his mirror brushing her scalp severely, dropping strands of her hair all over the floor.

Okay. Drastic times called for drastic measures. They didn't have to go home, but they had to get the fuck out of here so he could think and get in supportive mode for his mate. *Where's that...?*

Tommy had just the thing to scatter overstayed company from his lair. He went to a dresser and pulled out a huge black rubber spider and screamed as he threw it on the bed. He had to hold his lips tight to keep from having an outright laugh as they sprang into action, screaming and grabbing their belongings.

Once they'd left him in solitude, he looked at the clock on the nightstand. Still nine oh five, which meant it had taken all three of them thirty seconds to escort themselves out. Record time. He'd have the housekeeper throw out anything they left. Whenever he finally came back, he didn't even want to smell their perfumes in the air.

Now, to get his arse to L.A...

He slept the whole flight. As soon as he landed he

checked his phone. Three missed calls and a voice message from Capri. He almost ran into something and busted his arse while trying so hard to play her message. *Hey, this is Capri. Sorry I missed your call. My um…my mom just got here. Yeah…so… Well, anyway, call me. Call me as soon as you get there. I'm booking a flight now, but I probably won't be able to get to the hospital until tomorrow. Okay? Call me.*

He replayed her message seven times just to hear her voice. How sick was that?

After smacking the phone upside his head a few times, he headed to his awaiting limo. He took one look at the long vehicle with the comfy floor and ample seating and changed his mind. He could never ride in one the same again. He decided to rent a sports car instead then headed to the hospital. He just hoped he wasn't too late. He hadn't lost anyone close to him since his mamó, and no one he'd ever been intimate with or shared children with, but he empathized with Spirit. He just couldn't imagine the hurt Spirit felt behind shattered dreams. Whatever Spirit and his wife had planned for the future would be a puff of dust soon. That was the sort of helplessness he didn't wish on anyone.

He knew he'd been right about how inconceivably wretched the situation was the moment he walked in the hospital corridor and saw Spirit hunched over in a seat. The weight of the world sat on Spirit's shoulders. It was visible, even to the naked eye. Family sat all around him, but Spirit sat there looking alone and trapped in his own despair. Tommy nodded at Savior and Divine where they sat next to Spirit's mum holding each of her hands.

Tommy swallowed the lump in his throat. He'd

never seen Spirit so broken, and this was just the beginning. The fact that they were all out here meant his wife was still in the room, hanging on by whatever thin thread still held her to this world. Tommy put a gentle hand on Spirit's shoulder. That was all. Spirit didn't even look up. He just dropped his head and sobbed.

"I'm here for you, brother." Tommy gave Spirit's shoulder a squeeze.

The sobbing continued a moment longer before two men in scrubs walked up to them. "We've done all we can do," one of them said. "I'm sorry. If you want to say your goodbyes…" He left the end of the statement open to interpretation.

Spirit's ex-girl, Irene, walked their son over to Spirit. His other two children were brought over by various family members as well. Spirit took a deep breath and stood.

Tommy eyed Spirit as he used his bare hands to wipe tears from Spirit's face. "I'll be right here." He'd wait in the corridor sitting area for Spirit to return. There was no way in hell he was going in that room where death was expected to descend at any moment. He couldn't handle that again. He'd watched his mamó grab death's hand and wave farewell. He didn't want to be that close to it ever again.

Nearly thirty minutes later, Tommy heard Spirit's wail that could be heard down the street and he knew it was done. Tommy wiped the corner of his eyes, saddened by his mate's pain.

When Spirit emerged another twenty minutes later he said, "She's gone."

Tommy opened his arms to Spirit's big, distraught body, and let the big teddy bear soak his shirt with tears. There was nothing else he could do. Though Tommy had flown from halfway around the world to render support, he'd never felt more useless. Divine and Savior joined the hug, encompassing Spirit as well, as they stood in the corridor and cried like newborn babies.

Later on, as Tommy tossed and turned restlessly in his hotel room, he thought of Capri. What if it had been her in that hospital being downgraded to the morgue? What would *he* do? All these years later, he still loved her. Her soft hair, her cheerful smile, her thoughtful eyes, her exuberant laughter. More than anything, Tommy wanted Capri. He wanted to hold her hand, to talk to her about any and everything, to watch her listen as he played her favorite songs. He wanted her to know he wanted her. He needed her to know. He'd been absolutely miserable without her. He'd been surrounded by girls he didn't know, people he didn't like, and projects he had no passion for. He'd traded the possibility of something real with her for this phony, famous rock star image and lifestyle that he didn't even care about anymore.

Even though they didn't talk all the time anymore or cuddle themselves to sleep, he couldn't imagine life without the possibility of that ever happening again. Moments like this showed where the rubber met the road. It opened his eyes to what was most important in the world: love. Once it was gone, it was gone. Capri wasn't yet gone from the world, and neither was he. There had to be something, some way to finally get them on the same page at the same time with the same goals toward loving each other forever in mind.

He'd find a way before it was too late. Spirit was in

pain now, but only because he'd actually been one of the few to know what true love really was. He'd given and received it in kind. Tommy wanted to have that with the one he loved, minus the car accident, of course. But he'd take the road that led to Capri and follow it wherever it would lead. That's what he'd done with his love for music. That's especially what he needed to do with her.

He'd called her back and left a message giving her the somber update. He really wished he could talk to her before she arrived, but oh, well. He comforted himself to sleep with the thought he'd finally see her again tomorrow. She wouldn't escape him this time.

The next morning, he arrived at Spirit's house bright and early. As early as he could stand, that is, shortly after eleven. Fuck it. It was the best he could do.

Spirit opened the door with a haunting smile on his face. "Morning, stubborn. I told you we have plenty of room for you here last night, but did you stay here? Nooo."

Tommy had needed to get away from all the mourning to collect himself and start fresh today. "I'm here now, aren't I?"

Spirit slapped his back playfully. "Yes, you are, indeed. Come on in. We're all at the table having brunch."

Tommy followed him to the immaculate dining area, a room that showed Spirit's wife's exquisite taste in decorating and designing. Tommy looked at his phone's screen as it buzzed with a new message. A text from Capri: *What's Spirit's addy?*

He grinned in spite of the non-joyous occasion and texted it back to her. She'd be here soon. She'd make it all better. For him, at least.

Brunch was a craic, filled with light chatter and good food. Spirit's fans, neighbors, and clients had already begun bringing food items and condolence gifts. Tommy kept glancing back at the foyer and at his phone for any signs of Capri. It sure was taking her long enough to—

The doorbell rang and Tommy hopped to his feet. "I'll get it!"

He rushed to the door and nearly exploded with excitement when he saw her standing on the other side of the glass. Jesus…she looked breathtaking in her black-rimmed glasses, simple black dress with shawl, and her hair pinned in a bun at the top of her head. He opened the door and pulled her to him for a big squeeze before they'd said a word. She held onto him and him to her for several moments before he heard a throat clearing.

Capri jerked back. "Oh. Tommy this is Barry. Barry, Tommy."

Barry??? What the fuck? She brought BARRY? To their circle of friends?! Sorry, but he couldn't hide his animosity. He wasn't good at being fake in his personal life. He just stared at Capri. He couldn't even acknowledge Barry yet.

"How are you doing, Tommy?" Barry, looking uptight in his three-piece suit, stuck his hand out to shake Tommy's. "I am such a huge fan of your work. You are truly a god of rock and roll. Tell him, Capri." Barry's grin widened. "She can tell you, I have all of your albums. She's told me so much about you, I feel I know you already. It's such a pleasure and an honor."

Bet there were some things she left out.

Tommy dragged his eyes away from Capri's ridiculous-looking face to look at the sand she'd brought to the beach. "Thank you, Barry. The pleasure's all mine." Not. But hey, the moment called for cordiality even when he felt like punching his fan, her boyfriend in the face.

"Capri!" Spirit rushed up to welcome her to his home. "Thank you for coming. It's good to see you."

"I'm so sorry I didn't get here sooner. So sorry for your loss."

Capri reached up to hug Spirit and all the air in Tommy's body drained through his mouth. Her left hand wore an engagement ring. He looked at her in shock. She hadn't even told him. Not a peep. Not a whisper. When had she started to hate him that much that she wouldn't tell him she was going to marry this white collar son of a bitch?

Tommy excused himself then went to the lavvy. He couldn't...he just couldn't...

He started hyperventilating. His Capri was marrying some other fella. In what universe could that be allowed to happen? Since when did she ever want the ball and chain of marriage anyway? Hell, if that was all she wanted, Tommy could give her that. He could give her anything that little opportunistic geezer in there could only dream about.

There was a knock at the door. "You okay in there, Tommy?"

"I'll be out in a minute, Spirit."

"Let me in. Now."

"Fuck off, twat. You've got your own stuff to deal—"

"I said let me in."

Tommy opened the door, stepped back to the sink

and crossed his arms. "Can't a man take a shit in peace around here?"

"I asked you an important question once. Do you remember what it was? 'If given the opportunity, would you do whatever it took to be with the one you loved?' Do you remember that?"

Tommy swallowed and held his chin stiff. "Did you know about this? Did she tell you and not me?"

"I knew she was seeing the old fart, but this is my first time seeing the ring too. I didn't know, I swear."

"How could she do that to me? To us?"

"Where were you last night, Tommy? Were you sleeping next to her or some more of those no-strings attached standbys? 'Cause if you weren't with Capri last night or even trying to be with her, you did it to yourself. You might as well had just given Barry the ring and told him to ask her to be his wife."

"But she never wanted marriage and the whole picket fence thing."

"People change. She's thirty now. I'd give anything to have my wife back," Spirit's voice caught. "I'd do whatever it took to be with the one I loved. Would you?"

When Spirit exited the lavvy, he took Tommy's mojo with him.

The rest of brunch, the rest of the day, the rest of the night all went by in a haze of blandness. Tommy couldn't repeat one conversation he'd had. He couldn't remember one thing he did or saw. He'd been fixated on the ring on Capri's finger and that she was planning to marry Barry.

Could and should he do whatever it took to get her away from Barry and...and what? Be with him? Was he really bloody ready to give her the same thing and more that Barry was offering? Could he handle it?

Marriage.

Commitment.

Normalcy.

Trust.

Stability.

Love.

At least he had one of them covered. As far as the rest went, Barry may have been better suited for the job. Tommy's knee-jerk reaction was to steal her away and make her his, but was he really a better man for her all the way around? Good sex and friendship would no longer be enough. That ring on her finger made that clear.

He decided to stay at Spirit's mansion for the night, maybe all the way up until the funeral. Then he'd make his way somewhere. Maybe to a remote island in his own living hell. Who the hell would care?

After another night nearly spent entirely of tossing and turning in bed, he got up and had a few whiskeys before making his way to Tommy's baby grand piano downstairs. He always had a difficult time sleeping alone, but he was more restless than usual. His heart was heavy and needed a tune-up. He began to play softly so as not to wake anyone. Once he was done with the second song, he rested his head on the keys, feeling a little better. Music always soothed his troubled soul. Whiskey helped too.

Someone clapped behind him.

His heart dropped as he turned to see Capri standing in the doorway.

"As soon as I heard the chords, I knew it was you playing."

He looked away hurriedly. He couldn't bear to

look at her and know he couldn't touch her. "I didn't know you and Barry were staying here. I would have gone back to the hotel."

She eased next to him on the piano bench. "I know it must have come as a big surprise to you. I didn't mean to do it like this." She looked up at the ceiling. "Goddammit. Everything had just gotten so confusing and awkward between us. I just didn't know how to tell you."

Tommy turned to her, eying her long, thin black gown. He'd always known how to get her to say things she didn't intend to say. He could lift her gown now and... Fuck. No, not fuck. No, no fucking. He'd meant fuck, he couldn't believe he was thinking about fucking her at a time like this. He leapt off the bench to put more space between them. "Do you love him?"

"What?"

"You need a hearing aid to go with those spectacles now? I asked if you love him. Does he make you come when he's inside you? Do you have a good laugh at yourselves from time to time? Does he make you think about things in other ways than you've been programmed to think? Does he play music for you that transport you to another plane?"

She stared at him in the moonlight glowing through the wide picture windows opened to the patio and pool out back. "He makes me happy. That's all you need to know."

"Does he now?" He started walking toward her on the bench, speaking low and predatorily. "You mean you like watching his cumface as much as mine? You have as much fun with him as you did me?

"This isn't a competition."

"Isn't it? Though I must say that wanker has me at a disadvantage seeing how you never told me you'd become one of those women who wanted to be married. I didn't know the stakes had been raised."

She laughed. "As if it would have made a difference. What are you, thirty-two now? You have to see me with a ring on my finger before you start thinking about trying to win me?"

"What if I said I always wanted you back and I just didn't know if you'd take me seriously?"

"You say *back* as if you've ever had me. Fucking me senseless is not having me." She stood from the piano bench where he now stood directly in front of her. "And who in the world would ever take you seriously? You've done nothing but move from one game to the next. You think I haven't seen all the tabloids and paparazzi pics? Life is one big funfest to you."

He grabbed her arms, without a clue as to what he'd do next. He just needed her to understand… He just wanted her to feel… He just… He ended up doing what came naturally. He kissed her.

She fought to get away, so he tightened his grip on her and deepened the kiss. Before he thought his next step through, he grabbed both of her gown straps and ripped them off. She stepped back, eyes wide in surprise. "What do you think you're doing?"

"I'm going to remind you what you've been missing."

Her mouth dropped open as he pulled his running shorts down and exposed the part of himself he intended to use on her again.

"Tommy…" she warned just as she took off running to the door she'd come in through.

He caught up to her from the back and tackled her to the floor where she landed near the fireplace, her luscious arse pressed up against his groin. There was no fire, but the embers were still warm from earlier usage. Tommy intended to take her right here, right now. He'd create his own fire between her legs.

"Tell me you're not still attracted to me," he said as he held her neck down and ripped her panties off. "Tell me you haven't missed coming on my cock, and I'll stop."

"Please don't."

"Please don't what? Please don't stop?" He massaged her pussy, finding it already dripping wet. "You know when you say that, with your pussy coating my hand like this, I know you really want me."

"You sound like a rapist."

"Ah. But isn't that what you like? Isn't that your fantasy sex? To be ravished?" He stuck one of his fingers inside her and pumped it fast, priming her for the real pounding he was going to give that pink pussy. "Tell me you don't still love and want me, and I'll stop."

She tried to buck him off and swing to hit him with her arms. It was an awkward, useless cause that turned him on. "My wanting you is irrelevant. I'm getting married in the spring. Don't do this."

"Don't give you what you want? What sort of mate would I be then?" Ironically, this was exactly what she'd confessed to wanting. He put all of his weight on her, putting her flush with the floor before he started to enter her. "Aw, fuck, Capri. You make me want to come already. Jesuuuus." He'd intended to fuck her hard and fast, but he was too afraid any vigorous movement inside her would make him finish too soon. He had to keep it slow until he could get a reign on himself.

She moaned.

"It's so good, innit, Capri? You've missed it, haven't you?" he whispered in her ear as he held her arms down on the sides of her head. "You can't see my eyes when I doggy-style you, but you can hear my accent. You still love that, don't you? You know we belong together like this, you and I?" He still wasn't all the way in her, but he could feel her tightening up around him.

She kicked her legs in futility. "Tommy, I swear…" she took a deep breath, "you are the most selfish, horny, cocksucking…" Her voice trailed off when he used his knees to spread her legs wider. It made him slide right on in to the base of that sweet, tight, wet—

"Capriiii," he moaned. "Do you let him inside you raw like you do me?" Christ, he couldn't control himself. He was going to fucking come soon, and there was nothing he could do about it. "I've never been in anyone else like this. Nothing has ever felt so good." He withdrew and plunged in again. "Ohhh," he whimpered. "I want to come inside you so bad. Do you let him come inside you?" He squeezed her arms and pumped his hips. Fuck, fuck, fuck…that was so fucking good. "Can I come in you, sweetheart?"

She started shaking her head profusely. "You better not, Tommy," she panted. "I swear to God…" She moaned, defying her words. "I'm going to scream if you—"

He slapped a hand over her mouth at her warning

and proceeded to give her what her body was calling for. What they both wanted and needed. The way she started squeezing and convulsing and milking him a second later, made him want to put his seed in every molecule of her flesh. He lifted his torso off her back, letting his cock swing inside her like a mighty piston until he let it all go. Her hips rose off the floor to meet his thrusts as she moaned into his hand and came again.

His body jerked with each stream that left his body and went into hers. It still jerked for several moments later even after he'd had his longest, most intense orgasm ever.

He continued to throb inside her in that same position for several moments before he considered the aftermath of what they'd done. What *he'd* done. He pulled out of her, cautiously watching her turn over to face him.

"You selfish prick." Her face was defiant. "That's why you're going to be alone for the rest of your life and I'm going to be married with a family and a thriving practice."

"I won't be alone. I'll have you and that baby I just put inside you." He rose to his feet. "I just killed two birds with one stone. You got your fantasy out of the way, and I got mine."

She looked incredulous. "I've never thought of you as dumb before, but my. You've got to be the biggest fucktard ever. Do you honestly think I would be with you?" She stood up, brushing his hand away as he reached to help her up. She gathered her shredded garments. "What do you think they make the morning after pill for? We are no longer subjected to the whims of cocky bastards like yourself who like to get possessive and controlling when they see another man with what they could have had."

"Capri…" He reached for her again as she started to leave the room. "I love you. I love you more than anything. My feelings have never changed. Be with me. I can't live without you."

"You've been doing just fine without me, Mr. Superstar Rock God. Don't try to mess up my good life just because you gambled on yours and lost the best thing you almost had." She stormed out.

Tommy plopped on the rug in front of the fireplace and cried until he fell asleep naked with Capri's juices still drying on him. Maybe taking her hadn't been such a good idea a'tall.

CHAPTER 15
FIVE MONTHS LATER

Capri had been sitting at her office desk for a half hour straight, staring at the picture of her and Tommy on her desk. No matter how many different offices she had or how many pictures she took, this one would always be her favorite. It would always be the only one in her office. She'd always be sitting on his shoulders in it. They'd always be looking at each other, sharing smiles. The sun would always be shining, and they'd always be happy. In the picture, that is. Their light-hearted warmth and humor from those days would forever be framed on her desk, branded in her mind, chiseled in her heart. Unfortunately, those times were long gone in real life.

It made her sad. It made her feel downright depressed.

More so than breaking up with her fiancé did. She'd never thought it was going to work with him anyway. She'd agreed to be his wife because all the pieces had fit neatly together. He'd been the one she *should* have wanted. He'd invested time in her as a student, and he'd been there to help her professional career take off and flourish. He'd helped her work through some of her personal issues in counseling, and over time they had grown to be more than colleagues, more than friends. In truth, she had never found the passion she'd had with Tommy in the man she had prepared herself to marry. Her connection with Tommy had been one of a kind. *He* was one of a kind. Tommy was the kind of man she *really* wanted.

Damn her.

Capri had hoped she could get by on professional compatibility and common interests, but she needed passion too. She was reminded of that the last time she saw Tommy. It had been the first time she'd had an orgasm in years, self-induced or otherwise. And she was still pissed with him about that. Taking her attraction to him and using it against her… Throwing her hottest fantasy in her face when she'd least expected it… Confusing her with feelings of betraying her man and feeling guilty for enjoying what Tommy did to her… Fucking rapist. Making her want him all over again. She'd finally gotten over him after their disaster of a date and moved on until he'd…until he'd made her start to crave him again. She should have kicked him in his nuts and—

"I'm leaving for the day, Ms. Jackson. I've turned the office line over to the answering service. Is there anything else you need before I go?"

Capri shook her head without looking at her assistant. The one thing Capri needed, no assistant in the world could give her. That was Tommy.

She looked at her cell phone. He'd called her once every day for the past five months. He'd left messages every single time. At first, they were apologies. After the first month of that, the messages turned into songs. Then they became more diversified.

Sometimes, he just told her about his day and talked as if he was holding a conversation with her. Sometimes, he shared a memory from a happier time with her, and she would find herself laughing as she listened. Sometimes, he just told her how much he loved her and how he was just calling to hear her voice on the recording.

She never answered the phone. She also never deleted a message without listening to it first. She was looking at her phone because he hadn't called today yet. It made her wonder if her phone was working properly, though she knew that was irrational thinking. Of course, it was. She was just excited about listening to his newest message. What funny memory would he have her recall today? What part of his day would he share with her? What new song would he play that she had inspired?

She leaned back in her seat to stretch. Maybe she should just cut the phone off completely to avoid this cycle she had gotten on with Tommy without even trying. But then, she wouldn't be available if her mother needed to get in touch with her. Her mother's transition back into society had gone relatively smooth. They didn't need any setbacks over Capri being so caught up in Tommy that she closed herself off from everyone else to avoid him.

Her cell rang. She held her breath and leaned forward to see the caller ID. Sasha.

"What's up, girl?" Capri said, more jovial than necessary…because she didn't feel guilty about hoping it was Tommy calling. Noooo.

"You're extra cheery today."

Capri clicked her pen open and shut repeatedly. "It's been a good day. Can't complain. And yours?"

"I just called to give you the deets on your boy."

"Save it. I don't want to—"

"Tommy's going to be on Fallon's show tonight," Sasha said, ignoring her. "You should check him out. I hear he has new, solo music."

"Good for him."

"Capri, you did kind of tell him you wanted to be raped."

"That was not the context of our discussion. It had been years prior. And I was trying to be faithful."

"Okay, look. I'm not trying to make light of what he did, okay? I'm not. He was wrong. Plain and simple. But outside looking in—it just seems like you should give him a chance to apologize and see where you guys go from here." She yelled in the background to tell one of her children to get off the counter. "Where was I? Oh, yes. Capri, it's you and Tommy we're talking about here. You were BFFs. You survived a threesome and…me. I'm not saying this would work for all couples. I'm just saying it could work for you two. I've always thought you and Tommy had something special. Always. And…well… never mind."

"What? Just say it. You're already on a roll."

"And…if it took Tommy pinning you down and fucking you good to make you drop that man old enough to be your daddy, I say hooty hoooo! Thank you, Tommy. You were never going to be happy married to that man."

"Well, why don't you tell me how you really feel?" Capri said sarcastically while clicking her pen. Click, click.

"I could repeat everything for you, but girl, I gotta go. Jeremy's dragging the dog by his tail and Lena's eating out of the doggy bowl. Watch him tonight on TV, okay? Bye."

Pffft.

Watch Tommy on TV, my ass.

But later that night as she curled up on her bed all by herself, she turned the TV on. She cut it off a few times before committing to watch *The Tonight Show*. It wasn't on yet, so she popped popcorn and waited. When her phone rang, she didn't want to answer whoever called in case they caused her to miss Tommy on TV after everything she'd done to prepare for it. She'd decided to let it go to voicemail before jumping up at the last minute to answer it. She realized it might be Tommy. After she answered it, she kicked herself. She had only meant to listen to whatever message he left.

She didn't say anything in the microphone.

"Uh…Capri? You there?"

She still didn't say anything.

"Okay. That's fine. I'm just surprised you answered is all. Happy you took my call, just surprised."

She closed her eyes with the receiver to her ear. She could listen to him talk all night. She still wasn't ready to talk back.

"Is that the telly in the background?" He paused. "It is the telly. Good. Well good. Sasha got up with you then."

Aha. The traitor. Doing minion work for Satan.

"Don't be cross with her. Believe me, it cost me. I think I signed on to sponsor her son's guitar lessons for a year or something like that."

Capri grinned to herself. Served him right.

"I heard you called off your engagement. I'd be

lying if I said I was sorry. I'm not. I'm thrilled to death. But...I hope you're not planning to go out with anyone else. I'm ready to be serious about us. I'm begging you to give me a real chance. I'm so fucking sorry. I don't know what got into me. It will never happen—"

She cleared her throat.

"Okay. I get the hint. No talking about that right now. Cool. Got it." There was rustling on the phone. "You watching, Capri? My segment was recorded earlier. It's coming on now. Watch it to the end. It'll have you in stitches. I'll ring you back once it goes off." He hung up.

Tommy's interview with Fallon was actually funny, just like he'd said it would be. Tommy had even found a way to make the bat robbery a joke. Not that she ever doubted whether he could be funny. Taking something serious had always been his issue.

"So tell me, the man who calls himself Godd, is there a special someone in your life? Every woman on my staff would kill me if I didn't ask that," Fallon said.

Tommy's cheeks turned pink, which wasn't hard to do since he'd been spending so much time in the UK. His skin had lost some of its regular tan. "Yes."

The audience responded with *Awwwww*.

Tommy crossed his legs. "But she doesn't know how special she is to me. I love her more than anything, but I [BEEP] up bad." Good thing Tommy's interview was previously taped. "I did something I can't take back. I'm just begging her for another shot."

Fallon looked at the camera and smiled. "How odd to have Godd come on the show and beg for...well, anything. Who could resist that sad face?" He looked back at Tommy. On cue, Tommy turned his lips upside down and gave the most pitiful *I'm lost, take me home* look ever. It even got a laugh out of Fallon. "So tell me, Godd, what makes this woman so special? You know what I mean? With all the women out there, why do you want this one?"

"She's a woman who sets her own rules instead of being one of the sheeple. She's open and honest with me and knows everything about me, every kink, every secret. I don't have to pretend to be something I'm not with her. You guys see this." Tommy did a general sweep of his full leather clad attire. "She sees this." He tapped his chest.

Capri noticed his platinum chocolate chip cookie charm dangling from his arm underneath his sleeve.

"Hmm. She must have seen more than she bargained for if you're on TV begging to get her back." Tommy shrugged as the audience laughed at Fallon's more-truthful-than-he-realized joke. "So what did you do to end up in the doghouse?"

Tommy's face turned sheepish. "I can't say. Not on national telly."

The audience responded with *Ohhhhh.*

Fallon looked back at the camera and mouthed *Yikes.* "But you wrote a song about it, right? It's on your new solo album?" He lifted the CD cover entitled "Godd's Confessions". There was a picture of Tommy looking like the skinny boy with expressive green eyes she'd met as a freshman in undergrad. "And you're going to perform it for us tonight?"

"I'd love to. Yes, this song called 'Flirty and Capricious' is nearest and dearest to my heart. It's about her, the love of my life, my best mate."

The audience *Awwww*ed again as Tommy went to the stage to perform. He started off singing and playing the piano then moved to his guitar. From there, he ended up on his knees. Once the music stopped, he spoke into the mic on his leather lapel. "In a world where being judgmental and hypocritical is the norm, not the exception, you are the brightest shining star." He repeated the line verbatim that she'd said to him years ago, strummed a few more notes for effect then ended the song.

Fallon walked onto the stage next to Tommy as the audience cheered. "'Godd's Confessions', ladies and gentleman. In stores next month wherever good music is sold." The station went to commercial.

Capri cut the TV off and stared at the black screen. She would not cry, she would not cry... A traitorous tear fell down her cheek. *Fuck you, Tommy.* She rolled over and went to sleep, ignoring her phone as it rang and rang.

First thing she did when she woke up in the morning was listen to his message: *I hope you watched the show. I meant every word. I'm going to be in your town next week. I'm not telling you this so you can skip town. I'm telling you, hoping you will consider meeting me for lunch, dinner, a pint, anything. I just want to have a chat. Think about what it would take to put me back in your good graces and let me know whatever that is. I'm willing to do what it takes to be with the one I love.*

The next day his message was about the time she'd raised the bat to beat the man trying to rob them. He laughed in the voicemail as he reminisced about Capri transforming from a lady to a thug in a matter of seconds. Hey, Capri had grown up in a rough neighborhood and had to be tough. Sure, she'd overreacted with the gun her mother kept in the nightstand on that awful night, but there had been plenty of times when her vigilance and willingness to give a beat down had saved an ass or two, including Tommy's.

In another message he talked about how he was trying to grow up and do grown up things. He now played acoustic guitar every Friday morning at a local nursing home for free. He hadn't realized how much he'd enjoy it, but he believed the elderly company had more of a healing effect on him than playing for them had on them. It was like spending quality time with his mamó again before she'd become deathly ill.

Capri continued to listen to his messages, but she didn't answer when he called. She didn't call him back either.

Finally, the day he'd said he would be in town came. Tommy, along with his whole band, was doing a charity concert at Mr. Steely's pub to raise money and awareness for Alzheimer's research. Capri decided to go to their reunion concert, and she was glad she did. They played all their old music, taking her back to happier, simpler times. After the show, she turned to walk to her car. Someone shouted at her.

She turned back to see Spirit waving her to the stage.

No security. No red tape. No *Stand Behind the Lines, Please* signs. She just walked up and grabbed his hand as Spirit lifted her to the stage. After catching up with him and seeing that he was doing okay, she went down the line to Savior and Divine and lastly, Tommy. He'd been patient. And alone. No groupies.

Huh. Weird.

But good. It made her feel good.

Her decision had been made. She would give him another chance. A real chance. One they could both appreciate now that they were arguably in better mental places in life. "Hello, Tommy."

"Hello, Capri. I'm glad you could make it."

Their hug was stiff, but nice. It was nice to see him again. To touch him. To talk to him.

"I've gotten all of your messages."

He smiled, and it had the same effect on her it always did. "I guess there's nothing left for me to say then. What are your terms?"

"Do you have plans for tomorrow?"

"Hanging out with you, I hope."

She smiled. "Good. I'll text you my address. There is something that will make all of this better. Can you come around one o'clock? I'm off every Saturday and Sunday now."

He couldn't contain his excitement. "Yes, of course. I'll be there."

"See you then."

She got back in the car he'd bought her years ago and went home to the house she'd bought for herself. She needed to prepare for his visit tomorrow.

When her doorbell rang at ten after one, she answered it wearing a sheer black cat suit, leaving nothing to the imagination. It fit her snugly in all the right places.

Tommy stood on her porch, staring. "If this is some kind of test, I promise I will never touch you again without you asking me to first."

"Come in." She turned so he could follow, knowing her ass was on display for his lustful eyes.

He hesitated before walking in. "This is quite

lovely," he said as he looked around at her house and avoided looking at her. "Not as lovely as the one I'd gotten for you that you wouldn't keep, but still lovely."

"Some tea?" She handed him a teacup.

He eyed it before taking it.

"I wouldn't poison you, silly. I killed someone before out of misunderstanding, not malice." She rubbed a nail down his arm and circled him. He'd grown his messy mop of hair back out, and she took a second to run her fingers through that as well. "Besides, I'm not upset with you. Not anymore. I invited you over because I'm ready to move past what happened at Spirit's house."

"You are?"

"His wife had just passed. Emotions were high. We've never been good at expressing our feelings, have we?"

He shook his head. "I'm ready to try and do better though." He sipped the tea. "Good tea, thanks."

She nodded. "I am too. I miss my BFF. I want to bury the hatchet."

"In my back?"

"No," she laughed. "Metaphorically speaking."

Tommy relaxed somewhat. "How many pounds of flesh is it going to take?"

"Just a little."

"Are we talking revenge here? Payback?"

"You know me so well," she smirked. "I've decided there is a remedy—a cure, if you will—for what has been broken between us. There must be punishment and consequences for your actions." She picked up a rope off the coffee table.

He stared at it then at her before setting his teacup

down. He held out his wrists. "I said I'd do whatever it took."

She smiled. "Good boy. Take your clothes off first."

He moved in a rush to disrobe.

"Slowly," she said as she smacked his ass with the rope. "My back was to you last time. It's been a long while since I've seen you."

He took off his jacket, jeans and shirt with leisurely care. Once he was naked, she directed him to her bedroom upstairs. She made him get down on all fours and crawl all the way there. Once inside, the windows were covered with black velvet curtains and the bed had four solid, wooden posts. That's where she began tying his wrists together—right in front of that big bed. She tied his ankles together also.

"You got a wee thing for rope, I see. Anything to do with what you witnessed when you were fifteen?"

She paused as if contemplating. "Maybe." Once he was bound according to plan, she stood back to look at her knots. "Can you get out of them?" He tested the strength of the ropes. Nope. He was going nowhere until she decided to let him go. Perfect. "Stand there. I'll be right back. Don't go anywhere."

"Ha. As if."

When she came back in, he looked at her suspiciously. "What's that behind your back?"

"Something you'll like." She cut off the light overhead and turned on the red bulb lamp.

"Something I'll like?"

She nodded. "I know what you like."

"What?"

She pulled a gag from behind her back and whispered, "To be teased." She kissed his lips then stuck a red ball in his mouth and tied the strap around his head. He mumbled and fussed, attempting to express his disdain, but she ignored him. Once his mouth was securely muffled, she stood back and admired her handiwork. Now none of her neighbors would hear him scream. "You still willing to do whatever it takes?" she teased.

It took a few seconds, but Tommy finally nodded.

Capri could tell Tommy knew he was in trouble. How much trouble was still yet to be seen. Would she bring out a flogger, a crop, a whip? A dildo? Hell, was she twisted enough to scrape a knife across his skin? Judging by his erection, he wasn't immediately turned off by the unknown. Fact was, she had plenty up her sleeves, and it would surely be memorable.

"I'm going to make you come, Tommy."

He eyed her.

"Nod your head to let me know you understand."

He nodded.

"But first, I'm going to torture you."

His eyes got huge. Frighteningly so.

She grinned. "And after I make you come, I'm going to torture you again."

He started mumbling and acting out.

"I can't understand you, *sweetheart*." She threw back the pet name he'd called her right before he'd come inside her without permission. "That's the whole point of the gag," she laughed. "We're going to play a game. It's called 'Let's See How Long Tommy Can Go Without Having An Orgasm'. I promise you'll come in the end, after I say you can, but I'm not going to make it easy for you."

She shoved him on her bed and pulled the ropes to both ends of the bed. She tied them to the bedposts until he looked helpless and immovable. Without giving him a moment to collect himself, she pulled a toy from her drawer and used the Fleshlight on him painfully slow. She brought him to the brink of orgasm over and over again then stopped to laugh at how his cock bobbed and jerked without fulfillment. She got a kick out of watching his skin enlarge and retract, out of watching his hips buck and retreat, and watching his eyes roll in the back of his head whenever he thought he was close enough that she'd surely let him come.

She didn't. Because if she did, it wouldn't be torture.

His only breaks were the times she took breaks. His voice was hoarse after the first several rounds. Begging her to stop or let him finish did no good. His pleas were muffled and muted. She continued to drag the toy up and down his cock, giving him friction without release, laughing as he strained to get away and closer at the same time.

Whenever she thought he had gone numb from overstimulation, she mixed it up. She applied ice to his shaft and a warm towel to his cock head. Other times, she alternated with ice on his head and warm towels on his shaft. Either way, she kept him guessing. She kept him aroused. She kept him full to the brink of spillage. If fluid oozed out, she smacked his cock to shock it back into arousal instead of release.

When she tired of the Fleshlight, she used a small vibrator on the backside of his shaft and underneath his balls. His murmurs and moans turned into squeals. She abandoned that toy, dissatisfied with his reaction. Her intent was to torture him with pleasure, not pain. He hadn't hurt anything more than her feelings when he'd taken her. She wasn't trying to harm or kill him.

She realized every time she tickled his feet, it could be considered cruel and unusual punishment though. Too bad for him, it came in handy when she needed to bring his arousal level down a notch.

Sure, she fed him, helped him to the bathroom, and lay next to him and talked during intervals. But when he got comfortable and thought she might be done with him, she produced a new toy.

"This is a cock lock male chastity device, my dear. Someone as horny as you could stand to have one of these at all times." She held up the object for his inspection. "This is your plastic cage, and this is the lock key. I'll let you out to enjoy yourself every once in a while. Then back in you go. To the cage."

He started shaking his head.

She laughed. "Okay. Deal." She'd never thought of herself as sadistic. She certainly hadn't enjoyed ripping his cock with the zipper during their first physical encounter. But she enjoyed watching him squirm and strain now, relinquishing all power, all control. She continued his specialized teasing and torture until well into the night. Once she got too tired to continue, she locked his cock up and stretched out next to him. They fell asleep in their old spooning position. It felt like returning home after a long absence. She realized she didn't want to spend another night without sleeping next to him like this.

Her energy recharged and resolve strengthened, she awakened before him and used her mouth to awaken him. He was thrashing on the bed in moments, no doubt, hoping she was ready to let him finish.

Nope. She had the whole day off. And she used it to tease him. She alternated between teasing and locking him back in the cage throughout the day and night. His desire for pleasure had become his curse. Potty, bath, and dinner breaks came regularly, but her torture had gone on almost continuously outside of those intervals.

"I'll give you thirty seconds. If you can get off in thirty seconds, I'll let you come." Capri released his left hand instead of his right then hit the stopwatch. Watching him stroke himself fast and hard nearly made her come. "Ten seconds." Her breathing quickened as he threw his head back, bit his lip, and pumped harder. "Five seconds." She ran her fingertips through the gloss that popped on his skin as he pumped furiously. His muffled moans had to be the most erotic thing she'd ever heard. She was nearly out of breath when she said, "Two seconds...and stop." She snatched the Fleshlight back and watched him writhe on the bed. She tied his hand back up before he could make use of it. She locked his cock again then she stretched out next to him and got herself off while he watched. If she couldn't take it another second, she could only imagine how much discomfort he was in.

When she got too tired to tease him anymore, they assumed their natural sleeping position and dozed off.

The next morning, Capri left his cock locked, took the key with her, and made him promise not to leave the apartment when she left for work. Whatever plans he had for the day were considered cancelled if he intended to do what it took to make up his actions to her. She untied him from the bed, released the rope and ball gag…only to put them back in place when she returned. She unlocked his cock and used her mouth to tease him.

When his moans started to sound like cries, she figured he'd had enough. She released his gag. "You've endured three days of this. Are you ready to come now?"

"Yes. Please, Capri." His voice was so hoarse, he barely had one.

"Please, Capri what?"

"Please let me come. Pleeeease."

She put the ball gag back in place and stared at him lying there wide open to her whims. His hair was a damp mess and the bed looked like a hurricane had hit it. He looked as beautiful as he'd always been. A perfect vision of sin. And since she had reduced him to this sex-crazed puddle of aroused nerve-endings, what did that make her? Sin's master? Sin's partner in crime? Sin's pre-destined mate?

"You're not toxic, Tommy. You're you. And I'm me. And we're perfect together." She looked away to hide the vulnerability on her face. "So much for not being a cliché, huh?" She began to unlock his cage. "But maybe sex between best friends isn't just a plot device. Maybe it's as things should be. What if that was exactly what we needed to unlock the rest of ourselves for each other? What if that was the thing that set us free to fall *in* love with whom we already loved? Perhaps we complicated things by expecting our relationship to morph into something normal when we are extraordinary people."

He just watched her.

"Your parents may have gotten it right. They did a lot of wrong, hurt a lot of people, but they… I don't know. Maybe they loved each other so much they forgave each other and did what they had to do to make it work. That's why they're still together even though it looks crazy to everyone else. Maybe they are us...except we won't do anything behind each other's backs. We'll be open and honest about what we like, and what we want, and we'll enjoy it regardless of what other motherfuckers who aren't us think."

They stared at each other in silence for a while before Capri got up and went to the bathroom. She came back with a hairbrush. "I'm going to make you come now. And then I'm going to shove this brush up your ass."

His eyes got huge and he started shaking his head and jerking on the ropes.

"Shhhhhh. It has to be done. This is my requirement." She dried it off with a towel since she'd just washed it with soap and water. She couldn't trust a brand new brush to be completely clean for Tommy's virgin ass. "You've never been penetrated before, right?" She wasn't surprised when he shook his head. "Okay, then. I'm going to fuck you with this brush. After that, I'm yours. You're mine. We're going to be together no matter what. Is that still what you want? To be with me?"

He closed his eyes and exhaled. After a moment, he nodded.

"Good boy." She patted his head. "You'll walk away from this bruised and chafed, unable to fuck for several days...but you better thank me. You better be happy that you won't ever experience boredom with me."

He nodded.

She opened his legs and adjusted his ropes to keep

them open. "Oh, and… I'm on the pill now. Do you still want to come inside me?"

He nodded and grunted without hesitation.

Capri greased the brush handle with meticulousness before she shed her clothing and climbed on top of him backwards. She had only planned to make him come, but after watching him, she needed to give them both a release. Together. It had been too long since she'd been with him.

She slid down on his cock, taking an eager Tommy into her body once more. She rocked on him, absorbing his sounds and upward thrusts. He wouldn't be long so she had to be ready. She had to ready him, which was what she did with lube and her fingers. She lubricated and stretched his tiny muscle, using her finger to enhance each downward swing of her hips. She wanted to concentrate on her own orgasm, but she had to make sure she was careful with the tight part of his body that had only been opened to her.

She held the brush handle at what would be his entrance tonight and pushed.

At that moment she felt him throw his head back and jerk, she eased the brush handle into his rectum further and rocked back and forth on his cock as he came. She rode him hard, using one hand to stroke him, the other to massage herself. She kept on until she reached climax as well.

But she didn't stop there. She dismounted him after her first orgasm since she'd been with him five months ago. She replaced her pussy with the Fleshlight, pumping him ferociously with it. All the while, she stroked his ass with the brush. This constant stimulation after he'd already come and was extra sensitive... This was the real torture. The real power. Even after she'd taken his ass, this disregard for his muffled pleas for mercy, would be the part he'd never forget. She kept pumping and stroking until his whole body was soaked with sweat and his skin had turned a darker shade of red.

After many loooong moments, Capri stopped. She unbound him and massaged circulation back through his whole body, starting with the parts that had been tied up. He lay limp and exhausted while she cared for him. Once he resembled the Tommy she knew and loved again, she removed his ball gag.

She grabbed a bottle of wine and held it to his lips to sip. After sipping some herself, she rested her head on his shoulder and closed her eyes. "We need a bath."

"Mmhmm," he said lethargically.

She traced circles on his chest. "By the way, you were right. My mom and I have been going to counseling together. She said she regretted everything she'd ever told me. She wouldn't have changed a thing about taking my blame in the case, but she wished she hadn't told me to focus on work and to stay away from her. She missed having a relationship with me. She's proud of me, but if she had to do it over again, she would tell me to live life to the fullest."

He held up his right thumb to say *okay*. He'd only been allowed to moan, groan, and scream for the most part within the past three days. He'd have to get used to his voice again.

They traded the bottle back and forth and sipped in silence. When the bottle emptied, Capri took it to the kitchen trash and got another.

"Is marriage something you still want? Children?" He surprised her with the question.

"My father bailed on my mother after two years of marriage because he couldn't handle her severe mood swings. Guess he couldn't handle having a daughter either." She stroked his cheek. "I know neither of us can handle a spouse and children right now. Let's just give it some time and see what happens."

He raised her hand to his lips and kissed it. "You have the biggest, most beautiful areolas I've ever seen. Since they're mine now, we can take as much time as you need to decide." He planted his face between her boobs and made inhuman noises while he squeezed them.

"Shut up." She lifted his chin and leaned down to kiss his lips. "You have too much cock skin…but I love it. I love all of you."

"Enough to go on tour with me? Because if my muse—my new instrument of love—doesn't go, I'm going to cancel it."

She thought for a minute. "Yes, I do. I will turn my practice over to my progeny and go on your tour. I'm ready to see the world with you."

His face lit up like Times Square on New Year's Eve.

"Confession…" Capri said as she curled up next to him to cuddle. "I enjoyed you holding me down and having your way with me. I could never have created a more perfect set of circumstances to make that fantasy real."

"Confession…" he whispered, "these last few days have been so fucking amazeballs. Thank you."

She smiled. "You're welcome, mate."

\m/ ~ FIN ~ \m/

ABOUT THE AUTHOR

Wife to my best friend and biggest supporter.
Mother of two handfuls.
Attorney in Houston, Texas.
Author of sexy, wild, daring and risky books.

Let's keep in touch:

www.diceygrenorbooks.com
www.facebook.com/DiceyGrenor
www.diceyblog.wordpress.com
www.goodreads.com/DiceyGrenor
www.google.com/+DiceyGrenor
Twitter @DiceyGrenor

GRENO

Grenor, Dicey,
Best friends, fantasy
lovers /
Floating Collection FICTION
01/16

47396575R00149

Made in the USA
Charleston, SC
09 October 2015